MY FAMILY DAY

MY HOLIDAY TAILS

MARINA SIMCOE

My Family Day

This book is a work of fiction. Names, characters, places, and incidents are a
product of the author's imagination. Locales and public names are used for
atmospheric purposes. Any resemblance to actual people, living or dead, or to
businesses, companies, events, institutions, or locales is completely coincidental.
Illustrated Edition
Cover background image source: Depositphotos
Cover design and illustrations by Marina Simcoe
Spelling: English (American)
Proofreading by Jenny Sliger from Owl Eyes Proofs & Edits.

*This book was written entirely by the author. No generative AI or ghostwriters were
used.*

This book is a Science-Fiction Romance. It contains graphic scenes of intimacy.
Intended for mature readers.

❀ Formatted with Vellum

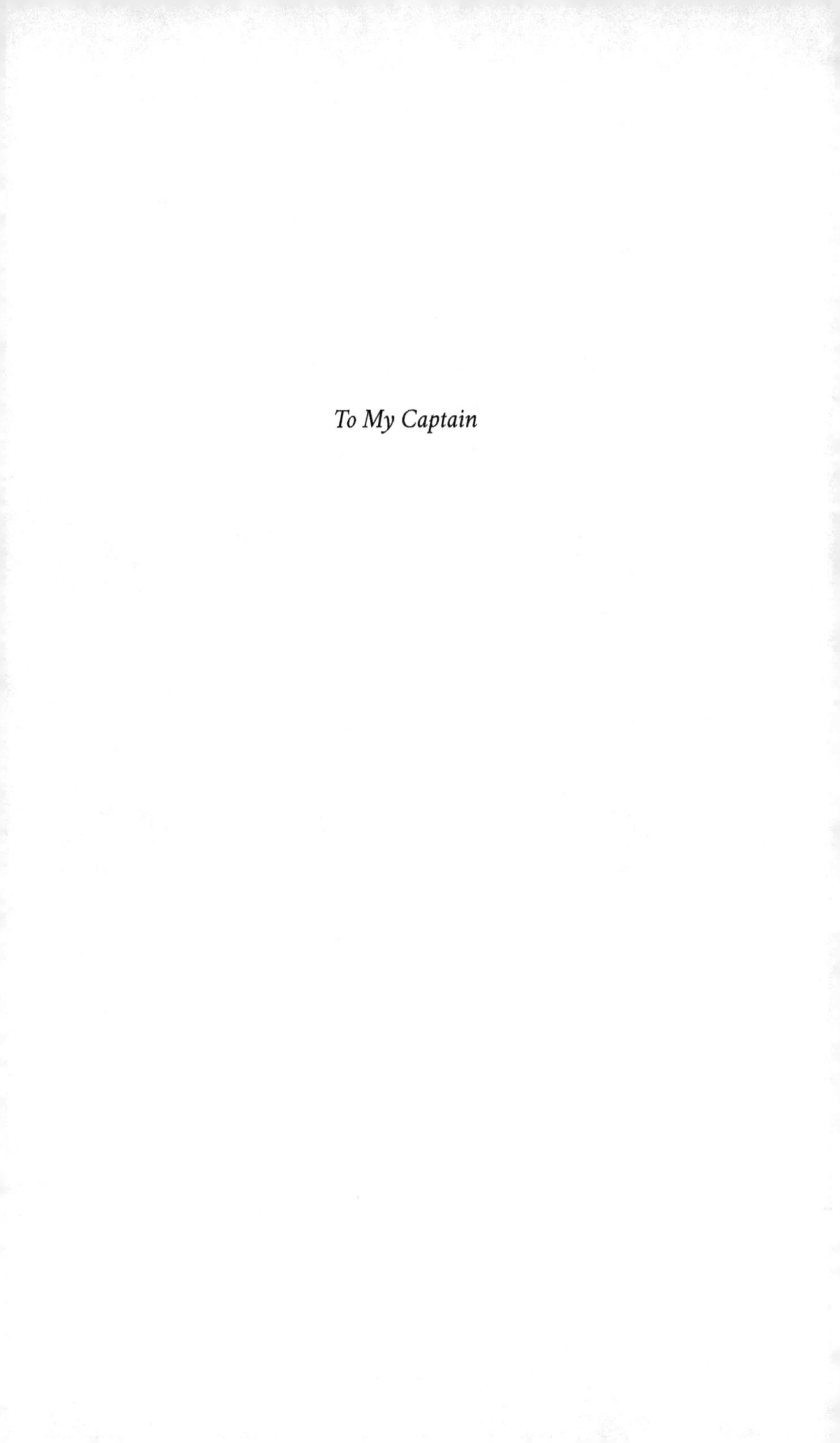

To My Captain

CHAPTER 1

ANA

"Bookkeeper Ana Hilal!" Alcus Hecear, a representative of the Earth-Voran Liaison Committee, hurried up the stone path toward the parked space shuttle that I was about to board.

I was a certified public accountant, but there was no direct translation of that designation in the Voranian language. Despite our fantastic translation implants, the literal meaning of my title didn't flow easily off the tongue either. As a result, my official title with the Voranian firm Interplanetary Enterprises remained simply "a bookkeeper."

Alcus Hecear trotted on his hooves to the space shuttle that would take me from planet Neron to planet Tragul.

"Bookkeeper Ana…" He ran out of breath, bending over and placing his hands on his knees. "I'm so…glad I caught you… before your departure."

"You look to be in much better shape than you actually are, Representative." I smiled sympathetically.

"Voranian genetic material is among the most superior in the universe." He grinned, catching his breath. "It doesn't mean one should neglect regular exercise, like I've done lately, sadly."

He ran his hand through the fur on his head, between the two long horns painted blue and pink. Gold and silver stars sparkled in the spirals painted along his horns. Since my arrival in Voran two weeks ago, I'd seen many beautiful designs on Voranian horns, but this one must be the most gorgeous yet.

"You're a busy man, Representative," I said. "It's hard to find time to exercise if you have so many new couples to help settle into their married lives."

The marriage program was the main collaboration agreement between the country of Voran on Neron and our Earth. Over the several years of its existence, however, a few smaller agreements had been signed and successfully executed between our nations.

For example, I came to Voran under an employment exchange program that allowed several professionals in requested areas of expertise to come from Earth to Voran to work while the same number of Voranians had traveled to Earth under similar terms.

Although when taking into consideration the fact that all professionals from Earth were women and every professional from Voran was a single male, the obvious goal of the exchange was still the potential for more future marriages. With the birth rate in Voran severely skewed—with about ten boys born for every girl—I couldn't blame the Voranian government for giving their men a chance to find a partner in life, either on their planet or on Earth.

"You must have your hands full," I sympathized with Alcus Hecear.

"Oh, yes..." Alcus Hecear exhaled, adjusting his white-and-gold uniform of the Liaison Committee. "Problems are abundant. But there is also joy in helping couples meet and potentially create something special—a future together."

I smiled warmly. "Well, thank you for taking your time to come and say goodbye. It's very nice of you."

"It's my job," he said simply.

As part of the delegation from the Interplanetary Enterprises where I worked now, I was going to Tragul on a business trip. Alcus Hecear didn't need to come here today to see me off, but he took his job very seriously and seemed to feel personally responsible for the well-being of all humans in Voran.

"Tragul is a beautiful planet," he said. "I have no doubt you'll enjoy your time there. But I need to make sure..." He grabbed his tablet from under his arm and turned it on. "It says in your application that you're not interested in marriage."

"That's right, I'm not."

I was surprised to receive a work permit despite my including that condition in my application. Apparently, my qualifications proved more important than my marriage potential, since the company accepted me anyway, and the government didn't put a stop to my arrival.

"I just got divorced last year," I explained to Alcus with a brief laugh. "I'm not really interested in acquiring another husband anytime soon."

"I understand." He nodded sympathetically. "Divorce rate on Earth is so much higher than it is in Voran."

Well, considering how rarely Voranian weddings happened when compared to Earth, how possessive Voranian men were in general, and how low their chances of remarrying after a divorce stood, I assumed Voranian couples had far stronger motivation to treasure their unions.

Not that I didn't treasure my relationship with my ex-husband when I got married, but I certainly should've thought harder before marrying him in the first place. I also had no business staying married to him for as long as I had. But he always acted so helpless around me that I honestly believed he simply wouldn't survive without me. Even now, almost a year since our divorce, he still texted me to ask where his pants were or where I put his shoes. It took me three years to realize he really wanted a second mom in his life, not a wife or a partner.

"If it is your preference, it will be honored, of course," Alcus Hecear assured me. "The men in your delegation have all been made aware of your wishes. No one will court you."

"Thank you." I exhaled with relief.

Fyna, the only Voranian woman in Interplanetary Enterprises, had warned me that men in Voran often looked at every single woman as a potential wife who needed to be courted and claimed quickly before another man swept in and proposed to her.

Fyna was married, with three children at one of the Voranian academies. She was also the one who had trained me in the Voranian financial systems for the past two weeks. I didn't work closely with any men yet, and now I wondered if that was intentional on my boss's part.

"Should I stay away from all men then?" I asked with a smile because the question sounded like a joke to my ears, but cultural differences weren't a laughing matter.

"No, we can't put restrictions on your socializing with whomever you like," Alcus Hecear replied. "I just want to caution you to be careful around Voranian men. Most of them don't grasp the concept of casual dating."

"Do you mean that if a male colleague invites me for a coffee, I should expect a marriage proposal soon?" I quipped.

The representative's expression remained serious, however.

"Yes. A proposal can be expected. You see? Something that a woman from Earth may take as nothing more than harmless fun can break a Voranian man's heart. It's best to avoid such misunderstandings and potential heartache that may result from them."

It was new to me to be told I might break someone's heart. Normally, it was *my* heart that was in danger.

"Well, thank you for the warning. I'll make sure to stay away from my colleagues. A workplace romance is frowned at back where I come from, too, so…"

A tall Voranian man strode along the path toward the shuttle. I tried very hard to keep my attention on Alcus Hecear and our conversation, but my focus drifted to the newcomer like the arrow of a compass would be pulled toward the North Pole back on Earth.

It was only when he came closer that I realized I actually knew this Voranian. His name was Esvar Baya Rotymus, and he was the owner and the director of the Interplanetary Enterprises.

And my boss.

I'd only met Director Rotymus in person once before. Along with the welcoming delegation of the Liaison Committee, he came to meet me right here in the Voranian spaceport when I'd just arrived on Neron. After that, I'd only seen him in video conferences. And frankly, the screen didn't do him justice.

Director Rotymus was at least a head or two taller than me, not counting his long, slightly curved horns that all Voranians had. Like all Voranians, he also had hooves. Only I'd never seen anyone strut so confidently as he did when he marched toward us. He also didn't seem to be out of breath at all. Apparently, despite the high demands of his job, the director still somehow managed to stay in better shape than Alcus Hecear or me.

"Greetings, Director Esvar Baya Rotymus." Alcus Hecear nodded politely.

The representative insisted on sticking with the most formal protocol, which demanded the use of all three Voranian names along with the person's title even when a simple "hi" would've been just fine, which made all his greetings that much longer.

His ability to memorize everyone's titles and triple names was also commendable.

"Good morning, Representative Alcus Hecear." Director Rotymus returned the nod. "Glad to see you, Bookkeep—"

"Ana," I said quickly. "Just call me Ana, please."

He gave me a warm smile partially hidden by his trimmed beard. Setting down his round suitcase, he took my hand in both of his in a formal Voranian gesture.

"It's my pleasure to see you, Ana." He tipped his horns downwards in a polite bow.

"The pleasure is mine." I became suddenly hyperaware of how large and warm his palms were and how gently they cradled my hand between them.

"Pleasant journey, Director Esvar Baya Rotymus," the representative wished.

"Thank you, Representative. I'll see you inside, Ana." The director walked up the ramp to board the shuttle, his hooves thudding against the metal with the same confidence that carried him across the stone path before.

I followed him with my eyes, wondering why I hadn't noticed before how tight his shirt sleeves were around his thick biceps or how his pants hugged his thighs and butt ever so nicely. But then again, he'd worn a long suit jacket in the office, and one I couldn't see his butt during a video conference.

"A workplace romance is very much acceptable in Voran," Alcus Hecear's voice snapped my attention back to the representative.

He clearly noticed my admiration of the director's *assets*.

"I'm sorry, I…" My face heated with a blush.

This was awkward. How could one explain themselves to an interplanetary official when caught ogling their boss's ass?

"It is perfectly alright, Bookkeeper Ana Hilal. A romance in the workplace is a wonderful thing. As long as it ends with a family unit being formed."

"And if it doesn't?" I cleared my throat.

"For casual dating, you may find the cultural norms of Ravils, the people on Tragul, a little more suitable. The ratio of males to females in their country is very similar to that on Earth, and the mating rituals in their society developed in a similar pattern too."

"Ravil men for fun, Voranians for marriage. Got it," I joked.

Once again, my humor missed the mark with Alcus Hecear, who remained as serious as always.

"I'm glad you understand, Bookkeeper Ana Hilal. But if you ever change your views on marriage, the Liaison Committee will be happy to assist you with finding a suitable husband in Voran. Have a pleasant journey."

With a last friendly squeeze of my hand, Alcus Hecear departed.

My tablet dinged with a message from Lucas.

"Hey, Walmart doesn't have the sausage I like. They said they discontinued it, like for good. How can they do that? Where am I supposed to buy it now? Do you know who else has it?"

I groaned under my breath. I should've blocked my ex-husband long ago. But a part of me still worried about him. Mentally, I never stopped feeling responsible for him. He still treated me as his emergency contact. Only in Lucas's case, every minor inconvenience was an emergency. I didn't even want to have children with him, because it felt like I was mothering a man-child that would never grow up.

Interestingly enough, Lucas proved to be perfectly capable of taking care of himself once I was no longer in the picture. He'd been living alone, paying his bills, and booking his own damn appointments. It'd just been so much easier for him to pile it on me when I was there to do it all for him.

I shook my head and turned my tablet off, trusting Lucas to find a substitute for his favorite sausage on his own. This wasn't an emergency I could handle from another planet, anyway.

"Ana?" Bree, our human flight attendant, poked her head out of the shuttle's door. "Time to board now."

"Sorry." I stuffed my tablet into my oversized purse and jogged up the ramp into the shuttle.

Our entire delegation was already seated in here. Other seats were taken by Voranian tourists traveling to Tragul and by the Ravils returning home to their planet. A seat to my left was free, but it was right next to the one occupied by Director Rotymus. He'd already made himself comfortable for the long flight, with a pair of headphones attached to his horns and a book open in his lap.

I moved ahead, hoping to find another seat in the tail section of the shuttle.

"Ana, we're about to take off. Please take a seat." Bree touched my shoulder from behind, pointing at the place next to the director.

At the sound of Bree's voice, he looked up from his book and gave me a polite smile.

Now it'd be rude if I walked past him, wouldn't it? It'd look like I didn't want to sit next to him. Especially when he'd already closed his book and moved the seat belts from the seat for me.

"Hi." I smiled back, plopping my ass in the seat and shoving my bag into the luggage compartment in the front.

"Please buckle your seatbelts," Bree instructed before going back to her seat in the front of the aisle.

I fumbled with the five-point harness.

"Allow me to help," the director's deep voice boomed from my left.

"Um...thanks." I held the two right belts together while he aligned the left two.

The director paused, as if waiting for me. I realized that to reach the fifth belt, he'd have to stick his hand between my legs.

And now, I got suddenly distracted, staring at his large hand covered in thick, gray fur up to his knuckles.

"Would you pass me the belt, please?" he asked evenly.

I blinked away the unexpected and extremely inappropriate vision of the director's hand slipping between my thighs. Something was seriously wrong with my imagination. The fact that I hadn't had a man touch me in over a year might have something to do with that.

"Sure." I hurriedly found the belt between my legs and handed its end to him.

Together, we managed to assemble the belts together and solve the puzzle of the buckle.

"It's worse than a baby car seat," I muttered under my breath, finally clicking the buckle closed just below my chest.

"A baby car seat?" The director gave me a questioning look.

I noticed how vividly pink his eyes were in the cool lighting of the space shuttle interior. I'd thought he had burgundy irises before, but now they had brightened to the loveliest shade of magenta.

"Oh, it's something used back home to transport infants safely." I laughed awkwardly. "How do babies travel in Voran?"

"I'm not sure." He smiled apologetically. "I don't have babies."

"Right. I don't either. I just had to buckle a friend's baby into her car seat once or twice, and it was…well, it was a nightmare."

Maybe I should've found a different seat after all. Clearly, sitting this close to the director turned me into a blubbering idiot. By the end of the flight, he'd probably regret having hired me.

"Well…um, thank you for helping me figure out the belt. I didn't mean to interrupt your reading." I gestured at the book on his lap.

"It's alright. I'd much rather talk to you than read this quite boring book."

"What are you reading?" I asked.

I could see the title clearly, but since I didn't actually know the Voranian language, I couldn't read it. As great as my translator implant was, it could only convey the meaning of spoken words, not the written ones.

"It's the latest update on all the trade agreements we have with the country of Ravie, complete with all amendments."

"It does sound like dry reading material," I sympathized.

He gave me a close look. "I'm sorry I didn't have much time to welcome you to Voran properly."

"No need to apologize. You came to the spaceport to meet me on the day of my arrival. That's more than many bosses would do for their employees."

He shook his head. "I should've been the one showing you around during your first weeks in the office, not Fyna, but I've been so busy lately, I only spent two days in the city in the last two weeks."

"Fyna has been great at showing me the ropes."

"She is an excellent bookkeeper, very good with numbers and knowledgeable about the law. I knew you were in good hands while I was getting the team and the paperwork ready for this trip. Have you been to Tragul before?"

He winced right after asking the question. The director knew I'd arrived in this part of the galaxy just two weeks ago. He had signed all my travel papers and knew I hadn't left Neron all this time. Now he must've realized how silly his question was and was likely kicking himself mentally for it.

The idea that my big, confident boss might feel just as nervous and awkward as I did helped me relax around him a little.

"No, I've never been to Tragul. How about you?"

"I've visited it several times. It's a beautiful planet, with a colorful jungle and a pleasant climate. You'll love it. Everyone does. Especially now that the war is finally over."

I read about the war that ravaged Tragul for twenty-three

years. Nasty creatures called *fescods* started it by invading Ravie, the only civilized nation on Tragul. After years of brutal fighting, the *fescods* took over the entire planet, then attacked Voran on the planet Neron. It took two more years of joint effort from the Voranians and the Ravils to push the *fescods* out of Neron. With further help from Earth, the *fescods* were finally defeated on Tragul, too, and Ravie had been recovering and rebuilding ever since.

"Did you visit Tragul during the war?" I asked.

"No. Only the trained Voranian Army went to Tragul during those years. My aptitude test at birth determined my career to be in business and finance, so I never went to the military academy. But when the *fescods* invaded Voran, I was allowed to join the Voranian Army in a supply and logistics capacity, which I did. For two years, I supplied our troops with equipment and provisions, often making the deliveries personally. I'd traveled to the battlefields and seen combat first hand." He sighed, his thick eyebrows moving into a frown. "War is ugly, Ana. It was pure joy when it ended. I went to Tragul as soon as I could. I wanted to see the planet we'd helped to liberate, and I fell in love with it. On my second trip to Tragul, I met with the governor of Ravie and realized I shared his vision of rebuilding the country."

"What is that vision?" I asked, mesmerized by his deep voice and the cadence of his narration.

"Ravie has big potential for investment right now," he said. "But instead of allowing foreign companies to move in and potentially redefine the Ravie's culture, customs, and even its landscape, Governor Eehie wants to help the local businesses to get back on their feet or get new ideas off the ground."

He spoke so passionately about it that I, too, felt invested in it already.

"I don't want to change Tragul or Ravie," he said. "I want to help the Ravil people build the life they choose for themselves.

That's how the Interplanetary Enterprises Foundation was born. I started out with my own money but then invited other businesses and individuals to join me. It turns out that many Voranians want to see Ravie prosper."

"It's a noble purpose," I agreed wholeheartedly.

"Now, you are a part of it, too, Ana. This trip is for us to identify the companies and businesses that need our support."

"Dear passengers," Bree announced through a speaker, interrupting our conversation. "Our shuttle has left the gravity field of Neron. It is now safe to remove your seatbelts and leave your seats if you so wish. Please feel free to join me and our service crew in the salon for refreshments."

I hadn't even noticed how the time had passed.

Director Rotymus unclipped his seatbelt and got up on his hooves.

"Would you like to move to the salon?" he asked.

I had to tilt my head all the way back to see his face high above me. In the process, my gaze traveled up his well-built body dressed in well-made clothes that fit him extremely well. Everything about the director seemed perfect—from his manners to his appearance to his motivation to do what he did.

His Voranian looks, complete with the thick gray fur, long horns, an arrow-tipped tail, and a pair of hooves, would've been a deterring factor for me just a few weeks ago. But while working closely with the Voranians, I'd gotten used to their unusual appearance. I'd even learned to identify individual visual characteristics between them. All such characteristics of the director were perfectly fine, too, from his size to his proportions, to those bright magenta eyes of his.

The more I got to know my boss, the more I liked him, which could present a problem if I wasn't careful. It was great to discover that my boss was a decent man worth admiration, but I promised Alcus Hecear to maintain a strictly professional relationship between us, and I fully intended to keep that promise.

I smiled at my dangerously attractive boss.

"No, thank you. I think I'd rather stay here."

I tried not to sound too disappointed, but a tendril of regret slithered into my chest. I would've loved to spend the entire trip in his company, but I had to be responsible.

"Would you like me to bring anything for you?" he inquired.

I mentally added chivalry to the list of Director Rotymus's many admirable qualities, which didn't make my task of staying away from him any easier.

"No, thank you. I stayed up late packing last night. I should catch up on sleep while I have a chance."

"Alright. Sleep well," he wished me with a parting smile.

As the sound of his hooves strutting down the aisle disappeared toward the salon, I put my seat in the horizontal position, then lowered the noise-cancelling hood over it. I didn't even feel sleepy, but I was determined to stay in the safety of the hood for the rest of the flight.

It'd taken mere minutes for my distant respect for Director Rotymus to flare into an intense admiration and even attraction.

At this rate, if I wasn't careful, I might end up climbing on his lap before the flight was over and seducing him into joining the mile-high club with me. Or the *light-year* club. Or whatever the heck it was called when space travel was involved.

CHAPTER 2

ANA

$\mathcal{A}$ knock came on the door of my apartment shortly after I had stepped out of the stone tub and put a bathrobe on.

"Coming!" I yelled, shoving my feet into my leather flip-flops before opening the door.

The most fantastic smell of baked goods hit my nostrils, making my stomach spasm with yearning.

A smiling Ravil man with a towel-covered basket in his hands stood on my second-floor landing. He looked older, but it wasn't easy to tell with the people of this nation.

Ravils enjoyed the reputation of being the most attractive race in the galaxy. And rightfully so. With their naturally fit bodies covered by short tawny fur, the voluminous golden manes of hair, and their bright green eyes, they were easy on the eye.

The smiling man fit right in with that description. Fit, tall, and topless as per the Ravil fashion, he was just a little wider in the waist, with just a few grooves of experience on his forehead, and some lines around his mouth that betrayed his age when one looked closely.

"Good afternoon, Ana," he said brightly. "I'm sorry I didn't get to meet you last night when you arrived, but I wanted to greet you as soon as you woke up. I'm Zaen, the owner of this building and the bakery downstairs. You met my wife Natlea last night."

"I did." I nodded, remembering the elegant, tall Ravil woman who showed me the apartment that the Interplanetary Enterprises rented for me for the duration of my stay on Tragul.

"Morning, Zaen. It's very nice to meet you." I extended my hand for him to shake.

He shifted the basket under his left arm, then shook my hand energetically.

"This is for you." He thrust the basket into my hands. "Welcome to Tragul."

The towel shifted, revealing the freshly baked pastries and a tall teapot with a thin curved spout.

"Oh, it smells amazing," I moaned. "Let me grab my payment bracelet."

"No need." He shook his head vehemently. "It's a welcome gift...um, a breakfast included with your stay for as long as you're here."

"Really? That's so nice of you. But you don't have to do it. I can pay."

"Please," he insisted. "Hosting a human woman in my house is the biggest honor we could've ever dreamed of. Lieutenant Emma Nowak helped end our long war. You are our guest of honor, Ana."

Emma Nowak was a soldier of the special unit that Earth had sent to help fight *fescods*. I had nothing to do with winning the war, but it felt impolite to reject his offering. Besides, it smelled too good to decline.

"Thank you. On behalf of all women of Earth." I bowed, pressing the basket to my chest.

He beamed, looking pleased. "I hope you had a good sleep."

"I did. I slept until noon." I smiled blissfully.

"Good, you're up just in time for the parade."

"What parade?"

"It's Family Day in Ravie," Zaen explained. "Today, we celebrate all families that got reunited after the war and all the new families that have formed since. There will be a parade down the main street, with music, then games and dancing on the town square, with lots of food. Our bakery is supplying bread and pastries. You should come, Ana."

"I'd love to. Thank you. I'll most definitely be there."

"THIS IS PRETZEL KVASS. It's brewed only in Ravie. I hope you'll like it." Director Rotymus put two wide glasses on the table in front of Fyna and me.

As I reached for my glass, my hand brushed against his. The soft tickle of his fur sent warm tingles up my arm, making me want to pet him. I bent my head down quickly, hiding a smile.

When I had messaged Fyna about the parade earlier that day, she replied immediately, *"We will all be there. It sounds fun!"*

The word *"all"* made my heart thud faster, and I knew exactly why. Because that implied that Director Rotymus would be coming too.

God, I was in trouble with this man already, wasn't I?

Wooden benches and tables had been placed along the short parade route. The route was short because the town of Tadolia, that Director Rotymus had chosen for our office, was pretty small. Short as the parade route was, however, there was enough space to seat the town's entire population and all its visitors along it.

The main town plaza was right behind us. Vendors had already set up their temporary shops under umbrellas and portable shelters with roofs of grass or leaves. One of them served the kvass that the director had brought for Fyna and me.

The remaining three members of our delegation joined us, taking the seats across from us at the table.

I took a drink of the cool dark liquid in my glass. It was a little sweet with bubbles of fermentation prickling my tongue.

"It's good." I nodded.

Director Rotymus smiled, looking relieved. "The taste of Ravil wine can be overwhelming for outsiders. Their beer often feels thick and heavy. But their kvass and fruit ciders are the best."

He took a seat on the bench next to me, making me hyper-aware of his closeness and the heat radiating from his large body.

The warm, humid weather on Tragul forced all of us to dress lighter. The director had to give up his usual dress coats in favor of the thin, short-sleeved shirt that hugged his muscular torso ever so nicely in all the right places.

A music band marched along the street, thankfully helping me shift my attention from my boss to the parade. The town mayor and his staff walked next, surrounded by a group of dancers in colorful costumes.

The vivid colors were what I loved the most about Tragul. Voranians loved colors and patterns too, both in their decor and clothing. But Ravils painted everything with bright, bold colors, unapologetically and without restraint.

The dancers' long, wide skirts twirled over the road. As they passed by, they gave space to the procession of local shops and businesses. I spotted Zaen and Natlea, who carried a giant baked creation shaped like something between a pretzel and an elongated wreath.

"Oh, those are my landlords!" I waved at them.

"You live above a bakery?" Fyna asked.

"Yes. I got a basket of delicious pastries for breakfast," I bragged. "But there wasn't anything that looked like the one they're carrying."

"It's probably not something they bake or sell regularly," Director Rotymus commented. "It's not just a pastry. It's the Ravil word for 'bread' baked out of dough."

I turned to him in surprise. "How do you know? Can you read Ravil?"

He nodded.

"Ever since my first visit to Tragul, I've been learning to read and write in the Ravil language. I may even be able to speak it, too, if my translator ever breaks." He smiled.

"Impressive." I gazed at him with admiration before remembering that I shouldn't and glancing away quickly.

"Oh, and there are *my* landlords!" Fyna waved energetically at a group of people passing by in the parade.

Judging by the sign they carried that depicted juicy hams and thick sausage links, Fyna's place was above a butcher shop.

"I woke up to the smell of meat in their smoker. I'm so looking forward to having it for dinner." Fyna laughed.

"What about you, Director Rotymus?" She turned to our boss. "What delicious things do you have in your building?"

"My apartment is in the same building as our office," he replied. "Nothing appetizing is made there."

"Oh, that's a shame. I'll have to bring you ham sandwiches for lunch then," Fyna offered.

"Apparently, I have a free breakfast for the duration of my stay," I said. "I'm willing to share."

"I'd love to have breakfast with you, Ana," he replied politely.

The tip of his tail flicked at his hooves, but his voice

remained calm and even. His words *didn't sound* like an invitation for anything, but the reply "It's a date then" was on the tip of my tongue.

Afraid that it would certainly come out as flirting, when I wasn't supposed to flirt with him, I snapped my mouth shut and fell into an awkward silence instead.

When I jerked my drink toward me, my pinky touched the side of the director's hand that he had rested on the table. The contact zapped through my body with unexpected thrill, immediately followed by alarm. I lifted my glass quickly and took a hurried drink, almost choking on my kvass.

This was ridiculous. Why couldn't I stay professional with my boss? I managed it just fine with all the other men in my office.

What was so special about him?

He treated me the same way he treated everyone else in the office. He'd brought a drink for Fyna, too, not just me. There was no preferential treatment of me on his part. After our accidental touch, his hand remained on the table, without a single twitch of his strong, long fingers.

He didn't flirt with me. He clearly didn't like me that way. I might be creating a problem that didn't exist.

The thought calmed me a little. I looked up at the director again…meeting his stare. It pinned me in place, robbing me of breath with its intensity. His eyes turned dark burgundy, despite the bright afternoon sunshine. He stared as if trying to reach deep inside my heart, needing to read everything I'd never voiced.

The music and noise of the crowd fell away. Other people at our table seemed to disappear, leaving the director and me swirling in the cloud of shimmering tension.

Oh, my God, I was in trouble. So, so much trouble.

"This music is invigorating." Fyna's polished hooves beat the ground to the rhythm of the fast music played by the band. "Let's dance, Director Rotymus. It looks like so much fun!"

He shook his head. "I don't dance."

"It can't be that hard to learn," Fyna insisted. She glanced at the group of Ravils at the edge of the plaza and nudged Director Rotymus with her elbow. "The mayor is waving at you. It looks like he wants you to come over."

The director's eyes left mine, and I drew in a lungful of air, finally remembering how to breathe again.

He glanced at the mayor and nodded.

"I'll have to go over there and talk to him." He got up.

I kept my eyes firmly on my drink as he moved away.

The parade had ended in the meantime. The band moved to the plaza behind us, officially turning it into a dance floor.

"Let's dance!" Fyna grabbed the male coworker closest to her, and they rushed off.

I politely declined the dance invitations from the two remaining men of our delegation, and they left our table, moving closer to the plaza to watch the dancers.

Left alone, I nursed my glass of kvass and tried to process where I'd gone wrong with Director Rotymus. I'd never seen him look like that at anyone before. Did I give him the wrong idea somehow, even as I had tried so hard not to?

What did he really feel for me?

And what was I going to do about it now?

"Dance with me," a male voice sounded from above me.

I lifted my gaze from my almost empty glass and squinted, met with bright sunshine and an equally bright smile of a Ravil man standing in front of me.

Ravils were generally pleasant to look at, but this one was simply blinding.

He stretched his hand out to me as an invitation.

"I...I don't dance. Not like this, anyway." I gestured at the plaza that had quickly filled with couples dancing to the light, exciting music.

"But your feet do." He tipped his chin, gesturing at my feet.

I hadn't even noticed, but I'd been tapping my feet in rhythm to the music. It was impossible not to. The excitement of the crowd was highly contagious, and the music was so light and airy, it made my body want to move regardless of what my brain thought.

I exhaled a short laugh, shoving my treacherous feet under the bench.

"Come on," the stranger encouraged, holding out his hand. "Let's give your feet what they really want."

"Well…" I glanced at the dancing crowd behind him.

Fyna had lost her Voranian dance partner somewhere already and now danced with a Ravil too. Zaen and Natlea were on the dance floor as well, dancing with a group of other vendors.

I didn't look behind me, where Director Rotymus had gone to greet the mayor. I didn't know if I could handle another dark-burgundy stare from him.

Maybe I should go dance, have fun, and lighten the mood? Maybe I could still fix the things between the director and me? Maybe we could still be simply friends and colleagues, with no hard feelings or awkward tension?

Maybe I could distract myself with a fun dance with a handsome stranger.

"Alright. Let's dance." I accepted the Ravil's hand. "Only you'll have to show me the steps because I have no idea what I'm doing here."

"I'll teach you everything I know." Flashing me another one of his stunning smiles, he led me to the dance floor and placed his hands on my waist. "It's very simple. Just two steps, a jump, and a twirl. Put your hands behind your back."

"Like this?" I clasped my hands behind me, like many other dancing women did.

"Just like that," he approved with a soft smile that showed only the very tips of the Ravil's sharp fangs.

Two dimples appeared on his cheeks, giving him an especially playful expression. His green eyes effortlessly pulled me in, commanding all my attention.

"Now follow me. Two steps to the right..." He led me in a dance, slowly at first to allow me to catch up and adapt to the rhythm of his movements. "Now, jump."

"Oh!" I gasped as he lifted me into the air in a wide leap.

With my hands behind my back, I had to rely on him for balance. Thankfully, he held me tightly. Landing back on the ground smoothly, he wrapped an arm around my waist.

"And now, twirl." He extended his arm, unwrapping it from around me and sending me into a spin.

As if launched from a slingshot, I spun across the floor. The band, other dancers, and the buildings around the plaza all blurred into a swirl of colors. My skirt flared in a twirl around my hips. I closed my eyes and unclasped my hands, spreading my arms wide. Yet I was rapidly losing my balance, unable to stop spinning.

A pair of strong arms caught me.

"I've got you," my dance partner purred in my ear, holding me to him.

Planting both feet firmly on the ground, I finally dared open my eyes.

The handsome stranger grinned at me.

"That was quite a spin, beautiful. How are you feeling?" he asked with concern.

"Dizzy," I admitted.

Afraid I'd tip over if I linked my hands behind my back again, I kept them up, because with his arms around my waist, there was nowhere to put my hands down but on him.

"Let's take it easy for a moment or two before trying again," he suggested, taking pity on me.

Gently swaying to the music with me, he noticed the peculiar position of my hands, and amusement warmed his expression.

"You can put your hands down, you know?" he said.

I lowered my hands a little, hovering them over his arms, then over his chest, then back over his arms again, unsure where to put them.

"Go ahead," he murmured. "Lay your hands on me, sweetheart."

Speaking in a deep, velvety voice, this man clearly had no qualms about flirting, and he wasn't hiding it.

"I don't think it's appropriate," I replied primly, "considering I don't even know your name."

"Orin," he said simply. "My name is Orin. And yours?"

"Ana."

"Here you go. Now that we've made acquaintances, my body is yours, beautiful Ana. Touch me anywhere you like."

"Wow!" I laughed. "That's all it takes? Talk about being easy."

He shrugged. "Why make it complicated?"

I kept my hands up, studying his chest, which was at my eye level.

Like all Ravil men, he was shirtless. The fur of his species was so short, it made their skin look silky from a distance. Up close, however, I could see the velvety texture, and I wondered what it would feel like to touch.

"You really want to touch me, don't you?" he teased.

"How can you be so sure?" I brushed him off, matching his tone.

"I can see it in your eyes."

I laughed, shaking my head. "No, you don't."

"Just think about it, Ana…" His voice dropped dramatically, as if narrating an epic story. "This might be your one and only chance to touch a Ravil. Just imagine, you'll leave here and go back to Earth, where you'll never ever have another chance like this. Do you really want to live with such a massive regret for the rest of your life?"

"Oh, however would I manage?" I laughed.

It was a hearty, carefree laugh that not many men could bring out in me lately, or ever.

Orin brought to mind all the best things about Lucas, my ex. The boyish charm, the fun-loving nature, the contagious enthusiasm with which Lucas followed me on any adventure. All those things that made me fall in love with him many years ago and that I would always miss.

Fortunately for me, I now knew that the initial attraction didn't always last and fun times were often short. I should simply enjoy this dance with a handsome stranger and not read too much into all these sparks of excitement flying between us.

"Well, I couldn't possibly set myself up for a life of regret. Here it goes..." I splayed both hands on his chest.

It felt soft and velvety as I slid my palms up, against the grain, and smooth and silky as I glided them down. I had expected touching him to feel amazing. I knew I would feel the hard muscles rolling under his skin. What I didn't expect was how fast his heart beat under my palms and the serious look in his eyes when I glanced up.

The smile left him as he studied my face intently.

We stopped moving completely, letting the couples glide and jump past us.

His heart thudded, and our eyes locked.

Maybe if I removed my hands from him, the spell would break, and I could breathe again. But I couldn't stop caressing his chest, enjoying the silky sensation of his body under my palms.

He shifted his hands from my waist up my ribcage until his

thumbs touched the underside of my breasts. Something hugged my ankle. His tail. It wrapped around my leg, with the soft tassel at the tip caressing my skin softly.

He licked his lips.

"I'm glad you took this chance, Ana," he rasped.

I was glad too. But I also wondered how many more chances I could take with him.

How far would I go?

It took all my willpower to finally remove my hands from him.

"Keep your tail to yourself," I said breathlessly.

He smirked. "Oh, but if you knew all the things this tail can do, you would beg me to keep it on you, beautiful Ana."

The brush of the fur tassel slipped just a bit higher. The squeeze of his tail grew a tiny bit tighter before its loop loosened from around my ankle and slipped away completely. I instantly missed its warmth.

"Are you feeling brave enough to try another twirl?" Orin asked, moving his hands back to my waist.

I took a bracing breath and clasped my hands behind me, taking the required dancing position.

"Let's do it. But I'm sorry in advance for the many times I'll probably step on your feet."

He laughed, tipping his chin at my feet.

"With those dainty sandals of yours? Go ahead, step all you want. My boots can take it."

"One step...two step," I counted in my head, following his lead. *"Jump and..."*

With my eyes open this time and my arms spread wide for balance, I landed back into Orin's arms perfectly.

"Well done!" He grinned. "You're the best human dancer I've ever met."

"And how many human dancers do you know?"

"Just you," he said, making me laugh again.

With me in his arms, Orin successfully navigated through the dance floor with minimal tripping on my part. When the dance ended, the music stopped.

With a crackling noise, the rusty loudspeaker mounted on a pole at the end of the plaza came to life.

"The ribbon of the Parade Queen is now ready to be harvested!" the announcement sounded over the crowd.

"What ribbon?" I asked Orin. "What does it mean?"

He grinned at me with a new flash of excitement in his emerald-green eyes.

"You're going to be the new Queen of the Parade, beautiful Ana," he declared, grabbing my hand.

"What?" I hurried after him as he dragged me to the end of the plaza.

"I will get you the ribbon." He gestured at the clearing in the park next to the town plaza.

A tall, thick pole rose from the middle of the open grassy area, with the town officials gathered nearby. Director Rotymus was among them, too, talking to the mayor animatedly.

A Ravil man with a yellow sash across his bare chest signaled for us to stay behind the line drawn on the ground at the edge of the plaza.

"Here, come here, ladies and gentlemen. Everyone wishing to compete, come to the line."

Orin squeezed my hand quickly before letting go of it.

"The ribbon is yours, I promise." He winked at me, jogging over to the line where several other men waited already.

I found Fyna in the crowd of onlookers.

"What's going on?" I asked her.

She squinted uncertainly. "I think they all want that ribbon over there."

I followed her gaze up to the top of the pole that was so high, its top almost disappeared in the sky, swallowed by the warm colors of early sunset. A long strip of bright material billowed in the breeze, hanging from the hook at the top of the pole.

"Do they have to climb the pole to get it?" I asked.

"Probably." Fyna shrugged.

"That doesn't look safe."

"It doesn't," she agreed, then gave me a curious glance. "Who is the handsome Ravil who is about to risk his young life in this crazy game?"

"Orin. And…that's all I know about him."

All I'd learned about my dance partner was his name and that he could probably do some amazing things to me with his tail, but Fyna didn't need to know that last part.

Taking his place in the line of the competitors, Orin gave me a wave and a smile that proved impossible not to return. It was just as hard to tear my eyes away from him. Excited and bouncing with energy, he was a pleasant, revitalizing sight to behold.

When I finally looked away, my gaze crossed with that of another man. Director Rotymus had caught my interaction with Orin, and his expression hardened. The director quickly said something to the mayor, then headed to the line of the contestants for the ribbon.

"What is Director Rotymus doing?" Fyna gasped in shock.

"I think he's going to try to get that ribbon over there," I said, with a heavy feeling sinking into my stomach.

"What does he need it for?"

"Maybe he wants to wear it on his horns?" I quipped in a voice squeaky from nerves.

And maybe it was true? Maybe the director's desire to get the ribbon really had nothing to do with me. Maybe he wanted to get it for another woman?

The other Voranian men from our delegation were happily chatting with Ravil women now. Without the severe gender imbalance of Voran, there were plenty of Ravil women on

Tragul. And they were gorgeous, with their green eyes and voluminous manes of golden curls.

Maybe the director met someone while mingling with the town officials. Or maybe he really wanted the ribbon to decorate his horns, since there was no one to paint them for him on Tragul?

I desperately clung to that hope as Director Rotymus took his place with the other men behind the line.

The man administering the game gave the signal, and the race began.

If there were any rules to this contest, they were disregarded by everyone. The men elbowed each other out of the way on their mad dash to the pole. Tails lashed between the legs, tripping the contestants. Someone tried to trip the director. Without even noticing, he stepped on the offender's tail with his hoof, making the other man howl in pain and regret.

With the grace of a cat, Orin slipped between the runners, getting ahead of the crowd and coming to the pole first. But Director Rotymus pushed forward, jumped up, and gripped the pole with his arms and legs ahead of the Ravil.

Orin clearly didn't expect such cutthroat competition. Shock registered on his face, then determination firmly set in. He jumped up, climbed higher, and yanked at the director's hoof, almost making him lose the grip on the pole.

The director slid down a bit. He kicked his hoof, hitting Orin in the shoulder.

Cursing, Orin pulled himself higher, climbing over the director.

I held my breath as they fought while moving higher and higher up the pole.

"I hope that ribbon is worth dying for." Fyna shook her head. "Because they would probably break every bone in their bodies if they fell."

"It's not worth it," I agreed, afraid to look at the two men climbing up into the sky but just as terrified to take my eyes off them.

With a desperate push at the very top, they both reached for the ribbon. The director's hoof slipped on the wooden pole. The hoof hit Orin on the shin. Accidentally, I believed. Orin growled, shoving the director in the shoulder.

Both slipped down the pole, randomly grabbing and clawing at it to slow down their fall. A short distance from the ground, they both let go of the pole completely and tumbled down in a mess of tails, limbs, and horns. A cloud of grass and dust rose in the air when they hit the ground with a thud.

"Oh, my God!" Terror paralyzed me.

"We need a doctor!" someone from the crowd yelled.

The town mayor rushed to the pole, followed by his entire entourage.

The dust cloud settled, revealing a grinning Orin and Director Rotymus, who looked just as happy for some reason.

Seeing them well and alive, the mayor stopped in his tracks.

"Well, and who is our winner?" the mayor asked, looking bewildered but greatly relieved.

Both Orin and Director Rotymus lifted their arms up, holding the opposite ends of the same damned ribbon.

"Um..." The mayor scratched the back of his head, glancing back at his people for help. "I don't think we've ever had that happen before, have we?"

The game's official rushed to his rescue. "Maybe we could do something to break the tie? Like another game? Who are the two ladies that you gentlemen meant the ribbon for?"

Climbing to their feet and hooves, both winners turned to face me.

"Ana." They pointed at me, each clutching their end of the ribbon.

All eyes turned to me now. My face flushed with heat under the crowd's attention. I felt responsible for this mess somehow, though I wasn't exactly sure how it was my fault since I'd never asked anyone for that ribbon.

"Oh well, it's easy then," the mayor said with a wide smile. "There is no need to break the tie. We have our Queen of the Family Day Parade!"

And that was it.

The game's official yelled the mayor's words to the crowd, and it erupted in cheers. Music blasted from the bandstand. No one seemed to mind the mess I'd inadvertently caused. On the contrary, people appeared to enjoy the spectacle.

"Gentlemen, please present your lady with your prize," the game's official waved his arm my way.

Director Rotymus glared at Orin, who smirked back at him, as they both approached me. Neither wished to relinquish their trophy, holding on to their end of the ribbon as if their life depended on it. They lifted their hands with the ribbon simultaneously, each yanking at their end. As they tried to put the ribbon around my head, however, they must've realized that they needed to work together to get it done.

Director Rotymus finally let go of his end of the ribbon to lift my hair with both hands, while Orin tied the ribbon under my hair on the back.

They both stepped back then, staring at me in admiration, and I felt my face burn even hotter.

"You look beautiful, Ana," Director Rotymus said.

"Simply stunning," Orin agreed.

I didn't plan for any of this to happen and had no idea how to feel about it all or how to act.

Two gorgeous men were staring at me like I was the best thing that had ever happened to them. Yet I had a feeling that if I weren't here, they would likely punch each other.

"Sadly, I can't say the same about either of you," I replied, running a concerned look over them both.

The director's neatly pressed shirt was ripped and smudged

in the front, probably from the friction against the wooden pole. Orin had grass in his mussed hair and dusty smudges all over his golden fur. They had just crashed down from quite a height.

"How are you feeling?" I asked.

CHAPTER 3

ORIN

I felt like an army of *fescods* had rolled over me. My arms and legs shook after the strain of climbing the pole. My side hurt after hitting the ground. My shoulder ached where the fucking Voranian kicked me. His hooves were harder than rocks, and the bastard had fought me tooth and nail for the ribbon. I supposed I should be grateful that he couldn't really use his horns to gore me while on the pole.

"I feel fantastic." I smiled at Ana.

Despite every part of my body screaming in pain, I wasn't lying. Looking at her made it easy to forget all the pains and aches.

It'd been so long since I had danced or even laughed, and Ana gave me the chance to do both today. I couldn't remember the last time I'd felt something other than fear, anger, or worry. And for just one evening, she had made me forget both the fears of war and all the troubles of the peace that followed.

"I feel better than ever, Ana. No need to worry," the Voranian lied.

Of course he lied. It couldn't possibly be true. I roughed him up pretty good on our way down the pole. The final fall also hadn't been gentle on either of us. But he put on a brave face, staring at Ana as if she was…the love of his life.

Chill spread through my chest, dousing the sunny feeling inside.

Were they a couple?

Was I too late?

Was Ana taken already?

"Oh, your shirt, Director Rotymus…" Ana fussed with the torn ends of the Voranian's shirt as he tried to calm her concerns.

Would a loving wife or girlfriend call her significant other "director?" I doubted it, letting hope bloom in my heart anew.

"Call me Esvar, please," the Voranian rumbled, clearly enjoying the touch of Ana's light fingers flying over his furry chest while tugging at the ends of his ripped shirt.

For the first time in my life, I wished I wore a shirt, if only for it to tear so that Ana would pull and tug on it, touching my chest the way she did the Voranian's.

They weren't on a first-name basis yet, I noted with satisfaction. Not all was lost here for me then.

The mayor sauntered to us, holding the flower sash of the Parade Queen.

"And here is our winning couple…um, the winning trio, I suppose." The mayor beamed at us.

In my mind, I vowed to cut this "trio" down to a "couple" before the night was over. The stuck-up Voranian *director* had almost snatched the ribbon from me, but he would not get this woman. Ana was going to be mine.

I took her right hand, taking my place at her side. Not to be outdone, the Voranian promptly took her left hand. She didn't take it away from him, which was a shame. On the bright side, she left her right hand in my possession too.

After the long but exciting ceremony of crowning the new Parade Queen, Ana was paraded through the main street with the entire town as her escort. Then the music and dancing resumed on the central plaza.

"A perfect time to continue our dance lessons." I tugged at Ana's hand toward the dance area.

That was my chance to have her all to myself again. Sadly, she didn't seem as enthusiastic to follow me this time.

"It's very late already," she said, adjusting her royal sash of golden flowers and purple ferns.

"The night is young," I insisted.

"Not when one has just arrived on this planet after a long and taxing journey," the Voranian intervened.

Who asked him to meddle?

"Not that I'd expect you to understand the complexities of interplanetary travel and the effects it has on living organisms," he added calmly.

I'd made the same journey enough times to understand the "complexities" perfectly well. Except that when I went to Voran and back during the war, I hadn't traveled in the comfort of a state-of-the-art Voranian space shuttle—like the director undoubtedly did—but in a rickety, outdated Ravil spaceship where the passengers were wedged between the cargo packs of supplies and provisions. But what would the pampered director know about that, of course?

"Way to reduce a woman like Ana to a 'living organism,' *professor*," I scoffed.

"I'm not a professor," he mumbled, looking confused and rather pissed.

Despite his infuriatingly calm composure, I was clearly getting a rise out of him.

"Then why are you trying to sound like one?" I snapped.

"I'm sorry, Orin. But I really feel exhausted," Ana intervened.

"I'll walk you back to the bakery." The fake professor sidled closer to her.

I couldn't let him take my chance away.

"I'll walk her," I said, shouldering him aside. "I'm going in the same direction, anyway."

The Voranian tilted his head with infuriating politeness.

"Well, if that's the case, I invite you to walk with *us*, provided Ana hasn't tired of your company yet. Have you, Ana?" he asked her with hope.

"We all can go together," Ana replied in a pacifying tone. "It's a nice walk."

Nice wasn't exactly accurate, not with the meddling Voranian tagging along. But Ana really looked tired, and I didn't want to upset her by fighting with him and keeping her awake longer than she could handle.

We went together as a 'trio' as the mayor had put it. The Voranian walked on her right, while I stayed on her left. Ana had threaded her hands in the hooks of our arms and rested them on our forearms.

As we walked, she subtly stroked my forearm with her fingers, the caress sending a rush of tingles through my body. I angled my head to take a look at her other hand that lay on the Voranian's forearm. She buried her fingers in his thick fur, but she was *not* stroking him.

"Where about do you live, Orin?" the Voranian asked.

He sounded polite as always, but I knew he was just gathering information to assess me as his competition.

Such an assessment wouldn't be in my favor, so I replied vaguely, "Not very far from here," then promptly switched the conversation to Ana. "How do you like Tragul so far?"

"From the little I've seen of this planet, I already love it."

I took my chance.

"I've traveled Ravie extensively and know it very well. I can show you all the best parts of this country. There is so much worth seeing."

"Really?" She stirred excitedly.

Anticipation buzzed through me. I'd walked, swam, and flown all over Ravie during the war—while feeling often angry, hungry, and scared. What a treat it would be to travel through my country during the peaceful times, with Ana as my companion.

"We can leave tomorrow if you want," I offered, holding my breath.

The Voranian was practically hurling daggers at me with his glare, but it only made my triumph so much more glorious...for as long as it lasted.

"I can't," she said with an apologetic smile. "I'm here for work, not on vacation."

"Every job allows you to take vacations, doesn't it?"

"It does. But I've only just started learning the ropes, so to speak. I don't want to take a break yet."

"A lot can be seen on a day trip too. Are you free tomorrow? I promise to have you back in Tadolia by the end of the day." I wouldn't give up hope.

"Oh, that'd be nice," she exhaled, with a small laugh. "But tomorrow is my first day of work on Tragul. And..." she leaned closer to me, with a playful glance at the Voranian, "I have a very serious, hard-working boss. I really don't want to disappoint him or to let our team down."

The Voranian stopped, and I realized we'd arrived at the bakery where Ana must be staying upstairs.

"Ana." The Voranian stood in front of her, making me essentially a bystander while they looked deeply into each other's eyes. "The weekend in Ravie is in two days. I'll be going to an art exhibit in the City of Ravie, the country's capital, by personal invitation from Governor Eehie. Please join me as my guest."

Fuck.

How did he ever so sneakily manage to ask her out before I did? Using my own idea of traveling the country too?

Clearly, the Voranian proved to be much stronger competition than I'd first thought.

"Ana," I rushed to salvage the situation. "Getting to know Ravie doesn't necessarily start from its capital. You'll need to see the countryside first, to meet its people, to—"

"The governor is one of the Ravil people too," the Voranian retorted coolly.

I clenched my teeth and stared straight at him, selecting the best target for my fists as my patience thinned. I couldn't introduce Ana to the governor because the governor had no idea about my existence, just as he didn't personally know the millions of other regular Ravils like myself.

But of course, some random Voranian enjoyed the pleasure of being personally invited to places by the leader of *my* country.

"It is a very engaging and informative exhibition." The Voranian took Ana's hand between his palms, even as her other hand remained in my possession. "The rescued artwork of Ravils' masters from the past several centuries will be displayed along with the creations of modern artisans."

"It does sound very interesting." Ana's face lit up with excitement, and my heart sank.

"Wonderful." The Voranian beamed. "I'll pick you up right after breakfast, unless you would like us to have breakfast together..."

Great. Now he was planning breakfast with her. My chances with Ana were quickly slipping away. I'd only just met this sweet, fun, wonderful woman, and I was already losing her to the stuck-up, boring Voranian.

Except that the longer he spoke, the dimmer the excitement on Ana's face grew, until worry replaced it completely. She nervously chewed on her bottom lip.

"Director...I mean, Esvar," she said quickly when he paused his tirade to take a breath. "Will it be just you and me going to the exhibition?"

"Yes. Is that a problem?" He blinked, looking worried now too.

"I'm sorry, but I have to make sure..." she said hesitantly. "Are you asking me out? Like on a date?"

My attention spiked. Did she *not* want to date him?

Because really, what woman would?

I knew his type—cold, detached, stuck-up, too full of himself, and boring. He was no match for a fun-loving, adventurous, smiling girl like Ana.

"Ana, my heart's deepest desire and my most daring dream is to earn the honor of calling you mine," the Voranian said, straight on.

I had to give it to him, the man had a way with words, and I could see the effect they had on Ana. She drew in a shaky breath, leaning toward him, which made me fear she would grant him that "honor" right then and there.

To my relief, she straightened and gently freed her hand from his large palms.

"I'm sorry, Esvar," she said softly, looking like every word pained her. "I like you. Very much..."

But...

There had to be a "but" there. I held my breath, straining my hearing in anticipation.

"But I'm not looking for anything serious like...uhm, a marriage, right now. I have to make it clear. I had a very good... a very *informative* conversation with Alcus Hecear."

"Ahh, Alcus." The Voranian's shoulders dropped at the sound of that name.

"Yes." Ana let go of my arm, too, and wrung her hands in front of her. "He warned me about dating a man from Voran. The last thing I'd want to do is to hurt you in any way."

"Alcus Hecear had a conversation with me too," the Voranian said grimly, running a hand over the fur on his head.

I kind of felt sorry for the poor guy. Sure, he was my rival, but I had been looking forward to defeating him fair and square by proving to Ana that I was the best man for her. Now, it looked like he was bowing out of his courtship before it even started.

"He did?" Ana looked surprised.

"Alcus informed all the men in the office that you weren't interested in a husband. He advised us to be friendly and professional toward you and to harbor no hope for more. However, if the only reason for your rejection is your concern for my feelings, I urge you to reconsider."

"But what Alcus said was true. I'm really not looking for a husband." She shook her head. "It looks like the right thing to do here is to decline all dates for the time being. I like you both, but I would never forgive myself if I caused either of you any pain."

What?

Did the fucking Voranian spoil it for *both* of us?

"Ana." I stepped forward. "I'm not from Voran. I don't have a clue who Alcus Hecear is, but I'm a very resilient man. You don't have to worry about hurting *my* feelings. I believe with all my heart that you and I can have a great time together for as long or as short as it would last."

"*Great time?*" the Voranian scoffed. "Is that all you think this woman is good for?"

I hiked my chin up in challenge, facing him straight on.

"What's wrong with giving a woman a great time? With me, Ana is free to be herself, which surely beats tiptoeing around your fragile, delicate *feelings.*"

"Nobody said I need anyone to tiptoe around my feelings," he snapped.

"Well, Alcus did."

"You don't even know who Alcus is!" He threw his hands in the air.

"Apparently, he's someone who looks after your fragile heart, because clearly you aren't man enough to take care of it yourself."

Ana lifted her hands.

"There is no point in fighting." She raised her voice, interrupting our bickering. "I won't date anyone. That's the only right thing to do."

That was such a *wrong* thing to do, in my opinion. But I felt helpless. I could kill the Voranian for causing this. His murder wouldn't help me get any closer to Ana, but it probably would make me feel a little better for a minute or two.

He reached for her hand again, but then wisely kept his furry paws to himself.

"Ana, you're free to make that decision, of course," he said, somehow managing to remain calm. Only a slight tremble of his fingers betrayed his nerves. "All I'm asking is for you to hear me out. Please?"

She nodded, the kind woman that she was. I leaned against the log that served as a support pillar of the awning by the main entrance to the bakery, waiting for what he had to say.

"Ana," he started. "I'm thirty-three years old—"

"Thirty-three?" I whistled. "Are you really that old, Voranian?"

Ana folded her arms across her chest, giving me a displeased look.

"His name is Esvar," she corrected sternly.

"Esvar," I repeated through my teeth, forcing a smile. "What a *lovely* name."

Disrespecting a man whom Ana obviously respected might be a direct offense to her. I had to rein in my dislike of the bastard or risk irreparably spoiling Ana's opinion of me.

"How old are *you?*" Esvar asked me gruffly.

"I'm twenty-seven."

"You're only six years younger than me."

"Yet so much more mature in my *feelings*," I couldn't hold back the barb.

Ana hugged her arms, glancing at the door to the bakery.

"I should go," she said. "It's getting late."

"Please let me date you, Ana," Esvar blurted out in what looked to me like a desperate attempt. "I appreciate your consideration of my feelings. But like I was saying…" he glared at me, and I kept my mouth shut this time. The sooner he said his piece, the sooner I could say mine. "I'm a grown man who makes his own decisions. And the truth is, I'd rather have my heart broken than never know what it's like to take you on at least one date."

She looked touched by his words, gazing at him softly, with her hands pressed to her chest.

What could I say? The Voranian really knew how to talk to women. Or maybe he had discovered the right way to reach this one particular woman, the woman in whom I happened to have a very keen interest myself.

"If he's taking you on a date," I said promptly, "then I request at least one date, too, please."

"Is that wise?" She looked concerned. "Wouldn't it be best if we just called it all off?"

"No," Esvar and I said in unison.

For once, we actually agreed strongly on something.

"You both want to date me?" She bit down on the tip of her thumb, contemplating.

'Yes," we said again firmly.

"But how will it work?"

Esvar glanced at me like one would look at a puss-sucking leech—repulsive but useful for a specific purpose.

"You admitted you liked us both," he said to Ana. "Maybe you can give us both an equal opportunity then? This way, no feelings will be hurt, since we both would have an equal chance to woo you."

"To *woo* me?" She smiled, casting her gaze down.

To woo her?

Who spoke like that?

Maybe it was a Voranian thing?

Either way, if it helped me to have Ana to myself, at least for one date, it would be all I'd ask for. One date, with just me and her, without the irritating Voranian lurking close by, would be all I needed to "woo" her. That'd be my chance to win her over.

"Will you really be okay with the two of you dating me at the same time?" Ana asked, moving her eyes from me to him.

"Sure." I shrugged. "Let the best man win."

It wouldn't take her long to discover who the best man was. I wouldn't even need to do much. The dull, boring Voranian would dig his own grave. How long could one suffer his company, anyway?

"Esvar, how would it make you feel if I went on a date with Orin?" Ana asked softly.

He looked at me like he'd rather eat a bag of rocks than see me anywhere near Ana. But he cleared his throat and nodded politely.

"I think it is a fair solution for everyone for the time being. It will give you a chance to get to know each of us more closely to help you decide which one of us you'll wish to continue dating."

"What if I decide not to continue?" she asked carefully. "As much as I like you both, I'm not planning to marry anyone anytime soon. I'm not ready for another marriage and maybe never will be ready. I just don't want you to see me as your potential wife."

"Fair enough." He nodded again, with an effort this time. "Dating can be casual, I've heard."

"I'm good with casual," I assured her. "Sometimes things spark, sometimes they fizzle. The only way to see how it goes is to start going."

Esvar curled his lips and winced.

Maybe I wasn't as great with words as he was, but I got my point across just fine—Ana looked pretty relieved now.

"Sounds good," she said.

The worry on her face eased, and a light smile played on her lips.

"It's been an intense couple of days for you, Ana." Esvar took her hand again, cradling it gently between his palms. "You need to get some sleep before work tomorrow. I'll see you in the morning."

Bowing ever so elegantly, he placed a kiss on her hand, letting it linger just a moment longer than was casual or polite.

I had to give it to him, the man was smart.

That was an effective move. Both understated, well-mannered, and fucking brilliant, judging by Ana's reaction. Her eyelashes fluttered. Her lips parted. Her cheeks glowed with a blush, and I would've sworn her heartbeat increased its pace too.

"Good night, Esvar," she exhaled breathlessly.

The look in her gorgeous dark eyes was still somewhat dazed when she turned to me.

"Good night, Orin."

If we were alone, I would've kissed her. Doing so in the presence of the Voranian, however, after him kissing her hand, would reek of desperation on my part. There was also a slight chance that kissing Ana on the mouth so soon would earn me a slap on the face from her, which would sting even more when witnessed by the Voranian.

Instead of kissing her on the lips, I wrapped my arm around her waist and pulled her to me, whisking her away from Esvar in a half-twirl.

She gasped in surprise, resting her hands on my chest when coming to a stop. Her eyes opened wide as she looked up at me.

I left her wanting and wondering for a moment, then pressed the lightest of kisses on her smooth, light-brown cheek.

"Good night, my beautiful Ana," I murmured just above her ear.

I would've bet my entire fucking farm that the blush on her cheeks was all on my account now as she backed toward the bakery door, stumbling over a step on her weakened legs.

I watched as she disappeared behind the door, then I turned around and left, not sparing a glance at the Voranian.

Oh, it was on, *Esvar*.

May the best man win.

CHAPTER 4

I barely remembered stumbling upstairs to my apartment. The sensation of both Esvar's gentle touch and Orin's tempting kiss lingered on my skin.

I removed the silk screen in the light wooden frame that covered the niche in the wall with my bed and hung the screen over the entrance to the balcony, just like Natlea had shown me last night.

The bed frame was low, barely three inches from the floor. A stretchy fabric replaced both the box spring and a mattress. The lack of bulky bedding helped keep cool during the warm Tragulian nights. But it did little to help me fall asleep tonight.

I tossed and turned in bed, going over what had happened that day in every detail. Either of these two men would've been enough to make me feel lightheaded and thrilled. But two of them at once? I felt overwhelmed and giddy at the same time.

My head was spinning, and I no longer knew whose touch I

missed the most or whose gaze sent more tingles of pleasure through my body.

With my feelings being scrambled into a hot, messy confusion like that, I still believed that the right thing to do in this situation would be to call off both upcoming dates. Walking away from both Esvar and Orin seemed like a simple, practical solution that would eventually restore peace in my mind and my body.

Except that walking away from the two gorgeous men who begged me to date them was impossible.

After the messy breakup and an equally ugly divorce from Lucas, I didn't believe I'd ever meet a man I would feel excited to be with again. And now, I met two. I was already looking forward to tomorrow when I would get to see Esvar at work again. And the thought of traveling with Orin filled my belly with fluttering butterflies.

Maybe once I got to know them better, I'd be able to make up my mind and choose one over the other? There was also a chance that one or both of them would fall out of "like" with me, too, after spending more time with me.

Maybe things would sort themselves out eventually? Without my stressing about them?

I managed to fall asleep before morning and woke up barely early enough to show up at work on time. Our temporary office on Tragul was in a large empty building at the very end of town. Wide and windowless, I believed it used to house barn animals during the war and looked abandoned now, save for the glowing sign of Interplanetary Enterprises over the large double doors.

Fyna was in the office already, working on a couch with her legs folded under her in a comfy, relaxed position. Her tablet lay on the portable stand in front of her, with the tablet's screen extended into a large holographic display above it.

My heart skipped a beat at the sight of Esvar making tea in

our break area that was only partially concealed behind a silk screen.

How was I supposed to act around him now? Keep things professional?

I cleared my throat. "Good morning, Director—"

"Esvar," he corrected with a warm smile. "Good morning, Ana. Have you had breakfast already?"

"No, I..." From my shoulder bag, I pulled out the pastries that got delivered in my breakfast basket earlier that morning. "I didn't have enough time to eat yet. I kind of...slept in a little."

Memories of last night rushed me again. My hand tingled in the place where his lips had touched it. I remembered the warmth of his breath and the tickle of his beard.

No one had ever kissed my hand before, and I couldn't believe how incredibly sensual and also arousing kissing a hand could be.

I wondered if he thought about that, too, when he splashed the tea a little while pouring it into a cup.

"Here. To go with your pastries." He offered the cup to me.

I accepted it. "Thank you. But you didn't need to make tea for me."

"I...um, I made enough for everyone."

"When did you have the time? How early did you get here?"

Fyna laughed from the couch on the other side of the screen. "It doesn't take him long to get to the office. He lives right here!"

I remembered he'd mentioned that last night. But the building appeared to have only one story from the outside.

"Where do you sleep?" I asked.

"There's a loft in the back," Esvar said. "It's roomy, comfortable, and extremely convenient, since it's right here. The only downside is that I don't get any baked goods or sausages delivered to my door." He smiled.

"I brought you a sandwich for lunch," Fyna yelled from the couch.

"And I'll make sure to share my pastry basket every morning. It's too much bread for me alone, anyway."

"Thank you," he said, looking at me.

I knew that workplace romance was not only allowed but even encouraged in Voran. But staring at my boss right now, I suddenly understood with perfect clarity why it was frowned upon back where I came from.

What would happen if the attraction ended between us? Would I need to find another job? Because I didn't think I could continue facing my boss daily if the butterflies in my stomach died and the relationship between us soured.

I was not looking for a husband. But I suddenly wished that this warm, gentle feeling I felt when I looked into Esvar's vivid eyes would last.

"Well…thanks for the tea. I'd better go start on those files," I mumbled, clutching my mug on my way to an empty armchair in the corner.

Making myself comfy in the chair, I pulled out a crate of applications for our financial grants and started sorting through them.

The electronic communication network was still rather spotty in Ravie. As a result, people often preferred to conduct business on paper, deeming it more reliable. I scanned each application with our office tablet to input the data into our system, then calculated the optimal amount of grant or a loan needed, and made sure to keep the original paper copies, too, just in case.

The applications that met our preliminary criteria would then go to the committee for discussion, with Esvar having a major influence on the final decision about which businesses will receive the grants from his foundation.

It was tedious work, but I felt rewarded already just thinking about how happy the grant recipients would be to have the help they needed for their businesses to survive and thrive.

Every now and then, I'd toss a glance at Esvar at his standing workstation. This was the first time we had worked in the same room, but over the next two days, I learned most of his work habits.

He preferred a standing position to sitting and would often turn on the treadmill under his standing desk, jogging at a brisk pace while crunching numbers. Despite having what one would call a "desk job," Esvar loved being on the move. At midday, he would take a pair of headphones and a dictation device and go for a run outside.

He claimed that moving helped him think. And it probably did, because he'd always returned with the device full of notes to upload to his tablet. With all that walking and running, no wonder he had that firm, fantastic ass that had caught my attention back on Neron.

Daydreaming about my boss's butt couldn't possibly be appropriate in any world or on any planet, but I couldn't get Esvar out of my mind, and it wasn't just his ass that reigned over my imagination.

On his part, Esvar tried to keep a respectful distance, patiently waiting for our date this weekend. But things weren't the same between us anymore.

When he made me tea, he always poured some for Fyna, too, or for the other men in the office. But he never looked at any of them the same way he looked at me when he handed me the cup. He'd hold the cup just long enough for our fingers to touch, and he'd keep his eyes on mine to let me know how much our contact meant to him.

Throughout the day, I'd catch his glances at me, and I knew that as much as I was learning about him, he was studying me too.

All these little things made every workday so much more exciting. The tiny sparks of affection excited me and filled me with effervescent anticipation that bubbled higher with every minute until the weekend.

When I returned home at the end of my second day at work, Natlea greeted me at the bottom of the stairs to my apartment with a giant bunch of bright flowers.

"These are for you," she announced, thrusting the bouquet into my arms.

"Me? From whom?"

"I don't know." She shrugged with a smile. "I found them at the main entrance."

"But where are they from?"

"Judging by the look of them, from the jungle outside of the town. These are wildflowers, and the jungle is full of them."

I turned the luscious bouquet, admiring the bright colors and the rich fragrance of the flowers.

"They're gorgeous. But how do you know they're for me?"

"There is a note." She pointed at the rolled piece of paper tucked into the bouquet.

It had brief writing on it in Ravil, which I assumed was my name. I pulled the note out and unrolled it, but I couldn't read a word.

"Would you mind reading it for me, please?" I asked Natlea, who lingered, probably curious about the note too.

She nodded, taking it from me.

"'To the most beautiful woman on Tragul. Can't wait to show you more of our planet,'" Natlea read out loud for my translator implant to pick up the meaning. "Who wrote this?"

I sighed with a dreamy smile.

"Clearly a delusional man. I wasn't even 'the most beautiful woman' back on Earth, far from it." I shook my head. But the smile refused to leave my lips. My face warmed with a blush when I thought about Orin's cheeky grin.

"Is that from the same man who made you the Queen of the Parade?" Natlea asked.

"One of them," I quipped, running up the stairs. "Have a good night, Natlea."

THE NEXT MORNING, Zaen delivered my breakfast basket along with two round grass-woven boxes.

"These just came for you." He helped me take the boxes in and put them on the table in my small kitchen area.

Today was my first date with Esvar, and the butterflies in my stomach grew increasingly more frantic as the time of him picking me up approached.

After thanking Zaen and bidding him goodbye, I poured myself a cup of tea and lifted the lid from the first box.

A large, round piece of paper covered the contents. It was a note with a single line of text.

I cursed myself for not looking inside the boxes while Zaen was still here. Maybe he could read Voranian? Esvar's strive to learn Ravil language made a lot of sense now. I couldn't read either of the languages that people around me spoke.

With no one to translate it for me, I had only one way to read the note. I grabbed my tablet and took a picture of the note, then activated the text-to-speech function.

"The safe choice," the tablet's program read out loud for my translator implant to convey the meaning of the note.

Except that it still didn't make much sense to me.

What choice?

The safe choice of what?

Well, there was one way to find out.

I moved the paper away and lifted a beautiful long dress out of the box.

It was a floor-length gown but in the style of a summer dress with wide sleeves gathered above the elbows and a deep, ruffled neckline. The light, black fabric was printed with large bright flowers, similar to those in Orin's bouquet that stood in a vase in the middle of the table now.

I'd asked Esvar what I should wear for our date today, and he had told me not to worry about it.

The dress would be the opposite of "safe choice" back on Earth. It was too bright, too big, too much in every way for almost any event, especially for an art gala hosted by the governor of the country.

But someone like me wearing it in Ravie made perfect sense when I thought about it. It was made in the style of current Voranian fashion but printed with the colors of Tragul—a perfect combination for a visitor from another planet who wanted to show respect for the local culture.

Esvar was right; this would be a safe choice.

Opening the second box with heightened curiosity, I found another note in it.

This one read, *"The one you'll like the most."*

I smiled, intrigued. Did the cocky man think he knew me that well already?

Well, let's see.

I put the note aside and lifted the second dress. It wasn't even a whole dress but a long skirt that flared out from the hips down. My breath hitched at its beauty. Blush pink on top, it darkened to deep magenta on the bottom. The wide, shimmering embroidery in pink beads and golden thread stood out against the dark hem.

A matching top was in the box too. Sleeveless and cropped, it reminded me of the scarves that Ravil women often wore tied over their breasts. The top was pink with rich floral embroidery done in gold and dark magenta beads in a stunning contrast to the bottom of the skirt.

The colors spoke to me. The outfit was bright, but the cut was elegant. The two-piece design was clearly inspired by the

Ravil style of clothing, but the outfit was still unique, fitting for someone who came off planet.

I tried it on, then spun in front of the mirror, making the long skirt twirl and the beaded embroidery sparkle and shimmer in the sunlight.

"The one you'll like the most."

Who could've imagined? Esvar already knew me well enough to guess it right.

CHAPTER 5

ESVAR

I tried to slow my steps when walking to the bakery that afternoon, but my hooves wouldn't obey, making me practically jog along the main street of Tadolia.

My heart soared with the anticipation of seeing Ana again soon. I loved having tea with her every morning at work and loathed the weekend because I missed her every moment she was not in the office.

I ran up the stairs to her apartment and knocked on the door, my body buzzing with barely contained excitement.

This was a date. Not another day at work where I had to contain my affection for her. I was officially taking out the woman who'd been reigning over my thoughts every waking minute from the day we met.

Alcus Hecear didn't need to have that conversation with me about Ana. The last thing I wished to do was to hurt or even inconvenience her in any way. She said she wasn't ready for marriage, and I respected that. But I also couldn't miss or ignore the something special that had been slowly growing between us.

The door flew open, and a smiling Ana greeted me.

"Hi, Esvar."

"Ana…" I exhaled, getting lost in her brown eyes for an endless moment.

"You look…dashing." She bit her lip, taking in my outfit of light green pants and a pale-blue shirt with short sleeves.

It was hard to wear proper formal attire in the warm and humid weather on Tragul. Most Ravil men wore no shirts. It was impossible to find a proper shirt at the local stores. Luckily, I brought enough of them with me from Neron. A short-sleeved shirt from light, breathable material without a dress jacket over it would never pass for formal wear back home. But here, wearing any shirt at all was as formal as a man could dress.

"Thank you. And you…"

Lost for words, I slid my gaze down the delicious curves of her body draped in the rich ombre shades of pink—the color that suited her so impeccably well.

"I knew it." I grinned, pleased with her choice of outfit.

It fit her perfectly, and the color matched that gentle blush on her cheeks that I wished I could kiss right now. I wished I could do many other things to her, things that would include getting her out of these clothes.

My pants grew uncomfortably tight at those thoughts, and I cleared my throat, adjusting my stance.

"You guessed well," she agreed, stepping out onto the landing and closing her apartment door behind her. "I love this outfit. But how did you know I would?"

"I knew you liked the color. It's similar to the color of the dress you wore to the parade. And…well, I love how it brings out the glow on your cheeks when you look at me the way you're doing right now."

Yearning to touch her, I stroked the ridge of her cheekbone

with the back of my fingers. Her smile grew bigger as she briefly pressed her cheek to my hand.

"It tickles. Your fur." She giggled, and it was all I could do not to grab her in my arms and kiss her right then and there.

It was torture to hold back my urges around her. But the pleasure of all these sparks of affection between us filled me with thrill.

"Well, should we go?" She threaded her hand in the crook of my arm, and I led her down the stairs, then out of the building and onto the street.

I loved the way she buried her fingers in the fur on my forearm, as if searching for warmth, comfort, and protection, all of which I would gladly give her for as long as she chose to be with me and beyond.

I led her back to the office building where I had left our rented aircraft.

"Wow!" She whistled, running her gaze up the smooth lines of the state-of-the-art flying machine. "That's a nice one. Where did you get it?"

"I rented it. It was just delivered from the City of Ravie this morning."

It wasn't easy to find a Voranian machine on Tragul, especially one that wasn't battle equipment or an army transport. But I chose it for safety reasons. I wanted a safe, reliable, familiar aircraft to fly the most precious-to-me woman on our first date.

"I'll keep it for the duration of our stay on Tragul," I said. "In addition to the transportation we already arranged to fly us to the meetings with applicants. It helps to have transportation readily available if we need it."

"It doesn't hurt that it's probably the prettiest aircraft on the entire planet, either, does it?" she teased, climbing into the passenger seat.

"It's important to have a reliable aircraft." I took my place in the comfortable pilot seat. "It saves a lot of hassle and even money in the long run. It's also considerably faster. The flight to the City of Ravie should only take us about forty minutes."

Sadly, the Ravil regulations didn't allow for an entirely hands-free flying mode. Otherwise, I would've held her hand for the entire flight. I would've loved to do more than just hold her hand, but there was a certain pleasure in taking things slow too.

Shortly after we took off, her purse buzzed. She took out her portable tablet and unrolled the screen.

"The signal must be good up here," she muttered. "I got a message."

"Who is it from?" I asked, worried if something happened to anyone on our team.

"Lucas," she groaned under her breath.

"Who?"

"My ex-husband. He's been an ex for about a year now, but still doesn't seem to grasp the fact that I'm no longer in charge of his existence."

"Were you in charge of that before?" I asked, curious about what marriage really meant back on her planet.

She rested her gaze on me with a smile.

"You're so adorable," she said softly, as if to herself. "Look." She showed me her tablet with a message written in a language I couldn't read. "He's asking me where the water shutoff is in the house because his kitchen faucet broke." She rolled the tablet up again, then dropped it back into her purse. "He knows it takes several days or sometimes weeks for me to get messages from Earth. By now, he's either already drowned in the house flood or put on his big-boy pants and called a plumber. Either way, there's nothing I can do for him, but he still does this to me all the time. It's like compulsory for him or something. If anything goes wrong in his life, he calls me to the rescue before he even manages to process a single logical thought."

"Like a small child calls for their father," I said, trying to remember the last time I needed someone else to solve my problems. It was probably when I was a toddler and couldn't reach something because of my limited height at the time.

"Exactly!" She slapped her knee. "He might've accepted I'm no longer his wife, but he obviously believes I will forever be his mother." She shook her head in frustration. "I should probably just block him. But a part of me worries that he may get himself into a dangerous situation when he'd only have one chance to call someone, and he'd call me out of habit, and I wouldn't be there to save him..." Her voice trailed off, then she exhaled a brief laugh. "I guess that's only enabling him on my part, isn't it?"

"Sounds like it," I said carefully.

I didn't want to be judgmental, but the easiest way to deal with an irritating issue is to remove the cause of irritation, which would be her ex in this situation.

She seemed to mull it over for a while, silently gazing out the window at the landscape of the Tragulian jungle stretching below. The vivid colors of the local plant life would never cease to amaze me, and they seemed to fascinate her too.

"I can see why you fell in love with this planet, Esvar," she said softly.

"It was easy." I agreed, admiring the delicate outline of her profile against the brilliant azure-blue sky behind the transparent hull of the aircraft.

It felt even easier for me to fall in love with her. The hard part was keeping my feelings to myself.

THE BUILDING that the City of Ravie had allocated for the art gallery was just outside of the city center. It was a one-story, sprawling construction of log walls and a clay roof. Its many walls had large floor-to-ceiling windows cut in them. All the windows were currently opened, their white curtains billowing in the afternoon breeze.

We left the aircraft in the field nearby, next to those used by the other guests of the gallery.

"Welcome," a Ravil woman greeted us at the entrance with a tray of tall glasses filled with golden liquid. "Would you like some honey-flower wine?"

"Thank you." Ana took a glass.

I took one too, just to be polite, then leaned to Ana's ear.

"The carved columns at the entrance," I said to her quietly, "are historical artifacts from about ten thousand years ago."

"Really?" She whipped around to look back at the columns.

The ancient wood had hardened and darkened over time, absorbing the minerals from the ground where it had lain buried before being discovered by archaeologists.

"The carvings are so detailed," Ana marveled.

"The people of Tragul have always been great artisans. Their skills have only improved with time."

I'd already seen most of the exhibits in other galleries, museums, and even storefronts in the post-war towns where they had been kept safe before being brought here. It felt good to see them all assembled under one roof at last.

As Ana sipped her wine, browsing from one display to another, I watched her, soaking in every detail about this woman.

She glanced at me, catching me staring.

"How do you like the wine?" I asked.

"It's lovely." She licked her lips. "But syrupy sweet. I think it may be better served over ice."

"I'll get some ice for you." I made a move to leave in search of ice, but she stopped me by placing a hand on my arm.

"Don't go. I almost finished it anyway. See?"

She took the last sip, emptying her glass, then another woman with a tray took it from her promptly.

"Stay with me," Ana said with a slight squeeze of my arm.

Stay with me.

The words resonated through my chest with a rush of thrill. She had no idea how much I wished to stay with her. Now and forever.

I let her thread her hand around my arm as I bent it at the elbow. Pleasure tingled over my skin as she dug her fingers in the fur on my forearm in a now familiar gesture, as if we'd already spent long years side-by-side like this.

"Are you going to drink your wine?" She asked with a smile, pointing at the untouched glass in my hand.

"No," I confessed. "I really don't like it. I just took it to be polite."

She laughed.

"Your good manners cost you comfort, Esvar. Here. Let me help you with it." She took the glass from me and took a sip. "It's growing on me. It's sweet, but I like the flavor."

We browsed the gallery together. She asked questions, and I told her what I knew about each piece. Finally, she paused at the last exhibit—a wall mural of *fescods* taking over a Ravil town.

It was a dramatic piece with the *fescods* crushing buildings under their large bodies as they rolled through the streets. Horror on the faces of people running away—mostly women and children because the men had long gone to war. Women carrying babies away. Small children taking a stance against the much larger and more brutal enemy that the viewer already knew they would not defeat on their own.

"It's horrible..." Ana exhaled in a half-whisper.

"It's real," I said. "The artist is a young woman who barely survived the attack on her hometown. She painted this on a wall of a building crushed by *fescods* the morning after the attack.

She wanted this memory to live on as a warning because we often take peace for granted. "

"Are there any *fescods* left on Tragul?" Ana asked.

"There are some. But since their central mind has been destroyed, they are incapable of organizing into an army. Individually, they tend to stay away from cities and towns out of their inherent dislike for structures."

"They don't like structures?"

I nodded. "Scientists believe that the reason for it is that buildings or fences impede the *fescods'* ability to move freely, triggering their rage for destruction. Built as blobs of flesh with no legs to elevate them over obstacles, they prefer flat surfaces as their habitat."

A shudder ran across Ana's shoulders as she studied the mural.

"They're such repulsive creatures."

I shared that sentiment. Fortunately, I'd never come face to face with a *fescod*, but I'd heard enough stories about them to despise them with all my heart. Destroying their central mind might've diminished their potential for global destruction, but their individual viciousness remained. They were the only wild predators I knew who killed for the sake of murder.

Ana and I left the gallery building, walking out onto the lawn outside. Long tables covered with brightly colored tablecloths were set for dinner here, with a band playing a merry tune nearby.

People gathered along the tables, having drinks and chatting. I recognized Governor Eehie in one of the groups.

"We should go say hi and thank Governor Eehie for his invitation," I said to Ana.

But the governor had already spotted us.

"Esvar Rotymus!" He rushed to us with a wide smile on his face, but his attention quickly switched from me to Ana. "I did not realize *who* your guest would be. Welcome, Madame Ana Hilal!"

He gave Ana a big hug.

"You know my name?" She beamed, looking a little stunned.

"Of course I do! It's always an honor to welcome a human woman in Ravie," the governor gushed. "Please let me introduce you to my family. Come, sit next to us."

He dragged Ana to the head table where his entire extended family seemed to have gathered.

"This is my wife, Madame Eehie. And this is my mother. My father…brother…"

After a while, I lost track of names, faces, or how they all were related, but the energy of the gathering was contagious. Ana smiled, shaking hands and sharing hugs.

"I feel like an imposter," she told me quietly afterwards as we took our seats at the governor's table. "Everyone likes me just because I'm from Earth. I did nothing to deserve such nice treatment."

Ravils were a generous, loving nation. But she was right, the fact that a human woman played a major role in ending the hated war certainly played into the enthusiastic reception that Ana got everywhere she went.

"Just accept and enjoy it for now. We'll try to repay their generosity with our work for the benefit of Ravie."

"*Your* work," she corrected. "You're the one who's been doing this for many months now. I just came along a few weeks ago."

"I wouldn't be able to do it without you and everyone else on our team."

After dinner, the dancing started.

"Come dance with us!" Madame Eehie nudged Ana, who readily jumped up to her feet.

"I'd love to—" her expression dimmed as she glanced at me uncertainly. "I'm sorry, but Esvar doesn't dance."

She sat back in her chair, and regret crushed me. For the first time in my life, I wished I could dance.

"Oh, no worries, we have plenty of men here who do. My nephew can be your partner for this one." Madame Eehie gestured at a young Ravil down the long table. "Come Isan, you're too young to sit with the old folks down there! Come, take Ana for a twirl."

Ana glanced at me again, and I had no choice but to smile and nod. I would never force her to give up anything she enjoyed doing just because I couldn't do it with her. But it hurt to see another man take her to the dance floor instead of me.

It stung to watch him put his hands on her waist. It made my heart ache to see her smile up at him, even if it was just a friendly, polite smile, far from the ones she had given me.

Voranian men had a reputation for possessiveness, deservedly so. But we also had the most practice in exercising control. With so many boys born for every girl in Voran, most of us had to learn to deal with rejection often and early on.

With jealousy burning inside me like acid, I mustered a calm expression and a serene smile while watching my woman being led in a dance by a stranger.

Fuck it.

The first thing I'd do after returning to Tadolia was find a dance teacher. I'd learned to read Ravil language just because I disliked the limitations of the translator implant. I can damn well learn how to move my hooves to music, instead of giving up Ana to someone else every time she felt like dancing.

The dance ended, and the young Ravil led Ana back to her seat, bowed politely, then thankfully fucked off.

"Was it fun?" I asked Ana, proud of my ability to resist glaring at the back of the unsuspecting departing Ravil.

"So much fun!" She laughed, her cheeks rosy, her chest rising and falling while catching her breath.

Despite all my lauded self-control, I severely lacked the

ability to resist staring at the swells of her breasts pushed up over the edge of her neckline.

"Were you okay here alone?" she asked, covering my hand on the table with her palm.

Her fingers raked through the fur on the back of my hand, sending a rush of sensations through my body.

I cleared my throat, spreading my legs wider under the table in anticipation of the erection that was definitely coming. In some very basic ways, Ana made me feel like a teenage boy again, waking lust with every touch. I barely knew how my thumb had found hers and was now stroking her, too, in response.

She grabbed a glass of water and took a long drink, holding on to my hand like to a lifeline.

"When would you like to leave?" she asked softly.

"Do you want to dance a little more?"

"No. I think I ate and drank a bit too much for dancing." She smiled. "The food was so good, it was too hard to stop. I'm ready to go whenever you are."

And suddenly, I wanted it to be just me and her in the aircraft again, when I had her all to myself.

"Let's leave now then." I got up.

We said our goodbyes to the governor and his family, then walked back through the gallery building and out toward the field where I'd left our aircraft.

Her hand was in mine, her fingers gripping it tightly. I'd spend the entire evening reining in my longing for her touch. Doing it again for the entire flight back to Tadolia seemed like torture. I had to feel her. I needed more than just a touch of her hand.

"Ana..." I stopped, facing her.

She looked up at me. Her lips parted slightly. Her breathing halted as if in anticipation. I leaned closer, and somehow...my mouth ended up on her lips.

I tried to keep it light and gentle, limiting it to only a slight caress of her lips, but she moaned softly, and I lost grip on reality.

She ran her hands up my chest and then behind my neck. Her fingers dug into the fur on the back of my head. Her body pressed against mine. And I dove deeper, devouring her. This woman was made for me, and I claimed her with this kiss, for now and forever.

My knees grew weak. My hands slipped from her waist and found the places I only dreamed of touching before. I gripped her backside through her skirt, then cupped her breast. Her nipple hardened under my thumb, and I lost control.

I groaned, drawing her into me. My cock instantly grew hard. A wave of lust rocked through me as she pressed herself against it.

"Ana..." I moaned her name against her lips, my voice raspy with need.

She leaned back, searching my eyes. I had nothing to hide from her, and she must've seen it all—my need for her body and my longing for her heart.

"Let's go home," she said.

She never specified what *home* she meant—mine or hers, but the promise in her voice was enough for me. It made me feel like I'd been given a pair of wings.

Hugging her to my side, I hurried toward our aircraft as if my life depended on the speed of our getting back to a room with a bed where I could do all the things to her that I had only done in my fantasies so far.

I barely remembered how we got into our seats and fastened our seat belts. Reality rushed me like a bucket of cold water dumped over my head when the aircraft wouldn't start. No matter how hard I pressed the buttons or yanked at the levers, nothing happened.

"Fuck," I cursed under my breath.

"Is something wrong?" Ana asked with concern, and I hated to see her worried.

"I'm sure it's just temporary," I said, not feeling sure at all.

When it came to aircraft maintenance, I knew how to find

the best mechanics in Voran. Unfortunately, I knew very little about how to fix anything myself.

"I'll take a look." I opened the door and jumped out.

I hoped it was something small, something that could possibly fix itself somehow. Maybe if I tried to turn it on and off again…

"Well, hello there, *Esvar!*" The sound of this voice felt like a punch under my ribs.

I winced, turning to face the last Ravil I wished to see tonight.

"Um…" What was his name again? *Orin.* What are you doing here?"

The cocky Ravil swaggered toward me from the darkness that had settled over the parking field by now.

"I had some errands to run in the city."

"Did you now?" I squinted at him.

Shirtless as always, he had on a short leather vest with pockets filled with tools, which indicated he'd been doing some work or was planning to do it.

"What a coincidence to run into you like that." He smirked shamelessly.

"*Coincidence*, is it?"

He leaned to the side to peek over my shoulder, and the fur on the back of my neck rose, sending a possessive growl up my throat. Was he trying to get a glimpse of Ana?

"Aircraft troubles?" he asked.

"Nothing I can't deal with," I dismissed, faking confidence I didn't feel.

"Orin!" With a slam of the door, Ana jumped out.

She sounded genuinely happy to see the cocky bastard, and my heart sank with misery.

"Hi, Ana." A wide grin split his face with a flash of his fangs.

She ran up to him. For one terrible moment, I feared she'd

jump into his arms, but she stopped short of touching him, though still beaming.

"What are you doing here?" she asked.

"He had some errands to run that he couldn't possibly run back in Tadolia," I explained, my words dripping with sarcasm.

"Isn't it fortunate?" the scoundrel mused. "Especially since you seem to be having a problem with your aircraft."

"We're not," I said quickly.

"Aren't you?" He tilted his head. "Because it's not flying anywhere yet."

"It's fine."

"Is it really fine, Esvar?" Ana asked.

I could pretend in front of him, but I couldn't lie to her.

I rubbed my neck. Something was undeniably wrong with the aircraft. Finding a mechanic would likely be very difficult at this hour. I didn't know the city well enough to even decide where to start looking. Sooner or later, I'd figure it all out, of course, and would have it fixed and running again. Meanwhile, however, Ana would have to wait around, growing more tired and uncomfortable.

Orin propped his hands on his hips.

"Well, lucky for you, I'm heading back home now. Happy to give you a ride."

"No," I snapped.

"Thank you!" Ana said simultaneously with me.

Fuck.

"If you want to spend the night here in the field, Esvar," the bastard gloated, "I can just take Ana—"

"No, that's fine. We'll both go."

It was *my* date with Ana, after all. Sadly, it was ending in a way I didn't expect and certainly didn't plan for, but I wasn't ready to part from her yet, and I definitely wasn't leaving her alone with this shady opportunist who showed up out of nowhere.

"We'll stay together." I took Ana's hand.

Orin followed my gesture with his eyes. Frowning, he watched as I laced my fingers with Ana's, then turned away from us.

"Follow me," he said. "I'm parked right over there."

He walked to the end of the field.

"No way." I winced as we approached a rusty, beaten-up clunker. "Please tell me this isn't yours."

Orin planted his feet wide, taking a defensive position.

"It may not look like much—"

"Like much?" I echoed. "Are you kidding? How old is this thing? It looks ancient. In fact, it should be in a museum. It belongs in that art gallery we'd just been to, not in the sky!"

Ana caught her bottom lip between her teeth, looking apprehensive.

"Does it fly?" she asked cautiously.

"Exceptionally well," the cocky Ravil boasted. "Looks aren't everything, or that shiny, new thing over there wouldn't be sitting useless right now, would it?" He flipped his thumb over his shoulder in the direction of my rented aircraft. "I guarantee you that my bird will take you home safely and without delay."

Ravil technology was significantly behind Voranian in many areas, including the mechanics and electronics. The war had delayed their progress even more. Orin's aircraft looked like it had been built even before the war. It had also taken quite a beating in the years since.

Its hull had corroded in many places and had been patched up regularly with materials that had often significantly differed from the original. The thick seams of the exterior were held together by fat, round rivets—an ancient technology no longer even used in Voran in aircraft construction.

However, I also noticed that no rivets were missing. All had been dutifully replaced as needed. The hull repairs seemed to have been done with care and focus on the essential maintenance at the expense of cosmetic and decorative improvements. This thing hadn't seen fresh paint probably since it left the factory it was built in, but it had been looked after in all the ways that mattered.

"Are you really sure it can fly?" Ana hesitated.

Orin came up to her.

"Yes, beautiful," he said softly, lifting his hand to her face. "I would never offer if it wasn't safe. I'd never put your life at risk."

He touched her cheek with the tips of his fingers, and I squeezed her hand instinctively. She blinked and cleared her throat, dropping her gaze.

"Well, we should go then," she said. "It's getting late."

"We should," Orin agreed eagerly.

I knew his type. His good looks and charming smile likely hid a slew of insecurities. He needed female conquests to feed his ego, and Ana risked becoming one of his many victims. I couldn't let him hurt her.

Ana deserved so much better than him.

ORIN

I fucking saw them kissing.

I didn't come to the City of Ravie to stalk them. I had a meeting with my *cirine* seed supplier, which didn't go that well, and I just had to see Ana. Simply a glimpse of her smiling face would make the world feel like a better place.

My plan was just to stroll by the gallery building without anyone spotting me. Deep inside, maybe I'd hoped that their date sucked and that Ana was bored out of her mind and ready to run from the Voranian. If it went even worse than that, if I caught him putting her in danger in any way, his horns would end up as a trophy on my wall.

What I saw, however, robbed me of breath and rooted me in place.

I saw her look up at him with an inviting smile. I saw him sway on his hooves, as if getting weak in his knees. And then, I saw their lips connect.

It started slowly at first, gently as if they both tested the waters. But it didn't take long for the kiss to grow more passionate and increasingly more intense. His hands strayed way past the decency line, and I had a dreadful feeling that she would've let him go even further.

A better man would've probably accepted the defeat, turned around, and left. But I'd been dreaming about this girl every night since we met. I'd been thinking about her every day while awake too. She'd become my one ray of sunshine in the hopelessness that had been moving in on me from all sides.

I couldn't let her go.

Fuck it.

I marched to the aircraft parking field nearby. It wasn't hard to spot the machine that belonged to Esvar. It was the only Voranian aircraft on the field, new and shiny like a freshly minted coin. It was just like him to show off.

What a phony.

Ana deserved better than him.

The Voranian was still tossing murderous glares my way, but Ana had already made her decision to come with me.

"Here you go, darling." I opened the passenger door for her to climb into my aircraft.

The old door screeched, making me cringe inside. I kept the aircraft in good condition, but it hadn't carried a passenger since the day I bought it. So I hadn't thought about adjusting the door to make it operate more smoothly.

Ana didn't comment on the awful sound, placing a foot on the first step of the steep ramp to climb in.

"Let me help you." I put my hands on her waist and lifted her in.

She smiled, grabbing my wrists. Blood rushed through my body, flushing me with heat. After days of dreaming about her, I was finally close to her again.

"Excuse me." The fucking Voranian tried to shoulder me away.

I was not in the mood to *excuse* anything coming from him.

"Sorry, bud," I said, closing the passenger's door after Ana. "There's no more space in the front. You'll have to get in the back now."

I swung the hatch open. I'd removed the back seats long ago, converting the back of my aircraft into a cargo space.

"You're lucky. I have a couple of bags with *cirine* seeds in there. The seeds are considerably softer than the *cirine* fruit that will grow from them next season. Hop in, Esvar, and make yourself comfortable."

He poked his head into the cargo space. "Do you really expect me to sit on those bags?"

I loved the uncertainty in his voice. It was pure joy to finally knock some snot off this overly confident prick.

"Unless you prefer to spend the night in the city?" I shrugged. "The closest aircraft mechanic shop is about forty minutes away. On foot. Not sure if you can make it any faster on your hooves." I tipped my chin downward.

His leg twitched, stomping a hoof that, I'd bet my farm on it, he wished to plant in my ass right now. My fists itched to fight him, too, but he held back, and I made the effort to do the same.

"I believe it's against the regulations to carry a passenger in a cargo compartment," he gritted through his teeth.

"It probably is," I agreed. "But what can we do? Leaving you here all alone would be heartless on my part."

I leveled a stare at him, waiting for him to stomp his hooves and walk away. He looked like the type who would deem it below him to board my aircraft in any capacity, but especially when forced to travel in the same comfort as a sack of grain.

If he walked away, I would have an hour to spend alone with Ana. My heart leaped with excitement at that chance.

Unfortunately, the Voranian must've also considered that, and the prospect of Ana spending any time with me didn't appeal to him. He glanced at her window as his frown deepened.

"Fine," he conceded, climbing into the back of my aircraft. "I just want it to go on record that this is probably the stupidest decision I've ever made."

"Aww, don't sell yourself short, Esvar," I murmured, not hiding my smirk. "I'm sure there have been many stupid decisions in your life."

One of them was the decision to go after my woman, asshole.

I patted his back on his way in, and he flicked my hand away with his tail.

"And watch those horns, will you?" I warned. "I'd just polished the ceiling in there."

I never polished anything in the cargo space, but the look of deep resentment on his face as he tried to fit his ass between the seed bags was priceless.

"Thank you so much for coming to our rescue," Ana said as I steered the aircraft back toward Tadolia. "It's such a lucky coincidence that you happened to be in the city."

Esvar stirred in the cargo area.

"Right, what a *coincidence*," he echoed sarcastically.

I turned the aircraft a little too sharply, making him tilt and scramble for balance. Keeping busy with trying to stay on the seed bags left him with fewer opportunities to stick his nose into my conversation with Ana.

"I'm glad I was there to help." I patted the controls of my aircraft. "This old bird has never let me down. Not all that looks pretty is reliable."

Esvar kept quiet this time. Maybe he was still busy trying to wedge his ass between the bags again, or maybe he had nothing to say in the face of his failure to get his fancy, shiny aircraft off the ground.

"What were you doing in the city?" Ana asked.

I scrambled for an answer. Ana had become my happy place, the one I'd go to in my thoughts to distract me from the gloomy prospects of losing the farm that had been in my family for generations. Telling her I'd been scavenging for *cirine* seeds all over the country for weeks now, borrowing and begging to buy the minuscule amounts that I still could barely afford just so that I didn't miss yet another planting season, I feared, would spoil the giddy elation I always felt when next to her.

"I come to the city to shop," I replied vaguely.

"For a new aircraft?" Esvar chimed in from the back, unwisely.

"Why would I need a new one when this one flies so well?" I shrugged.

"I wouldn't call it *well*," he grumbled.

I glanced over my shoulder to find him with his arms stretched out and his hands gripping the cargo straps. I pulled on the controls, making the aircraft sway to the right and sending the Voranian fly off the bags.

"See how well it handles maneuvers?" I grinned. "Remind me to give you the name of the mechanic shop I use. They may find you a bird that can actually fly, instead of just sitting in the field. Looking pretty isn't always useful for an aircraft, Esvar."

"It seems to work for some useless men I know." Esvar growled under his breath, climbing back onto the bags while holding on to the straps for his dear life.

"Are you okay, Esvar?" Ana worried.

"I'm fine, sweetheart." His voice softened and his expression relaxed, as if he were sitting comfortably in some tearoom with her, not hanging off my cargo straps with his ass swinging over the bags with *cirine* seeds.

It seemed Ana had the same effect on him as she had on me. She made even the worst of situations feel bearable.

I LANDED my aircraft in a field just outside of Tadolia.

Ana jumped out before I managed to get to her side to open the door for her.

"Thank you so much, Orin." She took my hand.

"Thanks for the ride," Esvar muttered, climbing out of the cargo space on his rather shaky hooves.

I had to give it to him, the Voranian had manners. After what I had put him through tonight, he had every right to punch me. Instead, he thanked me, giving me a polite nod.

Caught off guard by that, I ran a hand through my mane. Guilt rose inside me, unwelcome but real.

"Well, let me know if you need a lift back to the city tomorrow to fetch your bird," I blurted out before I could think better of it.

He gave me a suspicious look, clearly not expecting a genuine offer on my part. I pondered whether I should try convincing him of my good intentions, but Ana looked like she was about to bid me goodbye, and I wasn't ready to part from her like that.

"I'll walk you home." I shut the cargo door and offered her my hand.

That got Esvar's attention.

"Don't trouble yourself. I'll escort her home since it's still *our* date." He took her other hand.

"I thought your date ended with the fiasco on the landing field in the city." I couldn't miss the opportunity for a jab.

His beard moved as he flexed his jaw, giving me one of his glares that I kind of started to look forward to seeing. If he glared at me like that, it meant I must've said something smart or funny enough to annoy him, something he couldn't simply dismiss or ignore.

"Alright!" Ana raised her hands. "Either you both stop bickering right now or I'll walk home alone."

That shut him up, and I bit my tongue too. A moment longer spent with her was worth tolerating him.

The town's gate was closed but not locked. The tall, sturdy fence around Tadolia wasn't built to keep people out. It was constructed at the beginning of the war to deter *fescods* from taking over the town.

We closed the gate after us and walked down the main street, with Esvar on Ana's right side and me on her left.

She seemed content, walking between us. Excitement heated my skin under my fur when she laced her fingers with mine, holding my hand as if it was the most natural thing for her to do. Thrilled by that, I ignored her hooking her other hand in the crook of Esvar's elbow and burying her fingers into the fur of his forearm.

The town was quiet at this late hour. All the lights were off to preserve the scarce energy in our post-war country. But the stars were as bright as always, making finding our way to the bakery easy.

Ana stopped at the door that led up to her apartment.

"Well, thank you for everything. I had a great time, Esvar. And it was a real treat to have you join us, Orin."

I couldn't resist a triumphant glance at Esvar. I was a treat, an exciting, delectable dessert after the blunt, boring meal that was him.

"I can't wait for *our* date tomorrow." I leaned over and kissed her cheek.

A swirl of anticipation mixed with desire low in my belly. My arms flexed tightly around her, and my lips lingered on her skin for a long moment that felt tragically too short.

"Where will we go?" she asked, sounding delightfully breathless.

"That's a surprise." I winked at her with a smile. "I just have to ask you one thing, do you ride *marids?*"

"What are those?" She blinked, perplexed.

"You can't be serious, Orin!" Esvar stomped his hoof. "That's not safe."

"No less safe than riding *horses* on her home planet." Yes, I'd done some research about Earth and the customs of humans. That was my other reason for visiting the City of Ravie and its archives today. I had to learn more about Ana and the place she'd come from.

"*Horses* also aren't safe," Esvar insisted.

"I ride horses," Ana said. "My grandparents on my father's side had a farm in Turkey. I spent every summer there when I was a kid."

"You lived on a farm?" I stared at her in wonder.

Could she be any more perfect? When I thought I couldn't possibly like Ana any more than I already did, she said something as beautiful as that.

"Yes, I did. My father left Turkey to go to school, where he met my mother. My parents never had a farm of their own, but I dream about having one, one day. Maybe when I retire?" She laughed softly.

Now I imagined her on my farm, with a bright ribbon in her bouncy dark curls and a Ravil scarf around her breasts, her lips smiling and her eyes lit with joy as she rode one of my *marids* out of my barn...

Of course, for that fantasy to even have a chance to come true, I had to keep the *marids* fed and find a way to fix the old barn somehow.

"I'll be fine, Esvar," she said gently, letting go of my hand and placing both palms on the Voranian's chest.

He wrapped his arms around her waist. "Are you sure? *Marids* are different from your horses."

"All horses are different too. They all have their own personalities, you know? But I'm a pretty good rider. You don't have to worry about me, though I'm not sure if you're even capable of stopping worrying about others." She lifted a hand and ran it through the locks of fur over his forehead. "You feel personally responsible even in situations where it's not your responsibility at all. I love that about you. It's so new to me to find that level of responsibility in a man. But you can't manage everything for everyone. Sometimes the best thing is to let go and trust people to take care of themselves."

She spoke softly, caressing the side of his face. She talked to Esvar, but the tenderness in her voice reached deep into my heart. I'd give my life for just a few kind words spoken this gently to me too.

It didn't surprise me when he leaned closer to her. My chest tightened painfully when his lips connected with hers, but I wasn't surprised that he kissed her. There was no other action I would've expected from him after what she had said. I would've kissed the shit out of her too.

He kissed her for what felt like an eternity, and there was nothing I could do. I couldn't stop it without looking like a spiteful, insecure fool. I couldn't stare at them without looking like a pathetic pervert. But I couldn't leave, either, because I was so addicted to her presence already, I was willing to suffer as a sole witness to their kiss rather than walk away from her.

I'd like to think that he made the kiss last as long as it did specifically to make me suffer. But I'd be wrong. In truth, I knew I was the last thing Esvar thought about when kissing Ana. Because he would've been the last thing on my mind if I were in his place.

His hands ran up her back, pressing her to him. His tail

wrapped around her leg, the sneaky arrowhead tip slipping high under her skirt.

"Have a good night, sweetheart," Esvar cooed, finally ending the fucking kiss.

"Good night, Esvar," she half-whispered, looking slightly dazed and so deliciously frazzled when she looked at me right after.

For one terrible moment, I feared his kiss had made her forget, or even worse, regret my presence here. Never before had I felt so out of place, like they were a couple already, and I... well, I was just a pilot who flew them home after a date.

Then, a gentle blush colored her cheeks. A smile played on her lips that was both shy and sultry. And I would've given anything to know what was going on in her head when she looked at me while being held by him.

She blinked with a sigh, as if letting go of a thought she wished to hold on to.

"Good night, Orin." With one last caress on Esvar's arm, she opened the door and disappeared inside the building.

"Well, good night, Orin," Esvar echoed her words with a dismissive flick of his wrist in my direction.

I didn't miss the smug smile on his face as he turned on his hoof to probably head to some glitzy, posh place that cocky rich assholes usually scored for themselves while the rest of us struggled.

"Hey, Esvar!" I called at his back.

Maybe I wished to wipe that smirk off his face at all cost. Or maybe I was looking for a fight as the quickest and simplest way to deal with the longing tightening around my chest like a rusty chain and with the desire gripping my cock like a scorching hot pair of pliers. But I reached into my pocket and produced the shiny part I'd pulled out from the engine of his aircraft back on the field in the City of Ravie.

I didn't know much about all the fancy systems packed in that flashy aircraft of his, but I had figured out how to open the lid that covered the components of its twin engines, and I knew enough to find the part that he wouldn't be able to take off without.

"You'll need this tomorrow if you ever want to bring your bird back home," I said, tossing him the part.

He caught it. It took him a moment to realize what the object was. Then he slowly put it in his pocket and took a determined step toward me.

His self-control was admirable. Only his eyes betrayed his rage when he glared at me.

"You tampered with my aircraft," he growled. "You sabotaged my date with Ana."

"Well, to be fair, your date was what it was. I showed up only at the end—"

His furry fist flashed in front of my face before painfully connecting with my jaw.

What do you know? The Voranian knew how to punch.

I staggered back, barely keeping my balance.

One punch didn't satisfy him, however. He leaped at me, knocking me off my feet. I had expected him to attack me. I had wanted the fight. What shocked me was the ferocity and the skill with which he fought.

"You will cancel your date with Ana, right now," he gritted through his teeth, shoving his forearm against my neck.

Rage burned through my initial shock at that demand. How dare he?

"Not a chance!" I planted a fist into his ribs, making him groan.

I shoved him off me, but he hooked his hand behind my neck and yanked me to him, growling in my face, "You're not the right man for her. You're a lying, conniving piece of trash."

Indignation rose high inside me, fueling my rage.

"You don't know me. You know nothing about me!" I spat the words at him.

"And why is that? Why didn't you tell Ana anything about yourself? You had an hour in the aircraft with her on the way here tonight, and you wasted it on stupid jokes and useless chatter. You said nothing of substance."

My time with Ana was a reprieve. I didn't waste it. I savored every moment spent with her, drinking in her every glance and every smile. I took pride in my ability to make her laugh. The last thing I wanted was to talk to her about my depressing reality, which would surely chase her smiles away.

"Cancel your date with her." He pressed on my neck tighter.

I jerked my head, but he wouldn't let go.

"Fuck you!" I punched his arm and twisted out of his grip, climbing to my knees.

He shoved his fist against my jaw, making my teeth clank.

"Leave her alone!"

"Never," I grunted, fisting his fancy shirt on his chest. The flimsy material ripped in my grip.

He whipped his tail around my legs and yanked, making me crash sideways.

"I won't let you hurt her." He rolled on top of me.

"I'd rather die than hurt Ana in any way," I said sincerely, kneeing him in his side.

He howled in pain but wouldn't let go of me.

We rolled on the cobblestones of the main street, fists punching, feet and hooves kicking, tails whipping.

I ended up on top of him, choking him with his own shirt around his neck. "Ana wants a date with me, and I'll make it happen for her. I don't give a fuck how *you* feel about it."

"She'll hate you," he croaked, struggling for air.

Would she?

His words hit me like splinters of ice, chilling and painful. My grip relaxed, allowing him to draw a gasping breath.

"Is that what you're afraid of?" he asked somberly, catching my distress. "You're scared she'd hate you if she knew the real you. Is that why you don't talk about yourself?"

I shoved myself away from him, rolling on my back next to him and staring up into the starry night.

Fight left me. He could get up and stomp all over me with his hooves, and I wouldn't move a muscle to stop him.

I'd been fighting for every moment of Ana's time and attention. But what would she find if she gave it all to me? What could I offer her when I had nothing?

"All I know," I said, "is that I've finally found a woman I could spend the rest of my life with. I'm happy when I'm with her. And trust me, I hadn't felt truly happy since I was a kid. I didn't even remember what happiness meant before I met Ana. She makes this life worth living, and I'd be damned if I let her walk away without at least taking a chance to win her heart. You might as well kill me, Esvar, but I will not give her up."

I lay on the street, side by side with my biggest rival and most ardent adversary, staring up at the stars, as if we were camping out here.

Esvar rolled his head to face me.

"Where are you planning to take her tomorrow?"

I squinted at him suspiciously. "What do you need to know that for? It's not your business."

"Everything concerning Ana is my business. You sabotaged my date tonight. And I will end yours before it even starts unless you tell me where you're taking her. I need to know where she is when she's with you."

What an overprotective little prick he was.

"Are you planning on showing up there too?" I sneered.

"I'm not you. I respect the rules and Ana's wishes. But I need to know where she's going to be. And I swear if even a hair falls from her head while she is with you—"

"Starry Beach," I snapped, getting tired of him insinuating that I meant Ana any harm.

Starry Beach was the place of our last family picnic twenty years ago, at the beginning of the war. Father was still with us. *Fescods* were still far away—a serious but distant threat. My parents drank sweet wine after our meal. My sisters and I played in the ocean waves. That was the last time and place where I was happy. Now it felt like Ana was a part of that happiness too. She belonged to it.

"Ana is a grown woman, Esvar. You can't stop her from making her own decisions. And neither can I. She wants to spend the afternoon with me tomorrow. And yes, she can decide to dump my ass afterwards too." I sighed. "But it's her call to make, not yours or mine."

He stared at me as if trying to burrow through my skull and into my brain. But what I said was true, and I believed he was smart enough to figure it out too.

Finally, he pushed up to his hooves.

"Keep her safe," he barked, turning to leave.

"I will." I got up too.

He stomped away stiffly, tension visibly seizing his neck and shoulders. I doubted he'd get any sleep tonight.

I couldn't fault him for feeling protective of Ana. I even admired him for it. Under different circumstances, I could almost see myself respecting him.

That could never happen, however, as long as we both wanted the same woman.

CHAPTER 7

ANA

"How did it go last night?" Natlea asked me when I came down to the bakery that afternoon to bring back the basket in which my breakfast had been delivered earlier today.

"It went really well." I smiled as memories of my date with Esvar rushed through my mind with a burst of happiness in my chest.

"Are you seeing him again today?" She tipped her chin at the canvas bag over my shoulder and the straw hat under my arm. "Another date?"

"A date. Only with someone else," I confessed, feeling my face warm up.

She raised her eyebrows in surprise. Thankfully, the gesture seemed more teasing than judging. Not that it stopped me from judging myself.

I knew I'd done everything right when agreeing to this simultaneous dating arrangement. I hadn't broken any rules.

Both Esvar and Orin knew about each other. I wasn't sneaking behind anyone's back and wasn't lying to anyone.

Yet the feeling of guilt simmered in the background of my mind. One way to deal with it would be to choose one man and let go of the other. Except that I couldn't decide who to keep and who to let go of.

Esvar's kisses left me excited and needy last night. My body practically hummed with desire when I got up to my apartment. Even the warm water in the shower felt like a caress against my skin, arousing and exhilarating.

I remembered Esvar's passionate kisses, his hand on my breast, and the possessive loop of his tail around my thigh, and I longed for more. Unfulfilled desire had throbbed low in my belly, forcing me to slip my hand between my legs in the shower. But the moment I touched myself, I remembered Orin's large, calloused hand with his strong fingers intertwined with mine, and I imagined one of *his* fingers sliding inside me.

I jerked my hand away then, as if I'd touched a hot iron.

Imagining them both in the shower with me was the hottest fantasy my mind had ever conjured. Yet it also felt like a betrayal, like cheating on both men at once. It felt especially wrong because they clearly disliked each other.

Their mutual animosity was more than apparent. They barely tolerated each other, and if they did, it was only for my sake, it seemed.

"Who is the lucky man this time?" Natlea asked, smiling.

"Orin. I met him on Family Day."

"Is it the handsome fellow you danced with that day?"

"As if all Ravils aren't handsome?" I laughed.

"Some are more than others. That one is particularly cute, I'd say. Women were talking about him at the market the day after."

"Really? Why?" My curiosity spiked. Despite having seen Orin twice already, I still knew little more about him than his name.

"Well, they were mostly talking about *you*," Natlea admitted.

"What's there to talk about?" I dismissed with a wave of my hand.

"You're the first and only human woman this town has ever hosted. You were also the parade queen this year. People are curious about you, as well as about the young Ravil you danced with."

I didn't care to hear any gossip about myself, even if all of it happened to be positive, but I wanted to know more about Orin.

"What did they say about him? Isn't he from around here?"

"Apparently, his family is. Zaen and I weren't here during the war. But the butcher's wife said his family owned the *cirine* farm north of the town. She remembers them all from before the war, when Orin was just a baby."

"Where are they now? Still on the farm?" Orin never mentioned any of his relatives.

Natlea glanced aside as a veil of sadness crossed her face.

"No, his family is dead," she said.

"War?" I asked quietly with a hollow feeling in my chest.

"Yes, the war took his parents and his two sisters."

In Ravie, war wasn't a distant terror. Its tragedy had touched everyone in this country in some way.

"Does Orin have anyone left? Do you know?" I asked, my heart tightening painfully.

"As far as we know, no. He lives alone. But he doesn't come into town often. Only for supplies occasionally. He seems charming and friendly when he's here, but he doesn't talk about his life or his business with anyone."

I'd noticed that about Orin. Unlike many men I'd known, Orin was the opposite of self-centered. He never spoke about himself. When I asked him a personal question, he would always find a way to turn the conversation back to me or anything else rather than himself.

Zaen walked into the bakery with a pile of empty delivery baskets.

"There is a handsome fellow asking for you, Ana," he announced.

"See? Even Zaen finds him handsome." Natlea winked at me, taking the baskets from her husband. "Well, invite him in, Zaen."

"I did. But he has two *marids* with him. Are you going for a ride?"

"That was the plan," I said, putting on my hat.

Natlea seemed worried. "Do you know how to ride a *marid?*"

"I hope I do." I smiled, running out of the bakery with my heart pounding with anticipation.

"And there she is." Orin grinned.

For a moment, I could see nothing else but that wide smile of his with the cutest pair of dimples and a cheeky glint of his fangs.

"Hello, beautiful." He placed a chaste kiss on my cheek in greeting.

"Hi Orin." I cast a curious glance at the two animals he held by their reins.

Slightly taller than the average horses back home, the *marids* beat the cobblestones with their white, semi-translucent hooves. Each animal had six legs, dancing on them gracefully and impatiently. Their golden white manes and tails streamed in the breeze with a shimmer that made the animals appear mythical and ethereal.

"So, these are *marids?*" I asked, eyeing them with both shock and awe. "They're gorgeous."

"Ana, please meet Elet and Eca," Orin introduced them to me. "Elet is going to be your ride today."

He lifted his right hand, offering me the reins. I cautiously accepted them as the animal's big, guarded eyes studied me suspiciously.

"I don't think she likes me very much," I worried.

"Elet is a male. And a very mellow one. Unlike Eca here." He patted the other animal's neck.

"Is Eca a girl?"

"Yes, she is. A moody one too." He scratched behind the animal's short, round ear.

"Are they a couple?"

"I hoped they would be when I bought them last year. But it hasn't happened yet. Not for lack of trying on Elet's part." He snorted a laugh.

"Eca doesn't like him?" I lifted a hand and gently stroked my *marid's* long neck. His ivory-white fur shone with gold in the wake of my hand. *Marids* truly were magnificent animals.

"So far, Eca has adamantly rejected Elet's every attempt to claim her. I have to admit he's been rather clumsy with his seduction, and Eca has made it clear she wants nothing to do with him."

"Maybe he should ask you for help? You could give him some tips on seduction," I suggested teasingly.

"You think I'm good at that?" He moved closer.

His smile shifted from sweet and innocent to more sensual, almost sultry. Sunshine streaked his short silky fur with gold and made sparkles dance in his green eyes. A whiff of his scent reached me with the breeze. He smelled of something aromatic and sweet, good enough to eat. My breath caught, and my heart beat faster, sending a rush of heat through my body.

"Well..." I cleared my throat, gripping the reins of my *marid*, "As far as I can tell, none of your attempts have been clumsy."

As if to prove my words true, he slipped even closer to me in one smooth, graceful movement. Wrapping his arm around my waist, he pressed a sweet, gentle kiss on my cheek.

Just on my cheek.

I yearned for more, but he leaned away.

"I'm looking forward to our date, Ana. Very much," he said in a hot whisper just above my ear.

Our date had just begun, and I was already swooning and weak in my knees. Orin wasn't just good at seduction. With me, apparently, he was a true master of it.

"Let me help you up." He put his hands on my waist.

I really needed his help to get into the saddle, and not just because the *marid* was higher than an average horse back home. My mind was spinning and my legs felt weak after his kiss—the chaste kiss on a cheek. I could only imagine what kissing him in earnest would feel.

"How does it feel?" he asked.

It took me a moment to realize he was asking about me being in the saddle and not about the way his kiss had made my body hot and my mind reeling.

"Good." I shifted my butt to get more comfortable, then adjusted my grip on the reins.

He effortlessly jumped into Eca's saddle, then flashed me a smile.

"Ready to go, Ana, my fearless girl?"

Fearless?

I was a real mess inside when I flicked the reins, urging Elet to move ahead. It wasn't the *marid's* fault, however, but the Ravil's who rode next to me.

The *marid's* gait proved smoother than what I was used to, probably because of the extra pair of legs. The hooves thudded rhythmically on the cobblestones, and I got into the rhythm quickly.

"You're doing great," Orin praised.

"Thanks. I think it's easier than what I'm used to, actually."

"Are your horses more difficult to ride?"

"There is a little more sway in their gait, I believe. This feels more comfortable in comparison."

"Good boy, Elet." Orin reached into one of the baskets he had strapped to his saddle and pulled out something that looked like a long root vegetable curled into a coil.

He offered it to my *marid*. "Here, you deserve a treat."

Eca turned her head, flaring her nostrils as Elet happily crunched the vegetable between his tooth plates.

"Sorry, girl." Orin ran a hand through Eca's long mane. "You need to do a little better to earn the same treatment. You almost kicked me out of the saddle on the way to the bakery, remember?"

I watched his hand stroking the animal's mane and imagined it running through my hair. His fingers seemed strong but deft and gentle at the same time. I wondered how his touch would feel on my naked skin…

I blinked and forced my thoughts into a territory more appropriate for a first date.

"Where are we going?" I asked.

We'd left the town meanwhile. The *marids* trotted off the main road and onto a path that ran between tall trees and bushes with wide green-and-purple leaves.

"I'm taking you to one of my most favorite spots in Ravie and possibly the whole of Tragul," Orin said. "To the Starry Beach. Have you been to the ocean yet?"

"No," I gushed, excitement rising inside me. "I've only seen the ocean from the air so far but always wanted to see it up close. It's bright green."

"It is." He nodded, smiling at my enthusiasm. "It's only a short flight to the shore from Tadolia."

"I know. I always wanted to go, but I've been busy with settling in, and work, and…well, dating." I laughed. "Something I wasn't even planning to do on Tragul."

"Why not?"

"Well, I just got divorced last year. I feel content to stay on my own for a while."

"May I ask what disappointed you in married life?"

"Sure." I shrugged. I had no lingering trauma from my failed relationship, just some regret. "I don't have anything against married life, to be honest. I enjoyed many parts of it very much."

"Like what?"

"Being a couple. I like that—having someone at home waiting for me every night, spending weekends together, having someone to cuddle with whenever I wanted, and…well, sex was pretty good too. I do miss sex," I added with a brief laugh to cover up the awkwardness of the topic.

But if I couldn't talk freely and honestly about intimacy with the man I was dating, what would be the point in dating him at all?

"Why did you divorce?" he asked. "It sounds like you had everything people normally want in a marriage."

"Is that what you want in it too?"

He pondered my question for a moment.

"I haven't thought about marriage in much detail yet. But I believe that would be exactly what I'd want, yes."

"It all sounds good as long as it's with the right person," I agreed. "My ex-husband isn't a bad man. It just turned out that he wasn't the right man for me. And in a way, I was the wrong woman for him too. He needed someone to mother him, and I wanted an equal partner in a relationship. So…" I spread my arms wide, not letting go of the reins, "it didn't work out."

"Do you have any regrets?"

"My only regret is that I let it go on for too long. I didn't want to hurt his feelings by breaking up, so I kept trying to change the way I felt about him. In the end, it would've been easier on both of us if we'd ended it sooner. But I try not to look at those three years as time wasted. At least now, I know more about what I'm looking for in a relationship. How about you?" I asked in turn.

"Me?" He looked caught off guard, unprepared for the focus on him. "I…um, I've never been married."

"But you've dated, haven't you?"

Orin had more than just his good looks going for him. His playful confidence drew me to him stronger than a magnet. In addition, he was also kind and considerate. I couldn't be the only one who found him so irresistibly attractive.

"It depends on what you mean by dating," he replied evasively.

"The most conventional meaning of it, I guess. Two people who are attracted to each other spend some time together to see where it goes."

He glanced aside, taking his time before finally replying.

"No. The only kind of 'dating' I've had is the one where two lonely strangers get together briefly while one of them is on leave before he goes back to fight the *fescods*."

I fell silent, subdued by the realization of how different our life experiences had been. Even now, during the peace in Ravie, its tragic past was inescapable.

"Ana? Are you alright?" Orin bent forward, tilting his head to see my face as I dropped my head down.

"It's not about me." I shook my head.

"And that's the problem." He sighed.

I glanced at him for an explanation.

"That's exactly why I don't want to talk about my life," he said. "There's nothing light or cheerful in my past. But I love the sound of your laughter. And it kills me to see you sad."

"Life is not all about fun and laughter," I disagreed. "It's okay to share sad moments too."

He didn't look convinced but got no chance to reply. The trees parted as we moved ahead, revealing a bright strip of red sand edged by the lace of mint-green surf.

"And there is the ocean." Orin perked up, clearly relieved by the chance to change the topic.

Dark purple shrubs and soft grass descended almost all the way to the water, leaving only a narrow strip of wet red sand. The emerald-green water sparkled with the golden shimmer of sunlight reflecting in its waves. After kissing the land, the waves softly receded, leaving behind a lace of sea foam.

"It's beautiful!" I inhaled deeply, gliding my gaze over the enormous expanse of the ocean from the red strip of the shore all the way to the horizon where the green water met the cerulean-blue sky.

"Wait until you see Starry Beach." Orin gestured up ahead.

"What do you mean? This isn't the beach?"

He shook his head. "Not the one I'm taking you to. But it's not too long now. Are you hungry? Thirsty? We can stop for a drink and a snack."

I hadn't had lunch today, too excited for this trip to even think about food earlier. I could use something to eat now, but I didn't want to stop, not when we were close to our final destination.

"I'll wait. Let's do it."

He placed a hand on my knee, sending a wave of warm ripples through my body.

"That's my girl." He grinned, moving ahead.

We reached an outcropping of large, round boulders before dinnertime. They rose in our path, cutting off the grassy beach and spilling out into the ocean.

A tall tree grew between two terracotta-colored boulders. Its thick branches hung over the water, with their long, pale-blue leaves playing in the waves.

"This way." Orin moved an armful of the long ribbon-like leaves out of the way, revealing the narrow path that ran between the boulders.

"I would've never found it on my own," I marveled.

Orin nodded proudly. "It's hidden well, isn't it? Few people know this path exists. Many believe that Starry Beach is only accessible by air."

We followed the narrow, rocky path between the boulders. I focused on navigating it, keeping my gaze on the ground. When the boulders were finally left behind and I looked up, my breath caught in my chest in awe of the view that had opened in front of me.

The giant rocks descended into the ocean on both ends of the beach, forming a lagoon with soft waves that rolled onto the shore with gentle caress. The vivid palette of the vermilion sand, the mint-green water, and the bright terracotta rock formations was complemented by the muted shades of purple, blue, and pine-green of the vegetation framing the lagoon.

"How do you like it?" Orin looked at me with anticipation.

"I…I really love it, Orin. It's breathtaking. Everything I've seen of Tragul has been stunning. But this…this feels like a dream."

He beamed with pride and obvious relief at my reaction. Hopping off his *marid*, he reached for me.

"Come. We'll have dinner. I'm starving. I'm sure you must be too."

I propped my hands on his wide shoulders and slid from the saddle into his arms. But instead of letting go of me when my feet hit the ground, he hugged me to him tightly. I leaned into his large warm body, pressing my face to his broad chest.

His short, silky fur felt like fine velvet against my skin. His heartbeat quickened, thudding rapidly against my ear. My heart resonated with his, pumping blood through my veins faster.

I lifted my face to meet his intense gaze. My lips parted. With a hand under my chin, he leaned closer and silently claimed my mouth in a kiss, stealing my breath.

I gripped his belt as my mind reeled, spinning in a marvelous hurricane of emotions. Orin's kiss was soft, gentle, and incredibly sweet.

He leaned back abruptly, searching my eyes.

"It was…amazing," he exhaled.

"As I knew it would be," I echoed.

I often doubted things in my life, but not this. From the

moment I met Orin, there had been an unstoppable pull of intense physical attraction between us. I couldn't get enough of him.

Wrapping my arms around his neck, I brought him close to me again.

Hugging me tightly, he lifted me to him for another kiss. I ran my hands through his thick, short hair. Ravils often called their hair their "manes." And I could see why. Thick and luxurious, his silky strands ran between my fingers like a caress.

With my feet off the ground, I felt like I was floating. His hands explored my body. One cupped my ass, the other one slid up my back.

With a shuddering breath, he pulled away from me again, and I groaned in protest.

"I need to feed you before I fuck you," he rasped, shaking his head as if trying to get rid of the haze of lust that had descended over us both.

I was really hungry now, but I wouldn't mind the reverse order of those activities. It was a good thing that he could be the responsible one here, because when it came to Orin, I seemed to have lost all rational thought.

"Dinner," he said resolutely, untying a basket from Eca's saddle.

Reining in my desire, I helped him spread out a colorful, homespun blanket on the beach and set out the dishes he'd brought.

The food looked and smelled amazing. My empty stomach rumbled, making me grateful Orin had the presence of mind to call for dinner first.

"This looks so good," I gushed, making myself a plate.

It was new and exciting to have a man serve dinner to me. Normally, I'd been the one who'd planned everything when going on a trip, from meals to transportation to all the activities.

Tonight, I just relaxed and went along for the ride. And I enjoyed it immensely.

"Where did you get all this food?" I asked, spearing my utensil into what looked like a piece of dotted mushroom.

"I made it." Orin grinned, helping himself to a large slice of roasted meat.

I paused with my utensil in the air.

"You made all of it? These tarts too?"

I put the mushroom in my mouth, then reached for the meat tart.

"Yes," he said simply. "Do you cook?"

"I do. But living in Tadolia has spoiled me. With so much tasty food here, I haven't cooked once since coming to Ravie."

"Maybe we'll cook something together one day?" he suggested with a tilt of his head.

"We should." I finished the tart and took another one. "You have to teach me how to make these for sure."

"These tarts need to be baked in an oven."

"I believe I have an oven in my apartment, but I haven't really used the kitchen area yet."

"Not a regular oven." He shook his head. "These tarts taste the best when made in an outdoor river-rock oven, baked over *cirine* infused coals."

"That fancy, huh?" I took another bite of the tart, savoring its taste with a new appreciation for its complex flavors. "We should cook at your place then."

Usually quick to reply, Orin fell silent.

Did my lighthearted comment insult him somehow? Was it too forward of me to invite myself over to his place? I didn't mean to impose, but it felt like a natural next step for him to invite me over to see where he lived.

But he didn't do it.

Instead, he picked up a round pink fruit, then rolled it over his plate, looking lost in thought.

Eager to break the awkward silence, I took a long piece of vegetable wrapped in a thin slice of meat and took a bite, then closed my eyes in pleasure as fantastic flavors exploded all over my tongue.

"Mmm, this one tastes just as great as the tarts." I opened my eyes, meeting his gaze. "You're an amazing cook, Orin. Not that I needed another reason to adore you."

Delight spread over his handsome face.

"So, you adore me?"

"You're making it extremely hard not to," I confessed between bites. "I have a strong desire to know more about you, which is dangerous because the more I learn about you, the more I like you. So, you either have to tell me something terrible about yourself that would turn me off or...or I just don't know how to stop *this*." I waved a hand between us.

"The thing is..." he heaved a long, heavy breath. "I don't want it to stop, Ana."

"What if one day we have to? I mean, we have an unusual arrangement as it is. I'm dating Esvar too—"

"Oh, I'm not afraid of Esvar." He smirked, pushing up to his feet.

"I do like him a lot."

"But do you *adore* him?" He winked at me with a wide, disarming smile.

This was Orin as I knew him, using flirty banter and carefree smiles as weapons to battle the reality of life.

I enjoyed his flirting and loved his smiles. It'd be easy to just go along with the cheerful mood he was trying to maintain around me, to smile and flirt back, to have sex with him, which I was sure would be just as wonderful as his kisses. Then we would part ways with warm memories of each other.

And that would be it, wouldn't it? Because that was as far as I'd been planning to go with any man when I came to this part of the galaxy.

Melancholy filled me with that thought now. I no longer wanted just a light fling with Orin. I didn't want to think about parting ways with him.

"Let's go swimming," Orin announced brightly.

"Swimming? But I didn't bring my bathing suit." I got up too, shaking the crumbs off my skirt.

"You don't need it here. No one will see us." He took off his belt, then opened the closure of his pants.

"Um…" I raised a hand and quickly dropped it.

If this handsome man wished to undress, who was I to stop him?

He kicked off his boots, then yanked down his pants and underwear.

"Come with me." He propped his hands on his hips, standing proud and tall while giving me an eyeful.

I knew a beautiful man like Orin would probably have a nice dick too. But God…*he was* huge. Long and thick already, and he wasn't even fully hard yet.

As I stared at his impressive member, however, it started rising higher right in front of my eyes, swelling even thicker. The skin over his cock looked silky sleek, and I would've given anything to touch it.

"Come with me," he repeated in a very different voice this time—deep, raspy, and impossible to disobey.

As if of its own accord, my hand reached for the bow that tied the left shoulder strap of my dress.

I held no illusions about what would happen if I got naked with him. I wanted Orin, and I couldn't pretend otherwise. I wanted to have his strong arms around me, to learn the feel of his skin against mine, to have his large body move over me…

But I also knew it wouldn't be enough. Things with him had been flying at neck-breaking speed, and I had loved every minute of it. But my heart grew cold with fear that it might all burn out just as fast. I wanted him for more than just sex and for longer than just a few dates.

Orin stepped closer. His now fully hard cock bobbed between his muscular thighs, inviting and slightly intimidating in its massive size.

"Take your dress off, my beautiful girl," he murmured, but didn't help me, waiting for me to either get out of my clothes on my own or ask him for help.

I did neither. Holding the end of the wide ribbon that served as my left shoulder strap, I met his eyes.

"Let's make a deal," I said.

He lifted an eyebrow in surprise. "What kind of deal?"

Orin was only twenty-six, a year younger than me, but he'd been through a lifetime worth of pain and suffering already. I needed to know what sorrows he was hiding behind those smiling green eyes of his. What if I could help him somehow? What if I could make his life better in a long-lasting, meaningful way?

If only he would open up to me, but he'd been evading or deflecting all my questions so far. Bribery was the one tactic I hadn't tried yet.

"I'll take off a piece of clothing for every question you answer," I said.

A guarded expression fell over his eyes. "What kind of questions?"

"That'll be up to me what questions to ask. But you'll have to answer them all if you want me naked. Deal?" I yanked at the ribbon, untying the bow.

ORIN

The little vixen wasn't playing fair.

She dropped the ribbon that held up her dress on the left side, and I caught a glimpse of white lace—her undergarment.

Like the Voranians, humans covered their bodies in several layers of clothing, even in the warm climate of Ravie that required no clothing at all. On Ana, all these layers had a peculiar effect on me.

Women in Ravie normally wore only skirts. Some also tied a scarf around their breasts. I'd seen plenty of topless women in my lifetime. I'd never seen one who'd wear more than one layer of fabric on her torso. I would give anything to see Ana naked, but just glimpsing the layer of clothing she wore under her dress sent a rush of heat to my groin.

Fucking unbelievable, but I found myself lusting after the scrap of white lace peeking from under her neckline.

She intercepted my lustful stare and licked her lips.

"Do we have a deal, Orin?"

She could easily tie me up with that strip of lace right now and do whatever the fuck she wished with me, and I wouldn't be able to say no to anything.

"Yes," I croaked. "We have a deal."

Her chest rose with a deep breath, hypnotizing me with the swell of her full breasts above the constraint of that fucking lace.

"Good," she said. "First question. What kind of farm do you have?"

"*Cirine*. We grow *cirine* fruit."

This one wasn't hard to answer, but I sensed the questions might get worse with time.

And I was right.

"We?" Ana tilted her head, catching my slip-up. "Is there anyone else living on the farm with you?"

"I answered one question already. You owe me a piece of clothing." I tipped my chin at her dress.

With a wicked smirk like a villainess, she let go of the ribbon on her shoulder and untied the scarf holding her hair instead.

"Here you go. A deal is a deal." She dropped the scarf onto our picnic blanket.

I groaned in disappointment, running an assessing stare down her figure. A pair of sandals, two hoop earrings, a wide colorful bangle on each wrist... I sighed. A long night of questioning lay ahead of me.

She got hold of the ribbon over her right shoulder again, however, giving me new hope.

"Who lives with you on the farm, Orin? Who do you have in your life?"

Was it one question or two?

What did it matter? The answer was the same.

"No one," I said. My voice came out distant and hollow as I stepped away from her and toward the ocean.

It wasn't working. The date I'd planned so carefully had gone off track, heading for a disaster.

I'd tried so hard to keep it light because I saw how much she liked that about me. Ana always seemed to be so perfectly attuned to my moods. She easily responded to my smiles, and I wanted to keep it that way. But she decided to dig deeper, and now...

"I have no one, Ana. They're all dead. Is that what you wanted to hear?" I jogged down to the water. Alone.

"Orin. Wait!"

She yanked on the ribbon, untied it, and hastily got out of her clothes. All of them. She toed off her shoes and even dropped the bangles onto the blanket.

"Wait." She caught up with me in the water. "I won't push it, Orin. I don't want to pry. But I do want to know more about you. You don't have to talk about your past if it's painful. Tell me about the present. Or about your plans for the future. I'll take anything. Please."

My present was rather grim, my future bleak and uncertain. I really had nothing exciting to tell her about myself.

"Or just tell me anything you feel comfortable sharing with me at all." She wouldn't give up on me. "Anything. No matter how small. Like, what's your favorite food? Or color? What music do you like? Or what other dances do you know, besides the one you've taught me?"

I waded into the ocean up to my waist and stopped because the water reached up to her breasts here. I wrapped an arm around her to keep her safe in the waves, as small and gentle as they were here in the lagoon.

I didn't want to push her away with my silence or even worse—gruffness. I knew it wasn't just idle curiosity on her part. Her interest came from a good place. I should feel flattered and eager to share my world with her...if only there were something pleasant to share.

"*Ozeah* shell," I said tentatively.

"What is that?" she asked.

"My favorite food. I love baked mollusk in *ozeah* shell. But it's best when cooked right before eating it. I couldn't make it in advance to bring it for dinner tonight."

I looked at her, holding her to me. She deserved much better than what I could give her. She deserved everything. But I couldn't let go of her. I needed her more than air.

"You are my sunshine, Ana. My one ray of light. My one true happiness. And I want to be that for you too. Except that all I have to give right now is darkness, hopelessness, and despair. It's not fair. Not fair to you."

"You don't need to put on a brave face for my sake," she

implored. "I'm in a very good place right now, both physically and emotionally. So good that maybe I could take some of your burden off you? Share it with me, and maybe you'll feel a little lighter too?"

She was an incredible woman, more than I could've ever imagined. I didn't deserve her, but I would not give her up. I just couldn't.

I lifted her in my arms, taking a step deeper into the warm water. The vastness of the ocean was soothing. It made every problem look smaller in comparison. But it couldn't dwarf the huge, all-consuming feeling I held for Ana.

I nuzzled her hair. The ocean spray dampened her curls, weighing them down. Her naked body pressed against mine, warming my skin and my heart.

"I live alone," I said, unsure how far I would go but willing to at least try it with her. "All of my family died in the war, every single one of them. Dad went to fight the *fescods* soon after the war started. He never came back, and I hardly remember him at all. At fourteen, I joined a civilian resistance unit and left Tadolia. Things were relatively calm here, and I thought the *real* war was out there somewhere. I wanted to make a difference, to fight, to avenge my father. So I left the farm and my mother with my two sisters. But the thing about war is that it spreads everywhere, leaving no place safe."

I sighed, and she leaned her head against my chest. She hadn't said a word, but I felt her support and her affection, and it was enough.

"The war came to Tadolia too. *Fescods* attacked our farm first, destroying most of it and killing my mother and sisters."

"Orin, I'm sorry..." She wrapped her arms around my middle, holding me tightly.

This was the first time I'd spoken about my family to anyone. I'd always believed that even mentioning them out loud would destroy me, that it would blow my mind to pieces. But

Ana was here, holding me and keeping all my pieces together for me.

"I said '*we* grow *cirine*,' because I still can't think of the farm as just mine when it had always been ours. It belongs to my family. All of us. Even now, when I'm in the fields, I still feel their presence. But they aren't there, and that makes the place feel abandoned, even with me living in it."

She listened, and I didn't know how to handle it. Where did we go from here? Things were no longer the same between us. I feared they would never be the same.

It would've been so much easier if we'd just remained strangers who came together for sex and some fun. But we had moved past that point now. And it felt beautiful and poignant, but also so much more complicated.

How was I supposed to act around her now when I didn't feel like joking and smiling?

What could I say if I couldn't tease or flirt?

Thankfully, she didn't look like she expected me to do anything. She didn't say anything either, simply sliding a hand up my chest. It was a soft, gentle caress that said more than words ever could.

She was here for me.

She accepted me.

She wanted me.

Needing her closer, I lifted her higher in my arms. She cupped my face, peering deep into my eyes, as if trying to glance into my heart.

"You're not alone, Orin. I'm with you."

Those few simple words meant more than anything I'd heard from anyone in years. And they undid me.

"Don't ever leave me," I exhaled before taking her mouth in a kiss.

She didn't just kiss me back. It felt like she gave me air to breathe and a new reason to live. She was my sunshine, and I felt certain she could become my *everything*.

I carried her out of the water, swept the containers with food aside and laid her down onto the blanket.

She deserved everything in this world—all the nice, beautiful, expensive things. But I couldn't give her things. All I could do was just love her, and I would love her more than anyone ever did.

Tearing my mouth away from hers, I kissed the side of her neck, then along her collarbone and further down between her breasts.

She moaned sweetly, arching her back and stretching, basking in my affection like in sunshine, and I vowed to leave no part of her un-kissed.

"Tell me how you like it, my gorgeous," I murmured, cupping her breast. "Tell me what you want, and I'll do it. I'll do anything."

Kissing her right breast, I stroked the tight bud of her left nipple with my thumb, eliciting another soft moan from her lips.

"It feels so good, Orin…"

Lost in her scent and her body, I stroked up her leg with the tip of my tail.

She jerked and cried out in shock.

I did not expect that reaction.

"I'm sorry." I blinked, unsure of what I'd done that made her scream like that.

She rose on her elbows, giving me an apologetic smile.

"I forgot about your tail," she giggled softly. "I thought something wet had crawled out of the sand and up my leg."

Of course, humans didn't have tails. It was easy for her to forget that I did.

The fur tassel of my tail was still soggy with ocean water,

which surely didn't feel particularly pleasant when dragged over Ana's bare skin.

"Tell me if this is better." Moving my tail aside, I shook the water out of it the best I could.

"Oh my God, I've never seen anyone doing it before!" She laughed unexpectedly. "It looks so adorable. Shake it again. Please?"

"You like it?" I stared at her in amusement. Her laughter had already become my most favorite sound in the universe. I'd do anything to hear it again and again.

Lucky for me, it didn't take much to make this happy girl laugh. I shook my tail again for her. The wet tassel of fur at its tip spread out like a spiky pompom.

"This is just too cute." She giggled. "I can't believe how much humans missed out by not having tails."

And just like that, I could laugh and smile again. Except that with her, it no longer felt like a shield or a mask that I usually put on to hide my true feelings from the world. With Ana, I genuinely felt happy.

Kissing her smiling lips, I lowered her back onto the blanket.

"Now let me use my tail to make you scream for all the right reasons, my beautiful girl."

I felt a shiver of thrill run through her body as I slid my hand down her belly. Wrapping my tail around her knee, I used it to move her leg aside, opening her for me.

"Orin..." she breathed out as I trailed my kisses down her naked body.

"I want to kiss you everywhere," I murmured against her skin. "I want to kiss every single part of you."

Her furless skin felt smooth and cool after our dip in the ocean. Kissing her left a hint of salt on my lips.

She gasped softly when I placed a kiss on her lower belly, just above the tight little curls between her legs. She did have fur, as it turned out, even if only this small triangle between her thighs. I parted the dark curls, finding what I was looking for—the tiny bud above Ana's opening between her legs that was the epicenter of her pleasure. I flicked my tongue over it, quickly turning her little gasps into moans.

She curled her fingers in my hair, and I followed her tugs, using them to direct my licks and nibbles. When she pushed her feet into the blanket, thrusting her hips against my tongue, I sucked harder, giving her what she wanted.

"Ohh…" Breath rushed from her throat.

Her body tensed. Then, with a long moan of pleasure, her muscles spasmed.

Needing to see her face, I propped myself on an elbow and replaced my mouth with my thumb.

Her eyes were closed in ecstasy. Her lips parted with the moans I wished to commit to memory forever. Her body writhed in pleasure as she rode her climax.

Then, the most gorgeous smile lit up her face as she peered at me through her long eyelashes.

I pulled myself up her body, closer to her face.

"Careful!" She laughed. "I think the container with roasted meat is here somewhere, and I don't think it's closed. I can smell it. And it smells delicious."

I found the container and its lid.

"Would you like some?" I asked.

She sat up.

"No, thank you. I'm so full. And…so happy." She hugged me around my neck. "You make me happy, Orin."

I vowed right then and there to make her happiness my life's mission. If only she would let me stay by her side for the rest of my life.

"Would you like dessert, maybe?" I asked, trying to figure out which of the jars and baskets that I'd scattered around held the candied *cirine* and sticky nut mousse.

Climbing onto my lap, she rubbed the tip of my nose with hers. "Will you have some with me?"

I cupped her backside, pressing her against my hard cock. If it got any harder, I feared it'd grow numb or fall off altogether. But it was a pleasure just to hold her like this, to see her eyes shine under the stars, and to watch the teasing smile play on her lips.

"I already had my dessert." I slid my tail up her leg to the place that I had enjoyed devouring so thoroughly just a few moments earlier.

She squirmed in my arms with a needy whimper.

"Are you ready to do it again?" I marveled.

"It's been so long since I've been with a man," she said apologetically. "And you're so good at it. I'm sorry but...I'm not ready for this night to be over yet."

What was she apologizing for? I wished for this night to go on forever too.

"I'm yours, sweetheart, for as long and as often as you want me."

Heat rushed through my body. Lust gripped my cock in a vise of tension. My thoughts spun in a twister.

I couldn't wait to finally thrust into her...

The roar of engines above us exploded through my brain at the same time as bright light slammed against my vision.

Ana cried out in horror, gripping my shoulders. I tucked her into my side, ready to fight whatever or whomever invaded our peace so abruptly.

"*Fescod*s frequent this area!" blasted from the speakers of the patrol aircraft hovering over the beach. "Leave the space immediately!"

"Oh, my God..." Ana pushed away from me in search of her discarded dress.

I grabbed the blanket, sending the rest of the food flying

from it onto the sand. After shaking out the blanket, I wrapped it around her as the patrol aircraft descended.

"Thanks." She pulled the blanket tighter around her shoulders. "What's going on?"

"We'll have to leave," I said as my heart was weeping.

Every minute with Ana was precious. We were supposed to have the entire night ahead of us. But now, it was cut short. I couldn't possibly keep her in the area if there was even the slightest danger to her safety.

Raising a storm of sand with its propellers, the patrol aircraft landed on the beach, a short distance away. A security officer jumped out of the aircraft and headed toward us.

Shielding my eyes with my hand from the bright light, I took a closer look at the middle-aged man coming our way. Like many security officers nowadays, he wore the Ravie Army uniform with Tadolia's town crest painted on his safety chest plate. I recognized him as someone I'd seen in town once or twice from a distance but had never spoken to before.

Hunched over under the blanket, Ana hurriedly put on her undergarments. I stepped between her and the officer to shield her from his gaze, since it didn't look like she wanted him to see her in a state of undress. Personally, I didn't care what state anyone saw me in and didn't waste time looking for my pants.

"Are there just two of you here, son?" the officer inquired, coming closer.

He slid a casual glance over my bare crotch. I shrugged, and he didn't request an explanation either of my hard cock or the lack of pants.

"Yes, just the two of us, not counting our *marids*," I replied, giving Ana time to get dressed. "Where about did you see the *fescods?*"

"We didn't," he said. "But we got a concerning call from Tadolia. It's best for you to leave."

That the patrol hadn't actually seen any *fescods* was comforting. *Fescods* were hard to miss from the air because they usually left a wide path of destruction in their wake when rolling through the jungle. Knowing well how dangerous those creatures were, however, I had to get Ana back home as soon as possible anyway.

"We'll leave," I agreed with the officer.

I found my pants and boots, then got dressed and helped Ana put the dishes into the saddle baskets.

The officer scratched his bare chest under his protective plate.

"Not sure why *fescods* would come to this beach, to be honest," he said. 'There are too many rocks here for their liking."

Since the destruction of their central mind, the individual *fescods* spread all over Ravie. They no longer obeyed any commands or followed any logic. Most still had sporadic rage outbursts, which made them especially dangerous. It was possible that one or two would ignore the rocks and roll toward the beach aimlessly.

Either way, Ana was no longer safe here.

I whistled for the *marids* that had wandered off under the trees in search of saplings to nibble on. Eca came back right away, with Elet trotting close behind her.

"Can you take a passenger on your aircraft?" I asked the officer.

"Sure." He nodded. "Are you from Tadolia?"

"Ana is."

Years ago, the people in Tadolia knew everyone in my family. But I no longer came to town often, and when I came, I didn't socialize much with anyone. It was no wonder the officer didn't recognize me.

Ana came to me with a packed saddle basket.

"I don't think Eca will let me strap it to her saddle," she said.

"That girl seems to have her preferences, and I'm too new for her to trust me."

"Thank you. I'll do it." I took the basket from her. "The officer will take you back to town in his aircraft."

She darted a glance at the man then at the aircraft. "Why can't we go back the way we came?"

I strapped the basket to Eca's saddle. "With *fescods* in the area, it's much safer to fly than to ride."

"But how about you?"

Hugging her shoulders with one arm, I pulled her to me and kissed her temple. "I'll have to take the *marids* back to the farm."

"But that's not safe, you said so yourself." She looked alarmed.

"The officers didn't see any *fescods* in the area, sweetheart. Trust me, those things leave a wide path of crushed vegetation that would be easy to spot from the air, even at night."

"Can't I come with you, then? Since they aren't really here?"

The thought of any harm coming to her—real or imaginable —froze my insides with terror.

"It's safer for you to fly. Just in case. Please," I begged. "I don't think I'd survive if something happened to you."

She gave me a long, pensive look.

The officer cleared his throat, stepping closer.

"I'll come with you, son, to make sure you and your animals get home safe and sound. I've killed plenty of *fescods* both during the war and after. If these things get in our way, it's better to have two people to fight them than one."

I'd killed plenty of *fescods* on my own too. There was no need to inconvenience the man. But Ana took his hand in gratitude.

"Could you? Please? It'll make me feel so much better to know that Orin isn't alone." Grabbing her bag from the ground, she rummaged inside for her tablet. "Give me your messaging ID, Orin, please. I should have it anyway."

I ran a hand through my mane.

"I'd love to, but I don't have network access at my house. I just come to town when I need to use it. I'll be fine, Ana—"

But my reassurances clearly weren't enough for her. She grabbed the officer's arm.

"Are you coming back to Tadolia tonight?"

"Yes, but it'll be pretty late by then."

"Can you message me before going to bed? Please? Just to let me know that Orin is okay? Or you can stop by on the way home, too, if it's more convenient for you. I live in the apartment above the bakery—"

"I know where you live, Madame Ana." The officer smiled. "You are the only human in Tadolia. My colleague will fly you back home." He tipped his head at the aircraft waiting nearby.

She returned his smile, but it didn't chase the worry from her eyes. "Thank you so much for doing this. I don't care how late you get to Tadolia, please, let me know he's okay. I won't be sleeping."

"You should go to bed, Ana. You have to work tomorrow," I reminded her.

It wasn't how I planned this date to end. It pained me to say goodbye to her so soon. Her going to work tomorrow also meant she'd be in the office with Esvar again. I had *cirine* to plant and wouldn't get to see her for the entire week.

I lied when I said I wasn't afraid of Esvar. The thought of him taking Ana from me terrified me, even more so because of how possible that was. He met her before I did. They worked together and saw each other every day. He was her boss, for fuck's sake. They already had a history together when I still felt like an outsider.

She looked at me with her large brown eyes.

"I won't be able to sleep unless I know you've made it home safely," she said, and my heart overflowed with tenderness and gratitude.

It'd been so long since anyone cared whether I was dead or alive that I'd forgotten how important it was.

I took her face in my hands and kissed her right there in front of the officer. I'd do it in front of the entire world too.

Fuck Esvar.

Ana had to be mine.

CHAPTER 9

ANA

The following morning, Esvar and I were the only people in the office. One of my male colleagues wasn't feeling well and stayed at home. Fyna and the other two men left for the day to meet with several potential grant recipients.

"Your tea." Esvar handed me a clay mug of steamy, fragrant liquid.

"Oh, thank you so much. I really need it this morning." I took it from him, hugging the warm mug with both hands.

He didn't leave, standing in front of my armchair in our office with a frown of concern.

"Are you feeling well?" he asked.

"I'm fine." I nodded, setting the mug on the stand next to my armchair. "Just tired. A little."

I hid a yawn behind my hand.

"Did he keep you up late?" He sounded calm, but I raised my gaze to his face, catching his jaw move in annoyance.

"It wasn't Orin's fault," I defended my Ravil.

My?

Since when had Orin become mine?

But in a way, he had last night. He asked me not to leave him. I promised to stay in his life, and I fully intended to keep my promise. I just wasn't sure in what capacity I'd be staying yet.

I hadn't planned it, but it happened. Orin and I had passed the stage of mere acquaintances. He would never be just a fling to me anymore.

Was it right of me to wish for more with Orin? I doubted it. Especially since my heart beat faster as Esvar perched his butt on the armrest of my chair and his thigh pressed against my forearm. The warmth of his body seeped through the material of his pants and spread with tingles of excitement through my chest and belly. I knew I should move my arm, but the contact felt comforting. I leaned against Esvar while remembering my night with Orin.

What did that make me?

I had no answer to this question, but I had a feeling it wouldn't be a good one. Dating two men while growing closer to both couldn't possibly end well for any of us.

"It was extremely irresponsible on his part to take you to the beach," Esvar muttered, drinking his tea.

"How do you know where Orin took me?"

"He told me."

"You...talked? When?"

These two clearly didn't like each other very much. There was my fault in it, since I'd become the reason for rivalry between them. But I had no idea they'd met and talked behind my back.

"Kind of," he dismissed with a vague hand gesture. "We had a brief...um, exchange after he gave us a ride from the City of Ravie. He mentioned he was taking you to Starry Beach for your date. So I did some research—"

"You researched the place of my date with Orin?" I gave him an unimpressed look.

"I had to make sure it was safe. I don't trust that man, Ana." I made a move to protest, but he quickly added, "I admit I dislike Orin, but I also know that he cares about you enough not to hurt you, *intentionally*. Unfortunately, he acts carelessly sometimes."

I huffed in frustration. "Esvar, you don't even know him."

"But I know his type. Orin feels strongly and acts quickly." He stretched his neck and rubbed his jaw, wincing as if from a blow or a memory of it. "He needs someone to think *for* him sometimes. And maybe...maybe he needs someone to think *about* him too. He doesn't have anyone, does he?"

My attention spiked, and my defensiveness faded. Esvar proved to be even more perceptive than I thought because he wasn't wrong in what he said about Orin.

"No. He doesn't," I replied softly. "All of his family is gone. Killed during the war."

He nodded somberly, staring pensively at the tea in his cup.

I thought about what he had said earlier.

"Esvar? Why was it irresponsible of us to go to the beach?"

He looked at me. "Not you, Ana. But Orin should've known better about the dangerous species that are still present in his country. Some studies concluded that the ocean still holds an appeal for *fescods*. The scientists speculate it may be because the *fescods'* central mind used to be located on the bottom of the ocean. As a result, remnants of instinctual connection to it may still pull them to shore."

I took a long drink of my tea, pondering his words.

We saw no *fescods* last night. I flew home with one of the patrol officers while the other one safely escorted Orin back to his farm. The officer then messaged me later that night to let me know that Orin had made it home without incident.

Even if the studies were true, Esvar's worries proved unwarranted in our case.

"There weren't any *fescods* there last night." I said. "The patrol saw nothing, even from the air."

"I'm glad to hear it, but I figured it wouldn't hurt for them to check."

"Wait a minute." I stared at him as realization struck me. "*You* called them! Esvar, were you the one who sent them to the beach?"

He shifted his butt on my armrest uneasily.

"I didn't send them, per se. I just called the security office to express my concern. They mentioned that someone reported seeing a *fescod* north of Tadolia just last month. They shared my concern about your being on the beach. The decision to send the patrol aircraft was entirely theirs."

I set the mug on the stand and got up from my armchair. Pacing the floor of the empty office, I tried to sort through my feelings on this one.

On one hand, I couldn't be angry at Esvar for worrying about Orin's and my safety. Luckily, no *fescods* came to the beach last night. But if they did, the consequences could be dire.

On the other hand, it felt too much like an intentional interference on his part to cut my date with Orin short.

I speared my fingers through my wild curls that refused to be tamed in the hot, humid climate of Ravie.

"We had an agreement, Esvar. All three of us. I was supposed to have a date with each of you. But…" I pivoted on my heel to face him. "I can't help feeling that you sabotaged my date with Orin, and that's not fair."

"Then how about him sabotaging *my* date with you?" He pulled something out of his pocket and presented it to me.

"What's this?" I stared at the smooth, elongated piece of metal on his palm.

"*Cloedian* pin. An essential part of the molecular engine that powers every Voranian aircraft. Only a certified mechanic can insert it properly, but apparently any arrogant, insecure asshole can pull it out armed with nothing but a misguided belief that the most amazing woman in the universe should be his."

"Did Orin do that?" I asked, dumbfounded.

Not that I thought of Orin as an "arrogant, insecure asshole", but it sounded like something Esvar would call him.

"Yes, he did. Now I have to wait for my appointment with a certified mechanic—of which there aren't that many in the City of Ravie, I must say—to fix it before I can pick up the aircraft from the field by the gallery where we left it."

"How do you know it was Orin?" I struggled to believe it.

"He told me."

"He did? But why?"

Esvar shrugged, shoving the pin back into his pocket. "To gloat, I'm sure."

Breath left me in a disappointed sigh. This was not how I had hoped our arrangement would go, but I should have expected it. Between Orin's hot-headed confidence and Esvar's Voranian possessiveness, rivalry was unavoidable.

"Except that none of it is about me, is it?" I pondered out loud. "At this point, it's just a competition for you two, a contest to prove that you can best each other."

"Ana...what are you saying?" He stepped toward me, but I shrank back.

"I'm saying it's all about winning at all cost now, with a complete disregard of everyone's feelings."

"What? No. Of course not. It's not a competition," he protested.

"What is it then if not a competition? A mean and unfair one too? Just look at what you two are doing? You're undermining each other. You're sabotaging each other's efforts. You're lying—"

"We aren't lying," he said firmly. "Orin admitted what he did. And so did I."

I tugged at my hair, torn on what to do here.

"The only way to stop this is to...make a choice?" I didn't mean for it to sound like a question. I knew that making up my mind would be the right thing to do. I just didn't have the ability to choose between the two men I'd grown to admire, especially when choosing one would inadvertently hurt the other.

I believed that both Esvar and Orin were good, decent men. It was me who put them in a situation that brought the worst in them. I pitched them against each other, forcing them to compete.

Guilt rushed me.

"It's all my fault," I groaned, burying my face in my hands.

"Ana, sweetheart..." Esvar wrapped me in his arms, and I leaned on him, soaking up the comfort of his embrace. "It's no one's fault. It's not a crime to date two men. Women in Voran usually date several men at once. It's the norm in my country."

"Have you been with a woman who had more than one boyfriend?" I lifted my face to his.

"That's the only way of dating I know. The Voranians eventually split into couples. But before marriage, a woman almost always is courted by several men and dates them all simultaneously."

"How do they manage it?"

"They make it work. It just takes time. And some patience."

I rested my head on his chest while he stroked my back in slow, soothing movements.

"It feels like the only fair decision I can make right now is to stop dating you both and try to repair the friendships that we hopefully still have," I said.

His hand on my back stilled.

"Trust me—and I firmly believe that I'm talking for both Orin and me here—that neither of us wants you to stop dating us. Stopping it won't fix anything. Why push us away from you when you long to be close? I'm sure that Orin would fully support me on this."

"How can you be so sure?"

"Because as different as Orin and I are, we have one very important thing in common—neither of us wants to lose you."

"But someone will have to. Can't you see? I can't possibly be with you both. Even the Voranian women end up settling down with only one husband."

He stroked the side of my face gently, then lifted my face to his with a finger under my chin.

"You don't need to worry about that, though, do you? You said you didn't want a husband, anyway."

"Right," I remembered. "I don't."

My thoughts and feelings had grown too intense lately. Somehow, both my relationships already felt deeper than they should be at this stage.

"I'm not looking for marriage," I repeated the words I'd said so often in the months since my divorce.

"Exactly. So, take your time. Let the feelings settle a little. There is no rush." His deep voice flowed over me, caring and soothing.

"There is no rush..." I echoed, repeating his words like a mantra. My anxiety settled. Guilt shifted away a little too. "I'm so grateful to have you, Esvar."

"You'll always have me, sweetheart, no matter what. I'll always be there for you if you need me. That'll never change."

I exhaled a long breath of relief, swaying a little in his arms. He steadied me.

"Are you feeling alright?" he asked, studying my face with concern.

"Just a little tired. I stayed up late last night, waiting for the security office to tell me that Orin had made it home—" I bit my tongue mid-sentence, afraid that my mentioning Orin's name might start another argument.

But Esvar just held me in his arms.

"You really should rest, Ana. Lack of sleep never solves anything."

"And who's going to do all the work with everyone out of the office? I still have a pile of applications to sort through." I pointed at the box of files by my chair.

He brushed an unruly curl of hair away from my face.

"I'll tell you what, why don't you have a nap while I start on this box? When you wake up, we'll finish it together."

"By the time I walk home, then back here again—" I started.

"You don't need to go all the way home. You can nap in my bed." He pointed up.

I followed his gesture with my eyes, remembering that he lived above the office.

But was it wise to climb into Esvar's bed when my feelings were so tangled right now? Even if he wasn't going to climb in it with me?

"Come, I'll show you," he said, taking my hand.

I followed him to the ladder behind the office kitchen, then up to the spacious loft above.

"They said this building used to be a barn for *marids*," Esvar explained, moving aside a wooden frame with painted silk stretched over it to reveal his bed behind. "Up here in the loft, they used to store dried shrubs to feed the *marids* when they couldn't let them go outside because of *fescods*. I think they did a pretty good job of converting it to a living space."

"I think so too." I admired the painted paneling on the walls, the homespun curtains on the two small windows, and the thick, hand-knotted rug on the floor. "It's cozy in here."

Esvar placed a folded blanket on the bed.

"In case you get chilly," he said.

It was a very similar blanket to the one that Orin had

brought to our picnic last night. The one that he placed me on to have me for "dessert." It was a beautiful memory, but I blinked with a pang of guilt. It didn't seem appropriate to think about Orin when getting ready to sleep in Esvar's bed.

How did Voranian women deal with all these feelings in situations like this?

Or was I the only one so flaky and indecisive?

"Have a good rest, Ana." Esvar placed a sweet, light kiss on my cheek.

I lifted my face to his, not pulling away.

He paused his gaze on me, his focus sharpening. I parted my lips, wishing and waiting but afraid to act on it.

A corner of his mouth lifted in a smile of understanding before he leaned closer to give me a proper kiss on the lips.

"Sweet dreams, my darling," he murmured, finally releasing me from his arms.

"Does it mean our next date is still on?" I asked, catching my breath after his kiss had stolen it.

"I sure hope it is. My first dance lesson is tonight," he revealed proudly.

"You're taking dance lessons?"

He nodded. "There's a country dance in a town close by this weekend. Apparently, it's one of the biggest dance events this time of the year. I couldn't possibly let you miss it."

When he left to go back downstairs, I stared at his wide bed. Instead of climbing in it, I decided to just lay on top of the bedding and use the blanket that looked similar to Orin's for a cover.

Despite these precautions, I still caught Esvar's musky, masculine scent when I laid my head on his pillow. Warm and cozy, I snuggled under the blanket as thoughts of both Orin and Esvar floated in my sleepy brain.

When the doubts receded and only the truth remained, I

realized that my feelings for Orin and Esvar weren't actually tangled. I wasn't confused, never really had been.

My affection didn't flit from one man to the other. On the contrary, it had been steady and firm from the beginning, unchanged and growing stronger with every day and every date.

It just had never been for only *one* man.

I liked them both.

CHAPTER 10

ESVAR

"Hello, Director Rotymus. Ana is upstairs. She said you can come up anytime." Natlea, the baker's wife, waved toward the side door that led to Ana's apartment above the bakery.

I ran out of breath by the time I reached Ana's door, and it wasn't from climbing up the stairs. I ran the entire length of Tadolia twice almost daily. It helped me clear my head and improve focus. Normally, I wouldn't even notice the few stairs in my way.

Yet my heart kept pounding harder and harder the closer to the door I got, and it had everything to do with the woman waiting for me behind it.

Breathless with anticipation, I knocked on her door, then noticed a large bouquet of flowers perched in the corner of the landing. I picked it up just before the door opened and Ana greeted me with a smile.

"Esvar! Come in." She opened the door wider but stayed partially hidden behind it.

"Good morning, Ana."

As I entered, I realized why she tried to hide behind the door. She must've just had a bath. The thick curls of her dark hair were still damp, and a bright yellow towel was wrapped around her body.

"Are these for me? From you?" She pointed at the bouquet in my arms.

"No…I mean yes. They must be for you. But I didn't bring them. I found them by the door."

Why the fuck did I not think about bringing her flowers? It'd be so fitting—beautiful flowers for an even more beautiful woman. But back on Neron, men usually gifted women dresses or jewelry. So, I brought her a pair of pretty hair combs that I thought she'd like to have for her gorgeous, voluminous hair.

"Here, I hope you'll like these." I handed her the velvet pouch with the combs.

"What's this?" She took the pouch, untied the ribbon, and took out one of the combs carved from a translucent pink mineral and set with colorful gems. "Wow, this is beautiful. Too beautiful. Esvar… I'm not sure I should accept such presents from you."

I blinked at her in confusion.

"Why not? Is something wrong with the combs? You don't like the color? I thought you loved pink."

"I love pink, but…it's probably inappropriate for me to accept these. I don't know much about rocks, but even I can tell that these are expensive."

They were. But I still failed to understand why that was a problem.

"Is it a cultural thing?" I asked tentatively. "Don't men on Earth give presents to the women they date too? Because it's a very common occurrence on Voran. In fact…" I tried to contain my smile in anticipation of the joke I was about to make. "Remember what Alcus Hecear said about Voranian men's feelings? We're fragile creatures. If you reject my gifts, it'll devastate me. I may end up crying all night."

She tilted her head, looking at me with amusement before bursting with laughter.

I understood exactly why Orin had made it his mission to make Ana laugh. It was one of the most exquisite pleasures in life to see her happy.

"Well, I don't ever want to make you cry, Esvar. Thank you. I accept the combs." Pressing the pouch to her chest, she rose on her tiptoes and gave me a kiss on the cheek.

I would've loved to hug and kiss her properly, but the flowers were in my way.

Ana took the bouquet from me. "These must be from Orin. He's left me flowers by my door every morning this week. Sadly, he stops by way too early while I'm still asleep."

Orin.

Of course. He didn't get to see Ana every day like I did. Bringing her flowers must be his way of maintaining a connection with her.

Ana pulled out a rolled-up note from the bouquet.

"Yes. It is from Orin," she said, glancing at the handwriting on the top of the note.

"What does it say?" I asked, trying to sound casual and completely unaffected by the attention my woman was receiving from another man.

"We'll find out if you read it to me." She gave me the note. "I normally use my tablet, but you can read Ravil, can't you?"

I nodded, taking the note from her. "Are you sure you don't mind me reading what it says?"

I didn't want to learn possibly some very private things Orin might be writing to the woman he courted.

"I don't see why not," Ana said. "Orin doesn't usually write anything too personal. But if you find it inappropriate…"

"No, it's fine." Curious to know what he'd actually write to her about, I started reading, "*Good morning, my beautiful Ana. Another night spent without you and another long day before our next date. I can't wait to have you all to myself again. I've already packed for our trip. And since you didn't get to try any dessert last time at the beach, I'm making some candied berries and cirine tarts today. Personally, I'm more than happy to have the same dessert I had last time…* He can cook?"

I glanced up from the note, quite surprised to learn that about Orin.

Ana looked flustered, avoiding my eyes. The note didn't seem particularly personal or intimate to me. I would've written something far more beautiful and romantic for her. But something in it must have affected her more than I could understand.

She cleared her throat, tucking a strand of hair behind her ear.

"Is that all?" she asked, reaching for the note.

"No, just a little more left." I continued reading, "*I'd love to stay at the Razor Ridge overnight. Is there a chance you could take the next day off work? Tell that grumpy boss of yours I'll make some cirine tarts for him, too, and you'll bring them for him the day after we're back. He could use something sweet in his life to relax a little. He always acts like the world is falling, and he's the only one who can hold it up.*"

Ana giggled, and I gave her a look.

"What?" She laughed. "He's not that far off in his description."

I glimpsed my reflection in the big mirror on the wall by the door. Squared shoulders, tensed jaw, brows knitted into a perpetual frown… Maybe the farm boy was right on this one? I should try to relax and worry about things a little less, at least for tonight, while I'm dancing with my woman.

"Esvar." Ana stepped closer and cradled the side of my face in her hand. "Things aren't that bad in life to stress over them all the time, are they? But Orin doesn't know that you're already working on it. He has no idea that you're taking dance lessons. We're going to have fun today. I've been looking forward to dancing with you tonight all week."

The fragrance of the soap she had used in the shower mixed with the warmth of her skin created an intoxicating fragrance that enveloped me. I also became acutely aware that she wore nothing underneath that towel.

A wave of heat rolled over me, pooling in my crotch with an instant erection. I dropped my arms down, using Orin's note to hide the bulge in my pants—surely not the use he imagined for the note when he wrote it. But the thought of Orin, thankfully, brought my erection down quickly.

"You're going camping at Razor Ridge with him?" I asked, wrapping my free arm around her possessively, as if the Ravil was about to snatch her from me already.

She gave me a stern look but didn't pull away. "You're taking me out tonight, Esvar. Orin deserves to have a proper second date with me too. Promise me not to intervene this time."

"As long as he doesn't intervene in my date with you tonight," I countered. "Unfortunately, his annoying cockiness doesn't minimize his insecurities, forcing him to meddle."

I'd just gotten the aircraft fixed. The last thing I needed was for the bastard to tamper with it again.

"I hope Orin is too busy candying those berries tonight to chase us," I scoffed. "He has to make enough for me too, apparently. But he said he doesn't want to have any himself. Why would he say that?" I pondered, remembering her flushed cheeks when I read those lines to her. "Tell me, what did *he* have for dessert on your date on the beach?"

Her eyes opened wider. Her blush deepened. She bit her bottom lip, halting her breath for a moment.

"He ate me out," she exhaled. "*I was his dessert.*"

Fuck.

I probably should be enraged by that. Or tormented with jealousy, at the very least. But the mental picture of Ana with her legs open, ready to be devoured, sent such a powerful shot of lust through my system, I staggered on my hooves.

And now, all I could think of was me tasting her too.

Dropping Orin's fucking note to the floor, I lifted Ana in my arms. She squeaked in surprise, gripping my horns for support. Her towel opened, revealing her voluptuous breasts. My mouth watered. I wanted to kiss all of her.

With one hand under her delectable bottom, I supported her back with the other while sucking her nipple between my lips. She gasped, arching her back and pressing her breast into my mouth.

My hoof slipped on the rug. Afraid of losing my hold on her, I whipped around and pressed her back to the wall. New to her apartment, I wasn't sure where the bed was. The couch seemed to be too far away, but I had to have her without delay.

"Esvar..." she moaned as I rolled her tender nipple between my teeth.

The intense desire to devour her body, to taste every part of it, to nibble on her skin caught me off guard. Thankfully, she didn't seem to mind. On the contrary, she welcomed it. Whimpering and moaning, she pressed herself against me, and I couldn't hold back any longer.

Shifting her higher along the wall, I placed her thighs on my shoulders, bringing her pussy to my face. It was exactly where it belonged. I growled like a wild beast catching a prey, then buried my face between her legs.

"Oh...your beard," she moaned. "Fuck, it feels so good."

Another growl reverberated through my chest. If she liked the beard, I'd never shave it off. I dragged my chin along her inner thigh, making her squirm.

"Oh God, I want you so much, Esvar. I've wanted you for so fucking long."

Her words were like an arrow of lust sent straight to my cock. It got so hard, it bumped into the wall, making me hiss in both pleasure and pain. Half delirious from desire, I buried my tongue inside her. Pressing my nose into her lower belly, I sucked on her clit like my life depended on it. She gripped my horns, riding my tongue with abandon.

Her thighs flexed around my head, and I tilted my head back, moving away from the place where she wanted me most.

"Esvar! Why did you stop?" She yanked at my horns, so adorably displeased. "I was so close, and now it's gone."

"It's not gone, sweetheart." I dragged my beard along her inner thigh, making her squirm on my shoulders. "It's all there, building up and growing, and waiting for me to coax it out again. Only this time, it'll be even stronger."

I had no idea where I found the strength to slow down and hold back. Counting the seconds, I placed my kisses—first, in the midst of the dark curls between her legs, then on a petal of tender flesh in the middle, and finally, on the hot, hard bud of her clit.

She gasped, gripping my horns tighter. Her hips jerked.

"There you are," I murmured, stroking her with my tongue again.

Her breathing halted, then a shuddered moan tore from her chest as she came hard against my mouth. Her orgasm resonated through my body. My arousal spiked to unbearable heights. I shoved my hips forward, ramming my cock into the fucking wall and…came too.

"Fuck…" I groaned.

My legs gave in. Shifting Ana into my arms, I pressed my back to the wall and slid down to the rug on the floor.

"Wow…" Ana panted, catching her breath. Her body relaxed

against my chest, warm and cozy. "You were right. This was amazing. I never expected it to be this…intense."

"Why not? What did you expect?"

"With you? Something…I don't know…a little more tamed?"

"Tamed?"

"More constrained, subtle, gentle… You come off as a rather reserved man, you know?"

"Sweetheart." I buried my face in the crook of her shoulder, savoring this moment of closeness that felt like the apogee of all my prior existence. "I can be reserved and gentle. I can take it slow, eventually, if that's what you like. But this…this right now was the consequence of fourteen years of celibacy followed by weeks of jerking off to your image nightly."

She ran her fingers through the fur on my head, sending ripples of pure joy through my body.

"Fourteen years? You have me beat in the longest celibacy contest." She smiled. "Did you have a girlfriend back then?"

"I had two girlfriends in the academy, which is more than some men in Voran get."

"And here I thought I'd be seducing a virgin," she teased.

"Would it be better or worse if I were a virgin?" I wondered.

"Generally, I prefer men who know what they're doing," she said. "But at this point, I don't really care. I like you for you, Esvar, with whatever past you have." She stroked the side of my face tenderly, then squirmed in my lap. "I admit it doesn't hurt that you really know how to use your tongue on a woman. You blew my mind, darling. It was better than I could've ever imagined."

"Well, the tongue itself might have something to do with it." I smiled before sticking my tongue out—*all the way out.*

The tip of my tongue stretched down past my chest. One thing Voranians had over any other known species—we had the longest tongues.

"Oh my God, that's crazy!" Ana's eyes widened. She gingerly

touched the tapered tip of my tongue, sliding an appreciative gaze down its entire length. "I've heard about it, but I'd never seen it like this before. Never felt it before either. It sure explains a lot."

She shifted in my lap again, unwittingly rubbing her ass against my hardening cock. I sucked in a breath, bracing against the new wave of arousal heating my blood.

Ana noticed the growing bulge in my pants. "Oh, we need to do something about that. You're still hard, sweetie."

"Not *still*, but *already*," I corrected.

"What do you mean?"

I gathered my hooves under me and got up with her in my arms.

While being with a woman, I'd never climaxed outside of her body before. I'd heard from men back at the academy that some women found it flattering. They took it as a compliment that men found them so irresistible. Yet some women thought it was funny. I wondered what Ana's take on it was. Regardless of what it was, though, I wasn't going to lie to her.

"I came too, Ana, in my pants, against the wall. Hearing your moans and tasting your desire on my tongue, I..." I sighed with a swell of longing rising in my chest anew. "I couldn't help myself. It was the most arousing thing that had ever happened to me."

She didn't laugh. Biting her bottom lip, she ran a hand down between the squares of my abdominal muscles.

"You orgasmed too? The same time I did?" she asked, bewildered. "How are you so hard again already?"

"Sweetheart, around you, I'm perpetually hard." I brushed my hands down my pants and winced. "Now, if you don't mind, I'll have to use your bathroom to...um, clean up the mess in my pants. Then we should go if we don't want to be late for the dance."

Frankly, I wouldn't mind missing the dance completely in

favor of staying here with her for as long as she'd have me. But she nodded quickly and picked up her towel from the floor, then rushed to the bathroom in search of toiletries and fresh towels for me.

IT WAS a short flight to Dhiza, a town only slightly bigger than Tadolia. Dhiza's dance hall was constructed in the middle of the town's square, but the dancing mostly happened on the large wooden patio that circled the building.

We arrived shortly after the dance had started. Fast music was playing, and quite a few couples were already dancing all around the hall.

With Ana's hand in the crook of my elbow, I led her between the merchant stands that surrounded the dance floor.

I felt clean and presentable in my short-sleeve shirt and freshly rinsed and dried pants. Ana looked stunning in her pink-and-green dress with a frilly skirt and an embroidered ruffle around her bare shoulders. One of my gifted combs pinned a bright flower from Orin's bouquet to her dark curls. She was so breathtakingly beautiful, my heart ached with pride and longing whenever I looked at her.

The moment we approached the dance floor, a Ravil man materialized in front of us, as if out of nowhere.

"It's an honor to welcome you to Dhiza, Madame Ana." He bowed, acting like the mayor of the town, which he wasn't because I'd met the mayor of Dhiza, and this man looked nothing like him.

The word of a human woman living in Tadolia had gone out. Even people in other towns knew her by name.

"Thank you," Ana replied politely, allowing the scoundrel to squeeze her hand.

"May I have this dance?" He smirked with more confidence than any man needed.

Was that cocky smirk somehow programmed into all Ravil men's genetic material? Because it was a rare occurrence to meet one without it.

"Thank you, but I came here with my own dance partner." She beamed, looking at me.

The Ravil retreated promptly, which was very smart of him.

"Would you like to have a drink or something to eat first?" I asked, flicking my tail in rhythm to the music.

I tried to remember the steps that my dance teacher back in Tadolia had been trying to teach me all week. Shuffling my hooves to the music discreetly, I wondered how people managed to look so relaxed when dancing required so much focus and concentration from me.

Ana glanced down at my moving hooves.

"I think we should do at least one dance first. I can't wait to take you out for a spin." She grinned.

"All right." I headed to the dance floor.

"You should probably unwrap your tail from around my ankle unless you want me to trip," Ana whispered to me with a giggle.

I hadn't even realized I grabbed her ankle with my tail. It was an instinctive gesture that had probably happened in response to the Ravil trying to whisk her away from me into a dance, or in response to all the Ravil males watching us now. Well, I was the one by her side, not them.

My heart beat faster, and my hands felt cold, as did the tip of my tail, when I unwrapped it from around Ana's leg and moved it out of the way. The last thing I needed was to trip over my tail while dancing with the most important woman in my life.

"Ready?" I asked her in a voice that sounded like I was about to jump out of a moving aircraft with her.

She gave me a soothing smile. "We can start slowly, okay? Just sway to the music for a little bit to get into the rhythm."

Placing her hands on my shoulders, she let me hug her waist. The fast, energetic music was not suitable for slow dancing. The couples around us leaped and jumped, bumping into my shoulders now and then. I started moving my hooves faster, beating them against the wooden floor between the steps to keep up with the music.

The dance ended, and another one started.

"Oh, I love this one." Ana rolled onto the balls of her feet in anticipation.

I recognized the energizing music she had danced to with Orin on Family Day. I had been talking to the mayor of Tadolia when I turned my head to check on Ana whom I'd left sitting at our table, only to find her seat empty. Then I saw her in the arms of the Ravil—her cheeks rosy, her eyes glistening with excitement, her chest rising and falling with rapid breaths... At that moment, I would've given anything for her to look at *me* like that.

And now, this was my chance.

"Let's do it!" I gripped her waist tighter.

"Are you sure? It's not an easy one."

"Two steps, a jump, and a twirl, right?"

"Right, but..." She looked unsure but linked her hands behind her back as was required from the female partners in this dance.

"Sounds easy enough," I said.

Step. Step. Jump, and a twirl.

With a swirl of her skirt, I sent Ana away from me, then caught up with her in two wide steps to catch her in my arms.

"Wow," she exhaled, probably with relief. "You are a quick learner."

Encouraged by the success, I followed the pattern, trying to keep up with the neck-breaking speed of the music while avoiding crashing into the other couples.

Whoever said that dancing was relaxing must be out of their fucking mind. It took every drop of my concentration to watch my steps while keeping up with the tempo.

Step. Step. Jump. Twirl.

Ana laughed when I caught her again. She was truly enjoying it. And I tried to loosen up a bit too, gazing into her eyes instead of watching my hooves.

Step. Step...

The jump was next. I leaped up with Ana in my arms. My eyes locked with hers. My hooves landed back on the ground. One thumped against the wood of the patio as it should. But the other one...

The other hoof landed on something softer and definitely not flat.

Ana cried out.

My ankle wobbled, and I crashed to the floor in plain view of everyone.

Fuck.

"Ow, ow, ow..." Ana gasped, sitting on the floor next to me and gripping her ankle.

"Ana!" I crawled to her.

Other couples stopped dancing, forming a circle around us.

"Are you alright?" someone asked me, but it was Ana I was worried about.

"What happened?" A man crouched by her side.

"My foot," she said, wincing in pain.

Oh, no, no, no.

I'd stepped on her foot!

Kneeling, I hovered my hands over her sandal where an angry dark-red bruise was already blooming on each side of the middle strap.

I grabbed the closest Ravil by his tail.

"Call an ambulance!" I yanked him closer, screaming in his face.

He blinked at me in confusion. "We don't have that here."

Ana touched my hand. "Esvar, I'll be fine. I'm sure it's nothing…"

I took another glance at her bruise, a bloodied purple line edged the rounded outline of my hoof on her skin.

I hurt her.

I hurt Ana.

"Is there a doctor in this fucking town?" I bellowed to the crowd that had gathered around us.

A woman placed her hands on her knees, lowering her face to my level.

"We have a doctor. But it's best if you get Ana to the clinic first," she said calmly and clearly, probably trying not to agitate me any further, for which I was grateful.

Panic edged my vision with a blur. I couldn't let it explode, not until Ana was safe and had been looked after.

"I'll be careful, sweetheart," I promised her, gently lifting her into my arms so as not to aggravate her injury. "Make space," I barked at the crowd, afraid that someone might bump into Ana's foot and cause her even more pain. "Which way?" I asked the woman who'd claimed that the town had a doctor.

She made a face at my commanding tone of voice, but with a glance at Ana, nodded.

"Follow me. The clinic isn't far from here."

I carried Ana to the clinic that was located two streets over in a building that could've equally held a tailor or a barber shop. The front window was dark.

"Is it closed?" I asked the woman.

"Looks like it. But let's try." The woman knocked on the door with no answer.

"What's going on?" a deep voice sounded from the crowd that had followed us to the clinic.

A Ravil man stepped forward, and the woman smiled, looking relieved.

"There you are, Doctor. I brought a patient for you."

"Thank you, Illie." The doctor grinned with that signature charming Ravil smile.

I swore under my breath. This entire planet seemed to be populated exclusively by pretty boys.

"Are you the doctor?" I didn't care if he was the most handsome man in the universe, as long as he could help Ana.

"Yes, I am. I was at the dance, but I heard that someone got injured and figured this would be where they'd go next."

"How so very perceptive of you," I snarled at the good doctor. "Can we come in? Or do you see all your patients out here on the sidewalk?"

His smile didn't waver as he pushed the door open and invited us in.

I brought Ana into the small but neat front room of the clinic, then kicked the door closed behind me, stopping the crowd from spilling in after me.

The doctor gestured for us to sit down while he washed his hands. I lowered my ass into a chair, turning a little to allow for Ana's foot to rest on another chair.

"So, what actually happened?" The doctor asked, drying his hands on a white towel.

"I stepped on her foot," I confessed.

I did a horrible thing, and there was no way to make it sound any better.

"You stepped on her foot? With your hoof?" The doctor narrowed his eyes at me as if assessing a criminal.

I didn't mind. I felt like a criminal, anyway.

"It was an accident," Ana defended me. "He didn't mean it. He has just learned how to dance, and well…the Ravil dances can be quite difficult to master."

"They sure can," the doctor agreed. "Well, let's see how soon you can dance again, Ana."

"You know my name too?" she asked, not looking particularly surprised at this point.

"Everyone knows the name of the Tadolia's Parade Queen," the doctor said with that charming grin of his. "I had to work that day, but my wife and kids went to Tadolia on Family Day to see the parade."

Using a handheld device, he scanned Ana's foot.

The door to the clinic suddenly flew open, and another Ravil barged in. This one might be as pretty as the rest of them, but he was definitely far more annoying.

"Orin!" Ana exclaimed. "What are you doing here?"

"Spying on us, as usual," I scoffed. "What part of my aircraft did you rip out this time?"

"Calm down." Orin shrugged off my words. "I don't even know where you're parked this time. I always stop in Dhiza for fuel when flying to Tadolia from Chrystal River. I stopped this time, too, and heard them saying that a human woman was in the clinic, injured…"

He rushed to Ana, who remained sitting on my lap.

"What did he do to you?" he asked with a murderous glint in his eyes.

His hands balled into fists, and I knew I only avoided being punched because Ana was sitting between us.

She frowned. "It was an accident, Orin."

"He broke your leg by *accident?*"

"Nothing is broken." She rolled her eyes.

"Actually." The doctor cleared his throat. "The bone in your middle toe has a hairline fracture—"

"You broke her bones!" Orin roared.

I froze in horror, not even trying to fight the accusation. "I'm so, so sorry, Ana."

She squeezed my hand gently and turned to the doctor. "What's there to do about it?"

"Not much. Mostly, you should just rest. I'll give you tea for the pain if you need it, and we'll do a tight wrap with a cooling balm that will reduce the swelling and bruising."

The doctor went to the small room behind a glass door adjacent to the front room. The space behind the glass looked like a lab but seemed to also double as a kitchen. The doctor put a tea kettle on the stove and took a cloth-covered clay jar from a cabinet.

"What's the cooling balm?" I asked suspiciously when the doctor returned to us with the jar and a clean stiff cloth.

"It's an old but very effective remedy brewed from *zuphros* leaves." He opened the jar, filling the air with a strong, fairly pleasant fragrance.

"What pharmaceutical company produces it?" I demanded.

The doctor laughed.

"I do. My wife collects the leaves, and I brew it right here." He gestured at his little lab-kitchen.

Worry gripped my throat. Chances were this "brew" wasn't even tested properly. Untested, uncertified... Was this "doctor" even licensed?

He spread the pale-green substance over the cloth, using a spatula.

"It smells nice," Ana commented.

"How effective is it?" I asked, racked by doubt.

"Relax." Orin slapped my shoulder before removing the sandal from Ana's injured foot. "My mother used to brew this too. It helped a lot with all my childhood bruises."

Of which he surely had many, since this particular Ravil was born with hardly any sense of caution or self-preservation.

"Are there any adverse effects?" I asked.

Orin shrugged. "Not that I know of. Mother put it on all my bumps and bruises, and look at me, I turned out just fine."

"Well, I would argue on the contrary," I muttered under my breath.

"*Zuphros* leaf balm is perfectly safe," the doctor assured me. "It's been used as a folk remedy for thousands of years. It was also approved by numerous health committees for the treatment of Ravil, Voranian, and human soldiers who came to Tragul during the war. I had the honor of serving in the same area where the unit from Earth was stationed and learned a lot about human biology. Everything I will give you today is safe to treat humans."

Ana nodded, allowing the doctor to place the compress on her bruised foot. He wrapped it around tightly, then secured the cloth with flat metal clips around her foot.

"How does it feel?" the doctor asked.

"Good," she said. "Pleasantly chilly."

"It's good against swelling. I'll also make you tea to ease the pain. It'll help you sleep as well. You're not operating an aircraft to fly home, are you?"

"No," she replied.

"I'll fly her," Orin, the meddlesome Ravil, jumped in.

"Not in that rattling, rusty can you call an aircraft," I scoffed, earning a glare from him.

"My old bird delivered all of us safely home on the day when that shiny thing of yours proved useless," he retorted.

"It was only because you rendered it useless!" I lost my patience.

"Stop arguing. That's enough!" Ana's high voice cut through the air.

The doctor wisely left the room, going to the kitchen to brew Ana the tea he'd promised.

"Exactly, Esvar. Stop arguing," Orin chided.

"You too, Orin. Both of you." Ana tossed her hands in the air in frustration. "I can't stand listening to you fighting with each other, and I don't want to deal with men who act like children. I've had enough of that in my life. Stop it right now or I swear I'll hop all the way back to Tadolia on one foot. Alone."

I'd never seen Ana lose her patience like that before. She'd never yelled at anyone.

I kept silent. Orin finally shut up too, looking subdued.

But Ana wasn't done yet.

"Esvar is a responsible man and keeps his aircraft in excellent condition. It was *you* who disabled it." Ana pointed an accusing finger at Orin.

He drew in a chestful of air but…held it, probably finding nothing to say in his defense.

My satisfaction at seeing Orin defeated and deflated like that didn't last long as Ana turned her little finger at me.

"You too, Esvar," she scolded. "Stop putting Orin down. You're better than that. I know you are, or I wouldn't… I wouldn't *like* you as much as I do."

"Like" wasn't a word strong enough to make her blush the way she did when she said it. Did it mean something more to her?

Did *I* mean something more to her?

My heart soared in my chest, unfettered. I didn't even mind Orin's presence in the room with us. I grinned, actually, knowing he heard Ana too.

Orin darted his gaze between Ana and me.

The doctor returned with the tea. He handed her the mug, then gave me an extra packet.

"Give it to her before bed if she needs it," the doctor instructed. "It'll help her sleep through the night. Place a pillow or a rolled blanket under her foot to elevate it."

Orin frowned, clearly opposed to my involvement in Ana's bedtime routine in any capacity. But he said nothing, probably not willing to bring Ana's wrath on his head again.

I cleared my throat and straightened my shoulders. If Orin

could hold back his emotions and act as a mature individual, I certainly could too.

"I'll take you home, Ana," I said calmly.

Orin stirred agitatedly.

"How are you going to fly the aircraft with Ana on your lap?" he asked.

My aircraft had a spacious passenger seat, but Ana wouldn't be able to elevate her foot properly while sitting in it. Besides, I immensely enjoyed holding her on my lap. I'd love to do it all the way to Tadolia, which would be impossible with the controls in the way.

"We're not taking yours," I said firmly to Orin.

"I don't really care which aircraft," Ana said.

She looked tired. The tea must be working, making her sleepy already.

"No, dearest. We have to take our aircraft. There's no space in the front to stretch your leg in his. And I can't allow him to transport you in his cargo hold with some bags." I shuddered, remembering the flight we made in Orin's beaten-up machine from the City of Ravie. My ass still felt sore at those memories.

"I don't even have the bags in the back anymore." Orin sighed, looking sad.

Shockingly, he seemed to think as a rational person for once, even if it pained him.

"Fine," he said. "I'll fly your aircraft, with you and Ana in the passenger seat. This way, you'll make sure Ana is as comfortable as possible. You do have a comfy, fur-lined lap, after all." He grinned, slapping my thigh.

There went all his efforts to act as a grown man.

I shook my head. But Ana giggled at his words and shifted her delectable butt on my "fur-lined lap." I cupped her hip tenderly, immediately forgiving Orin for all his teasing.

After Ana had finished her tea and the good doctor loaded

us with enough refills and instructions, we headed out to my aircraft.

Orin held Ana while I got into the passenger seat.

"Alright, now come here, my darling." I reached for her.

"Guys, I can sit on my own, you know?" Ana protested, not very strongly though. "I feel fine. There is no need for me to inconvenience anyone."

"Isn't it the most comfortable position, though?" I gestured at my thighs that were more than ready to accommodate her backside once again.

"You can stretch all the way across and rest your foot on my lap," Orin chimed in. "Unless you want to send Esvar in the back, to punish him for jumping on your foot," he suggested ever so helpfully.

Guilt sliced through me again, but Ana stretched her hands to me.

"No," she said resolutely. "There is nothing to punish him for."

I accepted her in an embrace. Minding her injured foot, I carefully shifted her position sideways, with her shoulder pressed to me.

Orin jumped into the pilot's seat, then placed Ana's foot on his lap as he'd promised.

"Comfy?" He flashed her a smile.

She leaned against me, resting her head on my chest.

"Comfier than I've ever been." She yawned, closing her eyes.

"Let's get her home and in bed." I gestured at the controls impatiently, urging him to hurry.

"Niiice," Orin whistled, looking over the control panel. "All the knobs and levers match in color. And just look at all those screens."

"Please tell me you know how to fly it." I frowned as doubt took over me again.

I didn't want to free my lap from Ana. But I wanted even less for this hothead to crash us in the jungle somewhere.

"I know how to fly it," he repeated after me word for word, not easing my suspicions in the slightest.

"Listen, just tell me honestly," I said, "do we have to switch seats?"

"Calm down." He raised his hand. "I flew some Voranian equipment during the war. I'll figure it out. Where is the start button?"

He pressed on the control panel, then grabbed the navigation lever. The engines whirred to life softly, and the aircraft lifted off the ground smoothly enough for me to release the tense breath I held.

"See? Easy." Orin gave me a cocky shrug.

He proved to be a good pilot. I had to give him that, which of course meant that the bumpy ride I'd endured in his aircraft a week ago had been made bumpy on purpose, for my benefit.

With Ana snuggling against my chest, however, I felt peace and didn't want to spoil it by getting angry with Orin over the past. He navigated the dark night sky skillfully. The aircraft glided through the clouds like sliding through butter. And Ana dozed off, snoring softly in my arms.

CHAPTER 11

ANA

"There are the waterfalls. Can you see them?" Orin pointed at the jungle landscape outside of the aircraft window.

"Oh yes, I do!" I shifted in my seat for a better view up the wide river that cut through the colorful flora of the jungle like a silky orange scarf.

A pale-yellow mist rose over about a dozen high, narrow waterfalls. The mist shimmered in the light of the Tragulian sun, making the water appear to glow with gold.

"It's beautiful, Orin," I exhaled in awe.

He grinned, looking pleased by my reaction.

"It's one of the most beautiful places on Tragul, and it's just a short flight from Tadolia. It'd be a shame if you didn't get to see it."

Orin had planned to leave the aircraft on the river bank, then hike up the hill to another picturesque spot—a field of flowers that looked and smelled so wonderful, it promised camping in it to feel like paradise. Because of my foot, however, we had to skip hiking this time and stay by the river instead.

My foot was healing well. The bruise had paled overnight, and—likely because of the cooling balm—the swelling had hardly even happened.

After the quiet and enjoyable flight home, Esvar and Orin had jostled each other out of the way, trying to take care of me last night. In the end, I had to kick them both out of my apartment to get some sleep. Though what I really would've wanted was to have them both in bed with me.

Last night, on the flight home, I sat on Esvar's lap. His strong arms hugged me tightly. His heartbeat thudded rhythmically in his chest. The warmth of his body enveloped me, safe and comfy. I felt the happiest I'd ever been in my life. Then I realized it was also because Orin was there. He'd wrapped his large hand around my ankle, gently stroking my skin with his thumb. All three of us shared a peaceful, comfortable silence. It was sweet and perfect, and I'd missed that feeling ever since.

Now, I reached across to Orin and took his hand in mine, needing the gentle reassuring squeeze he gave me. All that was missing now was Esvar's palm wrapped around my other hand.

"Do you think having hooves makes it easier or harder to hike in the jungle?" I blurted out.

"What? Why?" He blinked at me. "Are you thinking about Esvar?"

It'd be stupid to deny it. It'd be dishonest too.

"I wonder if he likes hiking," I admitted. "He runs every day, but mostly on the even ground of the roads in Tadolia."

"Why does he run?" He looked genuinely confused.

"For exercise. To clear his mind and stay in shape."

"Ha! He should come to my farm then. I have enough work to keep him in shape forever. At least, it'd be more useful than running around aimlessly."

"Do you need help on the farm?"

"No," he said quickly. "I manage just fine. I'm just saying that if Esvar is looking for ways to stay in shape—" He stopped himself abruptly. "Why are we talking about Esvar?"

"Um…I'm not sure."

"Do you talk to Esvar about *me* when you're with him?"

"Yes," I admitted. "But I also think about you all the time, including when I'm with him."

He frowned in thought, flexing his jaw. He seemed more confused than concerned or angry. But I had no game to play here. All I could do was remain honest, whether or not he liked it.

"Well." He arched an eyebrow, regaining his usual expression of confidence. "Let's see if I make you forget all about Esvar by the end of today."

If only it were that simple. But he grinned again, and I was glad to see his frown disappear. I smiled back, saying nothing.

We landed downstream of the falls, near a long beach. Orin set up a tent from colorful canvas. He did it impressively fast, including putting up the awning over the entrance and arranging portable dining furniture on an outdoor rug.

"You've done this before," I noted.

"Many times during the war." He shrugged. "Most of my life was spent in tents, actually. Or in the trees, where *fescods* couldn't get us, though their allies, the *yirzi,* still could. Those fuckers are excellent tree climbers. But *yirzi* have been banished from Tragul, as you may know. I've checked the latest reports, by the way, there haven't been any sightings of *fescods* anywhere near this area for a long time. So, Esvar had better leave us alone this time. It's unfortunate that he even knows where we are."

"It's my fault. I asked him to read your note where you mention this location."

"Let's hope he keeps his nose out of our business this time." He stopped to kiss my cheek before unpacking a basket of dishes. "Though, I'm sure he has already learned more about this area than people who live close by even know. He just can't let anything go—" He stopped abruptly. "Why the fuck are we talking about Esvar again?"

"*You* started it this time." I laughed.

"Unbelievable." He shook his head. "This asshole just crawls into your head and stays there, doesn't he?"

"Your words, not mine," I quipped, then added in a more serious tone of voice. "But Esvar isn't an asshole, far from it. He knows so much about Ravie because he cares about this country more than any human or other Voranian I've ever met."

"Why does he care?" Orin asked with a guarded expression.

"Learning Ravie's history affected him deeply. He loves this country and genuinely wants to help. He created the program, Help Ravie Rebuild, specifically designed to support small family businesses."

"Help Ravie Rebuild? Isn't that the financial grant initiative by the Ravil government?"

"The government is supporting it fully. But the money comes from Voran. Esvar had fundraised for two years, ever since the end of the war. And he put a lot of his own money into it too. That's why we're here, to process applications and evaluate requests. Esvar didn't want someone else to administer it. The cause is so dear to his heart, he wants to personally make sure that the money goes exactly where it's intended—to the hard-working people who are at the root of rebuilding Ravie."

"Fuck. I didn't know that's where it came from." He scratched the back of his head.

"Why does it matter?"

"Because... Well... Alright, you're right. It shouldn't matter. But..." He ran a hand over his face. "Anyway, not a word about Esvar anymore, deal?"

It was Orin's date with me, but we'd been talking a lot about Esvar. I could see how that would upset Orin. It wasn't fair.

"Alright. No more talking about Esvar," I agreed, then

pointed at the dishes that he'd been taking out from the basket and arranging on our round inflatable picnic table. "What are these vegetables for? And is it meat you have marinating in this container?"

"That's our lunch." He grouped several jars and containers together on the table. "And this is our dinner." He lifted an unpacked basket and hung it on a tree branch.

"When it comes to food, you're remarkably organized," I noted.

"Not just food. Things generally tend to run more smoothly with some planning ahead. I've planned our entire day and *especially* the night." He winked. "So, if there is anything specific you think of doing, let me know, and I'll fit it in our schedule."

"I'll let you know, but I'm more of a spur-of-the-moment type."

That was true. Acting spontaneously came naturally to me, but I had always been the planner of all our trips and holidays with Lucas. Having a man now in charge of organizing the trip was refreshing. I enjoyed being able to kick back, relax, and let someone else handle the logistics.

"Just tell me if I can help with anything, please," I said.

He propped his hands on the armrest of my chair. Leaning over, he gave me a sweet, tender kiss on my lips.

"You sit right here, elevate your foot like this." He put my foot on top of a basket with some gear. "Comfy?"

I nodded. "Thank you."

He petted my calf. "Lunch will be ready soon."

After lunch, Orin inflated a small boat to take me down the river.

"Since the hiking trip didn't work out, I figured we'll go on a boat trip instead," he explained.

We followed the lazy stream, drifting with the current that allowed Orin to put down the paddles and point out some interesting plants or animals.

"A mud serpent, Ana. See over there? Wrapped around the fallen log on the riverbank?"

I squinted, finding a long orange shape wrapped like a thick noodle around a green log. The serpent raised its head and yawned, opening its round mouth the size of a hula hoop. Instead of teeth, its jaws were connected by a mesh of thin white membranes.

"It feeds on algae," Orin explained. "It gathers it in its mouth mesh by skimming the surface of the river along the banks. It then sucks it into its throat through the membranes."

"Sounds rather gross." I cringed.

"It does." He laughed. "But by doing that, mud serpents keep rivers clean for you and me to swim in."

"Are there any predators in the water?" I asked, trying to peer through the opaque orange water that wasn't clear enough for me to see the bottom.

"Predators? Sure. Only none that would attack you or me. In terms of predators, Tragul is one of the safest planets in the universe."

That, along with this planet's mild climate and hospitable people, made Tragul a wonderful tourist destination, especially for the Voranians, whose country was solidly covered with snow six months out of a year. Esvar wasn't only kind but also smart to invest in Ravie. Now that the war was over, this country had a bright future ahead of it.

"When I was a kid, we used to play with mud serpents," Orin said. "We'd wear them as scarves around our necks, and they would just keep on sleeping. They're so lazy. They spend their time either sleeping on logs like that one or floating down the river with their mouths open to collect the algae. Of course, they're almost always covered in mud, so we would get dirty too. Mother would get so angry when we came home, bringing all that mud in."

He laughed softly, reminiscing about his past, and I was glad he shared the happy memories with me, glad that they had survived despite all the dark days he'd lived through.

I dipped my hand into the river. Water steamed between my fingers. The minerals in it gave the river its distinct orange color and made the water feel silky and soft. I wondered how it would feel to dive into it.

"So, you said it's safe to swim here, right?" I asked. "Because I brought my bathing suit this time."

"You won't need one here either," he assured me.

"Oh, you just want to see me naked," I teased.

A wide smile spread across his face, displaying the tips of his two top canines. "I always do."

His eyelids dropped a little, giving him a deceptively relaxed expression. His bright green eyes glistened dangerously under his long eyelashes while he slowly dragged his gaze down my body.

Desire rolled through me in the wake of that gaze. I leaned back on my arms. The gesture pushed out my chest for his viewing pleasure. I wore the perfect dress for it too. Cut fairly low with a strip of ruffled lace around the neckline, it framed my cleavage nicely.

He cleared his throat, grabbing the paddles. "I'll get us back to the camp first. So you don't have to sit in the boat naked after the swim."

"Well, you'd better hurry then. Because I fear I may end up sitting here *wet,* anyway. Even without going for a swim." My voice turned sultry with the rasp of desire.

"Fuck," he groaned, energetically leaning onto the paddles.

Lust practically hummed in the air around him now. The muscles bulged in his arms as he splashed the paddles in the water much harder than was necessary and moved the boat against the current in determined, jerky strokes.

"With you paddling so hard, we'll get back to the camp in no time," I said innocently. "I may as well change into my bathing suit now."

From the small basket of snacks and emergency supplies that we brought with us, I took out my two-piece bathing suit and put it on the bench seat next to me. Then, I slid down the dress from my right shoulder.

Paddling frantically, he followed my gestures with his eyes so closely, it was as if his life depended on what I'd do next. I loved undressing for him on the beach last week, and now I knew exactly why. I enjoyed the rapt attention with which he watched me. The desire burning in his eyes proved infectious. It heated my blood too. Arousal swirled low in my belly, swelling hot between my legs.

I spread my knees open. The wide skirt of my dress draped between them, concealing my underwear from Orin's view. I sensed it's the "concealing" part that he liked so much about my little striptease. His eyes lit up in anticipation. His chest moved rapidly with his accelerated breathing.

I slipped the dress down from my left shoulder too, then freed my arms, shoving the bodice down to my waist. My black lacy bra came into view. I released a long breath and pulled up my knees, letting the skirt slide up with a flash of my panties.

My body was still covered much more than it would be by a bathing suit, but Orin's nostrils flared. He growled. Tossing the paddles to the bottom of the boat, he grabbed the anchor from behind his seat and hurled it into the water as if it were his mortal enemy.

"I won't make it to the camp. I want you now," he growled, lunging from his seat for me.

Need shot through me like lightning as Orin buried his face between my breasts. Supported by his arm around my waist, I fell backwards against the rounded hull of our blow-up boat.

He ran his hands up my thighs, lifting my skirt all the way up to my waist, then yanked my panties down to my ankles. He found my nipple with his teeth, nibbling on it through my bra.

The soft caress of his tail up my leg didn't alarm me this time. Instead, it sent ripples of pleasure along my skin.

"Open wider for me, sweetheart," he murmured, moving my knees further apart.

The tickle of the fur tassel at the tip of his tail slid up my inner thigh, then slipped between my legs.

"Oh, your tail..." I moaned, melting into the caress.

He tugged my bra in his struggle to get to my breasts.

"My tail is a naughty one, isn't it?" He stroked the fluffy end of his tail between my legs.

Searching for more stimulation, I lifted my hips. The hard bulge in his pants pressed against me. I welcomed the contact, rubbing against his cock through his pants.

He sucked in a breath, hurriedly fumbling with the closure of his pants. His other hand was cupping my right breast, stroking my hardened nipple through the lacy fabric of my bra.

"How do I get this off..." He tugged at the bra cup. "Has it merged with your body? Because I see no way to free you from it."

I exhaled a laugh, arching my back to reach the bra clasp behind me.

"Here you go." I clicked it open.

"You'll have to teach me that. Later." He took the bra off, then gazed adoringly at my naked breasts. "There is something about all the annoying layers of clothing you wear that drives me mad with lust. The more fabric I have to remove from your body, the more I want you. How does it make any sense?"

"Oh, you'll love our winters then. I wear so many clothes in the winter, you wouldn't even recognize me with all those *layers* on."

"I would simply combust while peeling them all off you." He thrust against me through his pants.

I gripped his tail at the base, trying to slow him down.

"I want you inside me, Orin. Now. Before you come in your pants like—" I stopped without mentioning Esvar's name.

It wasn't fair to Esvar to reveal the intimate details that had happened when we were alone.

It wasn't fair to Orin to bring Esvar into our intimate moment.

Yet maybe because I was so intimately attracted to them both, I itched to share all our moments between all of us.

The thought of Esvar with us warmed my heart and spurred my desire. I found the waistband of Orin's pants and shoved them down his hips. His cock sprang free—long, thick, and hard.

"Wow..." I blinked, staring at it. "Somehow, it looks even bigger every time I see it. And these..." I cupped his round, velvety testicles. "They're so cute."

"Cute?" He moved back, tilting his head to the side. "I don't think anyone has called those parts of my body 'cute' before."

"But they are." I squeezed his balls gently, enjoying the silky sensation of the short downy fur that covered his skin. "They feel amazing, too, like stress balls in a velvet bag."

He snorted a laugh, then groaned, "Mercy, Ana. It even hurts to laugh when I'm this hard."

"Really? I never knew that. We should do something about it then, shouldn't we?"

I circled his hard length with my fingers. He hissed as if I'd touched a sore spot, then moaned with pure bliss spreading over his face. I moved closer, eager to feel him inside me. Hooking his arm under my knee, he lifted my leg, and I guided the tip of his cock to my opening.

"Slowly, please." I tensed a little. "It may take some time for me to adjust to this giant member of yours."

He nodded, pushing in gently. "I'd rather die than hurt you."

I was too impatient to follow my own advice, however. My

body thrummed with need. Desire flooded me, making me dripping wet. I jerked my hips toward him, halting my breath from the stretch.

"Patience, my beautiful Ana." He kissed my face, sinking in just a little deeper.

The fluffy tip of his tail fluttered over my throbbing clit. Heat surged in me. My inner muscles spasmed. The sensation of Orin's cock inside me grew more intense. I no longer felt the stretch, not even the pressure, just the heat of heightened arousal and an intense need to come.

"Harder," I rocked my hips against him.

He groaned, pushing deeper. His tail worked me faster, rubbing against my clit. I closed my eyes as pleasure built up, then crested, taking me over the edge.

The moment I came, Orin thrust forward, sliding all the way in and making my orgasm seem to last forever. Swells of pleasure rocked my body, over and over again. He pounded hard. I raked my fingers through his hair, forgetting he had no horns.

He roared, coming inside me with a wild, desperate thrust. The momentum shoved me off the hull tube. Instinctively, I fisted my hands in Orin's hair, dragging him overboard with me.

The water splashed and then closed over us. I kicked my legs, trying to swim up to the surface, only I wasn't sure where the surface was.

Strong arms grabbed my waist and pushed me up. The stream broke over my face, and I finally gasped a lungful of air.

It all happened so fast, panic had no chance to register with me yet.

Blowing water out of his mouth and nose, Orin's head popped out of the river next to me.

"Are you alright?" he asked, shaking out his mane.

I moved my legs and arms to make sure all was well, and nodded.

"I'm fine. How about you?"

"I lost my pants," he stated.

I burst out laughing. It came slightly unhinged, with me being on edge after the sudden plunge. But relief already flooded my muscles.

"I can't believe you fucked me out of the boat, Orin! Literally."

"My beautiful Ana. It seems you fucked my brains out. I forgot where we were."

Something slithered around my leg under water.

I screamed, kicking at it.

"It's just my tail again," he said quickly, lifting both hands in a calming gesture. "I need to keep you close while I swim for the boat." He pointed back to where our boat remained anchored as the stream was slowly taking us away from it.

"These aliens and their tails," I muttered under my breath, allowing Orin to tug me along with his tail while he swam back to the boat.

"ARE YOU READY FOR BED, my beautiful Ana?" Orin asked after we'd finished dinner, put everything away for the night, and got ready for bed.

"Looking forward to it." I meant for it to sound light and flirty, but it came with a wisp of deep longing in my chest.

I didn't mind being single, but there were things about being in a relationship that I missed increasingly more as time went by. I was looking forward to having the man I cared about sleep next to me tonight.

It wasn't even about sex at this point. As much as I loved having Orin's hands on my body and his massive cock buried inside me, I felt excited about simply waking up next to him tomorrow morning.

Maybe I was ready for a stronger connection than just a quick fling after all?

"Are you coming, Ana?" Orin asked, standing by the tent.

"Just a minute, please." I made a wide gesture at the night-shrouded river. "I can't get enough of this view."

After sunset, the vivid hues of the landscape had changed to a more muted palette. The waterfalls streamed down the ridge like silver ribbons over black velvet. Clouds had moved in, leaving only a few bright stars still visible among them. They shone like diamonds in the wispy felt of the overcast sky.

Orin hugged me from behind, taking in the night landscape with me.

"Can one see Neron from here?" I asked.

"Yes. It's that most obnoxious bright star over there." He pointed at the biggest and the most brilliant star to the right. "It's always up in your face, hard to miss, kind of like the people who live there."

I playfully slapped his arm. "Hey, Voranians are very nice people. I've met quite a few of them."

"So you mean I shouldn't base my opinion of them just on one particular Voranian?"

"Are we talking about Esvar again?" I teased.

"Shit," he cursed under his breath. "No, we're not. Not again. Ask me about something else. Anything."

My thoughts had already veered off toward Esvar, however. He didn't look like an outdoorsy type, but I knew he loved Ravie. He wasn't afraid of trying new things, even dancing. I was sure Esvar would love to come camping with me. But not if Orin came too. Sadly.

The most upsetting thing about our situation was that Esvar and Orin probably would've gotten along just fine if it weren't for me. They could've even possibly become good friends if I didn't stand between them.

That was a depressing realization. I drew in a shaky breath, then asked the next thing that came to mind.

"Can you see Earth from here?"

"Not with all these clouds, sadly. Earth is much farther from Tragul than Neron. It's a smaller star, hard to find in the sky, even without all these clouds." Orin hugged me tighter, pressing the side of his face to my temple. "Do you miss home?"

The awareness of how far away I was from home never left me during my stay here. It was hard to believe that all my life prior, every person I ever knew, and every experience I'd ever had was now reduced to a single speck in the sky that wasn't even visible behind the clouds.

I loved my home and always would, but I didn't miss it enough to want to return yet. My adventure had just begun, and I felt more excited about the future than nostalgic about the past.

"No. Not really," I said. "My friends and family write to me regularly. It doesn't feel much different than when I moved out of my parents' home to the city a few hours away. And tonight, I'm happy to be exactly where I am, here with you."

I leaned against him, snuggling deeper into his embrace, and sighed as peace descended on me. It was an alien planet, but I felt at home here. And maybe it had something to do with the alien man holding me close right now.

"It's so beautiful here. I wish I could commit this to my memory forever," I said.

"Or we could come back here again whenever you want."

I turned around in his arms to face him.

"Thank you for bringing me here," I said softly.

His green eyes looked darker in the night. He kissed me, then pressed his forehead to mine, not letting me pull away.

"I've never brought anyone here before, Ana. And now, no

matter what happens, this place will forever be connected with you in my mind."

His tail slipped tightly around my waist, anchoring me to him. Yet I felt like I was flying. Soaring. Spinning out of control. Falling…

Falling hard for this man.

My intention had never been to hurt anyone. I used to believe I could stop it all before it went too far and the hearts would break. Now I feared I'd already missed the point of no return. No matter what was going to happen next, I was in for a heartbreak.

CHAPTER 12

ORIN

$\mathcal{W}$as I dreaming about the war again? I wasn't sure, but I woke up abruptly.

A loud screeching noise came from outside the tent. A thundering roar, then the snapping of metal.

"Ana! Wake up." I untangled myself from her limbs, limp from sleep. "Get up, sweetheart." I shook her shoulder gently before finding my pants and boots.

I had no idea what was happening out there, but whatever it was, it sounded bad enough for me to get Ana out of here.

"What's going on?" She sat up, rubbing her eyes and looking deliciously adorable.

She was dressed in her short pajamas that I would love to take off her right now and make her come for the fourth time tonight, but something wasn't right outside, and I had to find out what it was.

"Get dressed, Ana, I'll—"

I didn't finish my sentence as a muddy wave of water rushed under the canvas wall of the tent.

Ana cried out in shock, jumping to her feet.

"What's going on?"

"We need to get out. Now." I grabbed her arm and pulled her out of the tent just before its fabric walls collapsed.

Hard rain pounded the ground and pummeled the jungle canopy with torrents of water. The ribbons of the waterfalls had grown and merged into a wide continuous stream. It rushed over the Razor Ridge in a roaring current that bloated the river below.

My boat was gone, washed away along with the tree it had been tied to.

"Orin! Your plane!" Ana screamed, tugging on my arm.

My poor old bird had been pushed on its side with its hull smashed in and its long propeller blades bent and cracked. That must've been what made that terrible screeching sound that woke me up. As we watched, the stream pushed it even further off the bank.

"Oh, no! It's floating away." Ana made a move to run after the aircraft.

I stopped her by grabbing her around her middle.

"You can't stop it. If you try, you'll be swept away too."

"But what are we going to do?" She still looked slightly disoriented and dressed only in her pajamas and a pair of fuzzy socks that had soaked up a lot of water already.

I had to keep her safe.

I looked around quickly. The sky had already paled with the approaching morning, but it didn't seem like the torrential rain was stopping anytime soon. We had to get away from the swollen river that kept rising.

"We need to get to higher ground." I started hiking up the riverbank and into the jungle.

"But how about our stuff? *Your* stuff?" Ana clung to my arm as I half-dragged, half-carried her up the hill.

The stream had already washed away the tent with all of its contents. The rest of our campsite was being flooded as we spoke. I wouldn't be able to replace the things lost here for a very long time, maybe never. But if I lingered, we risked being carried away along with them.

"Leave it all." I yanked the basket of food from the branch where I'd hung it up last night before going to bed. "I'll have to get you to safety. Then, we'll worry about the rest. How is your foot?"

"My foot?" She looked around wildly, my question not registering with her at all.

I slung the basket with food over my shoulder, then grabbed Ana in my arms.

"What are you doing?" She hugged my neck so tightly that if she had the strength of a Ravil, I would've risked having my neck broken.

"We have to get to higher ground." I hiked up the hill, carrying her with me.

"I can walk," she protested.

Wearing only socks, with her foot injured, it wouldn't be a pleasant walk for her. Besides, it made me feel better to have my arms around her, to have her close to me like this, to know that no force of nature could rip her away from me.

"It's faster this way," I said simply.

She didn't argue again, but not because I'd convinced her. She seemed distracted by what was happening behind us.

"Orin, it's rising fast," she said in a hollow voice, clinging to my shoulders.

The flood was fast. Way too fast. A rainfall alone couldn't have made this flood as big and as vicious as it was, even if it had rained through the entire night. I wondered if the dam that was upstream on the other side of the ridge broke.

There was nothing I could do about it either way. I just hoped to be faster than the water and get us to safety before the stream could catch up with us. I didn't need to look back to know it was bad. The crashing roar of the river swelling out of control chased us. I ran, rushing to get to a place where I'd feel safe to stop and catch my breath.

The jungle closed around us. Grooves and trenches criss-crossed the uneven ground, possibly left from previous floods and rainfalls. I stepped forward, only for my boot to plunge into water that was both in front and behind us now.

I glanced around, searching for a dry path to continue up the hill, but the muddy, orange water rushed all around us, leaving me standing on the top of a small mound of dry ground that grew smaller and smaller with every passing moment as the river rose higher. The trench that separated us from the rest of the mainland grew wider, too, quickly filling with water.

I had no time to lose.

"Here's what we're going to do, Ana," I spoke quickly, wading into the trench. "I'll get as close to the other side as I can walk, then I'll give you a push so you can swim across to the other side."

"But how about you?"

A tree fell upstream, crashing through branches and tearing through the thick net of vines.

"I'll be fine. I'll swim right after you," I said in the most reassuring voice I could muster.

I waded up to my chest into the water, holding Ana in my arms.

"Ready?" I asked. "Swim with big, long, strong strokes, sweetheart. As fast as you can. And don't stop. Climb out, then run."

I lifted her a little higher. She stretched her arms in front of her, her face focused and grim.

"Now!" I pushed her across the stream toward the dry ground.

She worked her arms hard, swimming at an angle across the stream. The trench was deep, and the current was strong, but thankfully, this side stream hadn't spread impassably wide yet.

Unable to reach the bottom any longer, I swam too. The current carried us down the stream, but our efforts moved us across too. Ana was close to the other side when the fallen tree rushed toward us down the stream, tossed by the powerful current as if it were a matchstick.

It'd hit her.

She'd never make it to the dry ground.

"Faster, Ana!" I screamed, swimming to her side.

She panted, sputtering and spitting water out of her mouth. She was a good swimmer, but fighting the turbulent current wasn't easy for either of us. I grabbed her under her arm, pushing forward to give her more speed.

"Almost there, Ana!"

The fallen tree slammed into my side. A bone snapped in my forearm, sending a shot of blinding agony through my body.

"Orin!" Ana's voice sounded as if in a dream—faint and distant.

Water closed over me. And I no longer knew where was up or down.

CHAPTER 13

ESVAR

Ana was with Orin today.

Ana was with Orin today...

They were spending the night together too.

Every muscle in my body tensed at that thought. Restlessness buzzed through my chest, urging me to do something.

The ideal "something" would be to fly over to wherever the fuck they were and take my woman home with me. But I knew that would enrage her. I also knew that if Orin did something like that to me, I'd lift him on my horns with no hesitation. It was his time with Ana. The mature, rational part of my brain understood it'd be unfair of me to intervene.

I left my loft early that morning. And even though it was the weekend, with all my staff gone from the office, I stomped around our working area, searching for something to do. I needed to occupy my mind with something other than the images of Orin touching Ana's naked body, kissing her, driving his cock into her...

Fuck.

My own cock unexpectedly grew hard.

What was wrong with me?

The rage that another man could be touching my woman at that very moment burned through me, which was in line with my Voranian instincts. The arousal, however, was not something I could explain.

The mental images of Orin pleasing Ana made me wish to be there with them for all the wrong reasons. And here I was, hard as a rock and itching to touch myself.

Ridiculous!

I ran both hands through the fur on my head, tugging at it firmly. The sting at the roots at least somewhat distracted me from the lustful impulses.

I spotted the box with the few remaining unprocessed grant applications and grabbed it like it was a lifesaver tossed to me in the ocean. Dumping the contents of the box onto my desk, I set the running walkway under it on high. With my mind hopefully focused on the work, I wanted to exhaust my body too. Then, with any luck, I'd sleep that night without being tortured by the images of Orin fucking Ana in their tent. Or even worse, jerking off to them.

I went through each application carefully, imputing the data into our system, taking notes, and making calculations. Then, I searched and marked the location of each business on the map and added any relevant information about the owners and their work. It was a long and scrupulous process, but we had to be careful not to miss anything. These people put their hopes in us. Their livelihood was at stake. We couldn't afford to make mistakes.

I worked through the entire day, eating at the desk and only taking breaks for bathroom visits and for an hour-long jog through the town. I always went jogging on workdays. Running cleared my head. This time, however, it crammed my brain with more thoughts than I could handle, so much so that I was actually glad to return to the office and get back to work again.

All of that exercise, mental and physical, had achieved its goal. By the end of the day, I felt exhausted and was looking forward to a restful sleep.

"One more application, and I'll call it a day," I thought to myself, lifting a paper from the much thinner pile of the unprocessed applications.

Orin.

The name at the top of the application jumped out at me from the text.

I'd been thinking about that man way too much, much more than I'd ever thought about any man in a day. Was his name haunting me now?

I squinted at the text, rereading the Ravil letters carefully.

Shit. It was his name.

Someone with Orin's name had applied for the grant from our foundation. Someone of the exact same age as Orin... With a *cirine* farm that was located...just north of Tadolia.

Fuck.

I dropped the paper on my desk and stopped the running track.

It was Orin. It had to be him. It'd be too much of a coincidence otherwise.

Orin, the man who was currently on a date with my woman, was asking my foundation for financial help to help keep his farm running.

I stared at the wall blankly, trying to process this.

It wasn't surprising that Orin needed help. Many businesses struggled to get back on their feet after the war. A lack of labor and capital resources was often the cause. That didn't make Orin's application unusual or concerning.

What worried me was his motivation to date Ana.

Did he know who she was when he asked her to dance on

Family Day? Ana was the only human in Tadolia. It would've been easy for him to find out where she worked and why she came to Tragul.

Did he ask her out to get closer to the resources of the foundation?

Did he hope to gain her trust and use her sympathy to influence the outcome of his application?

Was he using Ana to get the money?

What a slimy, sneaky, lying asshole would play with a woman's heart like that?

Anger heated my blood, spreading through my body like molten lava. My first instinct was to fly immediately to the Razor Ridge and rescue Ana from the fraud of a man she was wasting her time on.

I made it all the way to the aircraft, then paused by its door.

It was getting dark. I didn't know the exact location of their camp. I could use the lights of the aircraft to search the ground for their tent. But would Ana appreciate such a drastic invasion from me? Again?

The mature thing would be to trust her instincts and her judgement. She was a smart, grown woman, capable of figuring out on her own what a piece of shit that Ravil was.

As low and cruel as it was of him to use her like that, I believed he wouldn't physically hurt her. Ana wasn't in any immediate danger that would warrant my showing up in the middle of the night and waking her up.

Forcing myself to turn around, I returned to the office. The best I could do was probably wait until Ana was back in Tadolia, then I could show her Orin's application and question his motives with her.

Or maybe I should just confront the bastard and tell him to stay the fuck away from Ana.

Oscillating between reason and my instincts like that, I couldn't calm down enough to go to bed. It'd be impossible for me to fall asleep when thoughts crowded my head, worries knotted my insides, and anger boiled my blood.

The best I could manage was to plop into Ana's favorite armchair and connect to the local television station. If I couldn't sleep and couldn't do anything to warn Ana at this hour, I could at least kill the time by watching something entertaining.

Sadly, there were only two television channels in Ravie that I could access through my tablet. One was the state media. The other one was a local station that broadcasted news and events of the area encompassing a few small towns, including Tadolia.

The limited satellite network of Tragul transmitted some Voranian and Aldraian content. Here in Tadolia, however, the feed from satellites was limited to communications only. No entertainment programming reached us.

After making myself a cup of tea, I settled in to watch the local program about preparations for a bake fair taking place two towns over the following weekend.

I tried to give the program a fair chance, dutifully following the narrator describing in every detail the production of the canvas material that was going to be used for the awnings over the merchants' tables.

Then, we moved on to the suspenseful selection of just the right outfit for the mayor's pet *elgril*, a rodent-like creature that had apparently been present at every bake fair in the area since the end of the war and had worn a different outfit for every single one. The finely dressed *elgril* was also on the jury that identified the best tarts and crowned the winning baker of each fair.

I wondered if Ana's landlord, Zaen, was going to participate in the fair and if he'd submit some of his tarts too. Then I wondered if they would be *cirine* tarts and, if so, I wondered where Zaen usually bought *cirine* fruit for his tarts.

By the time the show finally got to the categories of all the baked goods expected to be at the fair, my mind was no longer with it. It was with Ana. And with fucking Orin too.

What if I misjudged him even more than I thought? What if Ana wasn't safe with him after all?

Anxious worry rose inside me again, sending me to my hooves for the millionth time that night.

"...higher than expected rain volume for this time of the year is to blame for the breach of the dam," came from the screen of my tablet, snapping my attention back to the program.

The show about the bake fair was no longer on. Instead, a Ravil woman with a concerned expression pointed at the wall map.

"The following areas are affected..." She named several places that were mostly unfamiliar to me, until, "...Razor Ridge."

"What?" I stared at the screen, trying to make out the exact location on the map where the woman was pointing.

"...luckily, the flooding isn't expected to reach any populated areas," the woman continued.

"But there are people out there!" I shouted at the screen. "Ana is there!"

I ran outside, jumped into the aircraft, and started the engines. Before taking off, however, I remembered that I might be unable to contact anyone from the air, so I pushed my contact screen.

"Town security office," the sleepy voice of an officer sounded through the speaker.

I quickly explained the situation to him.

"I'm flying there right now," I said, pulling on the controls to take off.

"I'll send the emergency aircraft right away too," the officer promised.

I pulled up the map with the location of the Razor Ridge and directed the aircraft to it.

The sunrise was well on its way by the time I reached the

ridge. Water rushed over the tall rocks in a wide, relentless current. The river swelled, flooding the jungle and uprooting trees. Horror seized me at the thought that Ana was down there somewhere, possibly lost in the disaster.

I lowered the aircraft as far down over the raging river as I dared and turned on the floodlights. Illuminated like this, the scene of devastation below looked even more terrifying. Torrential rain poured down on my aircraft. The river below roared and churned, cutting into the jungle, and tossing around long, thick trees like playthings.

Starting from the top of the waterfalls, I slowly flew down the stream, hovering low over the river. I didn't know the exact location of Ana and Orin's campsite, but I feared that wherever it was, it might've flooded already. There was simply no space remaining anywhere along the river to accommodate a tent.

I cursed myself for not following my instinct and not coming here sooner. Ana would've been angry with me for waking her up and interrupting her date with Orin, but she would've been safe and sound now.

A flash of white caught my attention—a pair of white short pajamas.

Ana!

She ran down the stream, climbing over the fallen trees and crashing through the shrubs at the water's edge.

As my aircraft came closer, she climbed onto a fallen tree trunk and waved with both hands. She looked so small and helpless standing in the rain alone like that. My heart twisted in agony.

"I'm coming, sweetheart!" I shouted, knowing she couldn't hear me behind the noise of the weather.

There was no place for me to land. I circled around her, letting her know I had spotted her. Dense jungle surrounded her, with not a single break in the canopy for me to land the aircraft.

I turned down the river again, hoping to find a clearing close enough. I didn't need much space or even a particularly even ground to land, but I saw nothing even remotely suitable.

"Fuck, fuck, fuck…" I chanted under my breath, peering into the pale light of the early morning.

Worry wrecked me. With every passing moment, I was moving farther and farther away from the spot where I'd left Ana. I needed to make sure she was alright. I couldn't leave her, even if I had to crash-land the aircraft in the jungle.

I turned the controls sharply, steering the aircraft back upstream. A flat island caught my attention. It was close to the riverbank where I'd left Ana, separated from the main ground only by a narrow strip of water for now. It must've been a part of the mainland until recently, but the stream had already washed away whatever trees had been there, leaving only dirt and wet underbrush. In a little while, the entire island would likely disappear under water. But for now, it would work as a landing platform.

I brought the aircraft down promptly, jumped out, then waded across the narrow stream to the mainland. Rushing up the riverbank, I had only made it a short distance from the island when Ana came running toward me.

"Ana!" I exhaled with relief.

The crushing weight of terror eased off my shoulders when I finally wrapped my arms around her.

Soaking wet, out of breath, and with only soggy, dirty socks on her feet, she fought out of my embrace.

"Orin…" she panted heavily, sucking air in short, ragged breaths.

Right, Orin must be here too, somewhere.

"Where is he?" I asked.

"The river took him…" she sobbed, her tears mixing with rain on her face. "We were swimming across. He helped me, but then…a tree crashed into him and pushed him down the stream."

"When?"

She speared her fingers through her wet hair, looking devastated.

"Just now. Up there…" She waved up the stream.

Orin could be dead already. We risked ending up dead too if we lingered, looking for him.

"Esvar…we can't leave him," Ana pleaded.

I didn't want to leave him. Orin was probably a fraud and a scoundrel. Likely a liar too. I wanted him gone from our lives for good. But I didn't wish him dead.

Ana was my priority, however.

"Come." I lifted Ana in my arms and ran back to the aircraft.

The wet ground sucked in my hooves. I slipped on the fallen leaves. The long grass caught my legs. But I made it back to the island with my precious woman in my arms. I waded across the narrow stream toward the aircraft, opened the pilot's door, and put Ana in the seat.

"Stay here."

"What? But where are you going? Wait…" She made a move to jump right out.

I put a hand on her knee, her bare skin wet and cold under my palm.

"Stay here, Ana, please. Keep the lights on. If the water gets too close, push this button and pull this lever to take off. The aircraft will then hover over the river at a safe height until the emergency aircraft gets here."

"But—" she tried to protest, but I squeezed her knee gently.

"You'll be safe. All you'll have to do is push this button and pull this lever right here. Promise, you'll do it, Ana."

"I won't leave you."

"I'll be fine. I'll find Orin. You don't have to wait for us. Do you understand, sweetheart? None of this matters unless you're safe. Please? We don't have much time. Promise me you'll take off before it's too late."

She hesitated, biting her lip.

"Ana? Promise me, or I'll take you home myself, right now."

"I'll do it." She nodded quickly.

I brushed a wet strand of hair away from her face. She shivered in her thin wet pajamas, and I wished I could keep her warm in my arms. But while I lingered, Orin might be fighting for his life somewhere. I had to hurry if I wanted at least a chance to deliver him to her alive.

With a last squeeze of Ana's knee, I let go of her and grabbed a portable light source, a knife, and a long thin rope from the emergency kit in the cargo compartment. Then I waded across to the mainland, noticing that the water was at my hip now when it had only reached past my knee the first time I'd crossed it. If it got as high as my shoulders, the entire island would be under. If I wanted to make it back in time, I had only minutes to find Orin, and I had no idea where exactly he was. At this rate, the stream could've taken him way past the distance I could ever cover by walking.

If he was still alive at all...

Even if I managed to find him, it all could be for nothing. The poor Ravil might have drowned already. But I knew that neither Ana nor I would ever forgive me if I didn't at least put in an honest effort in finding the asshole.

"Orin!" I yelled out down the river.

My voice drowned in the roar of churning water, just as the jungle was slowly drowning in the river.

My light source proved unnecessary at this hour. By now, the morning sun illuminated the river enough for me to see the pale-yellow foam on the surface of the churning water and the debris carried by the stream.

"Orin!" I screamed again, running down the river bank as fast as the wet, slippery ground allowed.

Ana said that Orin had been washed away with a tree, and I peered closely at every log and trunk passing by.

A pile of uprooted trees and debris rose from the water up ahead, stuck and not moving with the stream. I shone my light source at it, inspecting the dark spots where the sunlight couldn't reach yet.

Clinging to a root, a Ravil fought against the stream that tried to push him under.

Orin!

His tawny-orange fur almost completely blended with the dark orange water. It was a miracle I'd spotted him at all.

I waded into the stream up to my waist, trying to get to him, but the current was so strong, it almost knocked me off my hooves. There was no way I could swim to him without being swept away or hit by a log myself.

I looked around frantically, thinking what to do. Unwinding the rope, I tied one end of it to the nearest tree that was still in the ground. I wrapped the other end around my waist. With a little luck and some effort now, the current would take me straight to Orin.

If only he had enough strength to hold on a little longer.

CHAPTER 14

ORIN

The roar of water drowned out everything, rendering me completely deaf to any other sound. I heard nothing but the storm and the frantic beating of my heart.

The raging current slammed into me over and over. I held on to the tree root with my left arm—the only arm I could use. Excruciating pain shot through my right arm. I didn't need to see it tossed by the current like a limp branch to know that it was broken.

Light suddenly blinded me.

Had the morning light made its way between the broken roots and branches?

No, the light seemed to come from the shore.

I closed my eyes, unable to see anything with it shining straight in my face. And when I opened them, someone was swimming from the shore toward me, someone with a pair of long gray horns and arms strong enough to combat the current or at least to make it work to his advantage.

Esvar?

Fucking Voranian.

What was he doing here?

Instead of anger or irritation, however, relief warmed me. I wasn't alone. The sight of his horns jutting out of the churning water came as a beacon of hope.

In a few long moments, he reached me.

"Can you swim?" he asked, spitting out water from his mouth and blinking the rain out of his eyes.

His dripping-wet fur plastered his skull.

"Where is Ana?" I squeezed between my chattering teeth.

"Safe."

That one word lifted a burden that tormented me far more than my broken arm. She was safe.

He gave me a quick, assessing look.

"Your arm?"

I winced. "Broken. I think."

Holding on to the root with one hand, he reached under the water with the other and pulled out his belt.

"What are you doing?" I smirked, then teased, "Esvar, honey, no need to take your pants off for me."

I tried to smile, but it probably came out more like a grimace of pain.

He remained dead serious, of course, like always.

"We don't have much time." He looped his belt around my shoulders, then gingerly brought my broken arm to my chest.

Despite his obvious effort to be careful, pain zigzagged through my arm like lightning. I screamed, tossing back my head and grinding my teeth.

"Here. It'll be better now." He buckled the belt, securing my arm to my torso.

"Yeah, fantastic... Thanks." The pain remained strong, but there was no way I'd let Esvar hear me complain.

"Let's go," he ordered, supporting me on the side of my injured arm. "Sorry, it'll hurt."

"No kidding." I winced from another shot of pain as I let go of the root to plunge into the current with him.

It hurt. A lot. It was a miracle I hadn't passed out. But with my arm now being fixed in one position, at least there weren't any more sudden jerks and jolts.

I worked my healthy left arm twice as hard while Esvar used his free arm to swim while supporting me with the other. Unfortunately, two arms were hardly enough to keep both our bodies afloat and moving in the right direction across the river. The current caught us, tossing us aside.

"I have a rope," Esvar granted through his teeth while fighting the raging river with me.

Reaching down, he fished out the rope attached to his waist and pulled. I grabbed at the rope, too, helping him pull us toward the shore.

With a loud crack followed by a crash, a tree tipped and fell, its roots washed out from the soft ground.

"Fuck," Esvar cursed. "That's the tree I tied the rope to."

The tree rolled into the water, quickly caught by the current.

"Get the rope off!" I reached underwater, searching for the knot around his waist.

If we didn't untie it right away, we were both fucked. The tree would pull us out into the middle of the stream and down the river. Esvar must've realized that, too, frantically tugging at the knot with me.

Turning in the water, the tree rolled downstream. The rope tightened, yanking Esvar forward. I gripped his shoulder with my healthy hand. There was no way I'd let him disappear on me. He had come all this way for me, and I wasn't going to let the river take him to his death now.

Instead of pulling us down the stream with the tree,

however, the rope remained stationary. It stretched from us to the shore, keeping us in place. I followed the bright yellow line of the rope with my eyes.

"Ana!" Esvar exhaled.

And there she was, standing at the water's edge and holding the end of the rope that she'd untied from the tree earlier and had already wound around a tall stump nearby. Rain pummeled down on her, plastering her thin clothes to her body and running down her face, but she waved at us energetically.

"Fuck, we have the best girlfriend in the world." I tugged on the rope, eager to get to her.

"One thing we sure have in common," Esvar agreed, pulling on the rope with me. "You and I have excellent taste in women."

SHORTLY AFTER ESVAR and I had climbed up the riverbank and onto the solid ground, the emergency aircraft arrived. It transported me to the medical facility in the closest town, where the doctor had scanned my arm and set my bones before allowing me to see Ana and Esvar, who waited in the front room of the hospital.

Dressed in dry clothes that had likely come from the hospital's donation bin and were at least two sizes too big for her, Ana still had a towel over her shoulders with her hair spread over it. Her hair was mostly dry now, but the streaks from tears on her cheeks seemed fresh.

My heart burst with the intense need to comfort her.

"Ana. Have you been crying, my beautiful?" I rushed to her.

But she stepped away from my open arms.

"I'm fine." She dried her cheeks with her hands quickly. "How are you doing? How is the arm? What did the doctor say?"

"I'll live." I shrugged, giving her a smile, despite the worry slithering into my chest. "But how are you? What's going on? Has a doctor seen you too? Have you been sitting here all this time? Have you had breakfast yet? Esvar, please tell me you fed her."

I'd expected Esvar to hold her, comforting her in my absence. But he was awkwardly shifting from hoof to hoof in the corner. Ana used to enthusiastically accept cuddles from him. What was different now?

Instead of feeling any satisfaction from this obvious distance between them, it irritated me. I would've far preferred to see Ana happy on Esvar's lap than upset and in tears like that. He should've taken care of her while I wasn't around to care for her myself.

"I'm not hungry." Ana waved away my concerns.

A nurse came in with a small cloth bag in her hand.

"Here is some tea for the pain." She handed me the bag. "You can go home now. Take it easy, don't overexert yourself. The doctor would like to see you in a week to monitor how the fracture is healing."

"Is Orin going to be okay?" Ana asked the nurse.

"He'll be good as new in a few weeks," the nurse replied brightly. "As long as he stays away from all natural or unnatural disasters, of course." She smiled. "The doctor will see him weekly for the next six weeks to make sure the healing goes as it should."

"Are you saying that all functions in his arm and hand will be fully restored?" Ana kept fretting over it.

The nurse nodded. "It's a fairly clean fracture, surprisingly, considering the circumstances. If nothing else happens to impede the progress, it should heal well, with full recovery. We'll see you in a week, Orin." She smiled at me, then left.

"How will you get here for your next visit?" Ana turned to me with a worried expression.

"I have a week to figure it out." I shrugged.

Weekly visits would be difficult to accomplish now that my aircraft had taken a dive into the river and disappeared without a trace. But no one needed to know that. With my arm in a cast now, there was nothing else for the doctor to do anyway. It'd heal eventually, with or without someone looking at it every week.

"Is a new aircraft just going to materialize in a week?" Esvar squinted at me with sudden suspicion.

"I said, I'll figure it out," I snapped.

"How?" he insisted.

"Well, that isn't any of your business, is it?"

He crossed his arms over his chest, his tail lashing irritatingly. "I'm afraid it very much is."

"What do you mean, Esvar?" Ana frowned. "It sounds like you're attacking him for some reason?"

"Not attacking, just clarifying something," the Voranian explained. He spoke calmly, but I sensed a concealed menace in his voice, like a storm hiding among the clouds. "I believe Orin has a hidden agenda here. Don't you, Orin? Do you date women with a certain goal in mind?"

"What the fuck are you talking about?" I lashed my tail against the rug-covered floor.

Did he hit his head on a tree while rescuing me? Because what he was saying made no sense at all.

"Why did you ask Ana to dance with you the day you first saw her?" he demanded grimly.

The answer to this question was simple.

"Because I liked her from the moment I first laid my eyes on her," I said.

"But did you know who she was before you met her? Did you find out where she worked before you approached her?"

That sounded very much like an interrogation, and I still failed to understand the reason for it.

"No!" My voice rose with indignation. "I didn't even know there was a human woman in Tadolia until I spotted her sitting at the table all alone and so obviously wishing she could be dancing instead."

"Esvar, what are you doing? Why are you questioning him like that?" Ana seemed offended on my behalf too.

"He's a scoundrel, Ana." Esvar advanced toward me, spitting words through his teeth like hurling stones. "He applied for a grant from our foundation. I found his application last night. He wants money. And, I suspect, he started dating you to increase his chances of getting the grant."

Blood boiled in my veins with anger.

"Fuck you!" I shoved against his shoulder with my healthy arm. I'd use the broken one too if I had to. Rage from the insult flared inside me, making me forget about both pain and reason.

How dare he! How could he put a dirty label like that on my relationship with Ana? Since the day I met her, she'd been the brightest, most beautiful part of my existence, and he tried to soil it now by accusing me of using her for…money?

I swung a fist, but he grabbed my wrist, blocking the blow I wished so much to place on his fucking face.

"You stay away from her!" He raised his voice along with his fist.

"Not a chance!" I twisted my wrist out of his hold and took another swing.

He whipped his tail, trapping my wrist with it this time.

"Orin, stop it!" Ava screamed, wedging herself between us. "Esvar, you too!"

The nurse ran into the room again, followed by two security officers.

"Disturbances like that aren't allowed inside the medical building," the nurse said quickly, darting her gaze from me to Esvar.

The security officers flanked us on both sides. One of them glanced at Ana, and she nodded somberly as if answering some unspoken question, then walked to the door.

"Sorry for all of this…" she said to the nurse. "I'm leaving now. Goodbye."

She glanced at Esvar, then at me.

The chill of realization spread through my chest. Was she saying goodbye to all of us? To me too?

"Ana, wait!" Esvar lunged after her.

Since he'd never released my wrist from the noose of his tail, he ended up yanking me along. I ran with him, trying to keep up.

She didn't stop. With her head down, she promptly left the room. Esvar and I ran after her into the clearing in front of the medical building with several aircraft parked to the right.

The rain had tapered to a drizzle by now, but the dark clouds still hovered low over the ground. Ana hugged herself, turning to face us.

"Ana, darling," Esvar pleaded. "I just didn't want you to go through a heartache because of *him*." He jerked on my wrist with his tail, lifting my hand as if it was somehow evidence of my perceived transgression.

Betrayal stung like a sharp needle. I knew Esvar owed me neither friendship nor loyalty—there was no love lost between us. But his accusations still felt like a stab in my back.

Maybe it was because I'd started to see him as a decent guy lately, especially after he'd braved the raging river to swim to my rescue… I'd even started to believe that I might possibly respect him one day. But then, he had to go and make up lies about me to the woman I treasured more than life.

I yanked my arm, shaking his tail off my wrist.

"Stop with the lies already," I hissed at him through my teeth.

Ana looked at me. Her big, dark eyes trapped me.

"Then tell him the truth, Orin," she said softly. "You don't need to play games with us. If you really need help, all you have to do is ask."

If only it were that simple, but I'd rather cut my one good arm off than ask anyone for help. I'd been doing everything myself, trying to get it all done on my own, and the weight of it all had built up to the point of crashing me.

I ran a hand through my hair. Even admitting it to someone was hard.

"The truth sucks, Ana. My farm is failing, and I have no means of keeping it going on my own. I've run out of options. But I never saw *you* as a solution to my financial problems. I admit I wasn't looking for anything serious when I first met you. At first, you were a very welcome escape from reality. But you've become so much more very quickly. When I'm with you, I remember how true happiness feels. The war might've ended two years ago, but only with you did I finally get a taste of peace."

Her eyes glistened with emotion. She swayed forward as if to run into my arms, but her feet didn't move.

Why would she not come to me for a hug that I was so eager to give her?

"Oh, Orin..." she breathed out. "I-I didn't know how bad things were with the farm. You never told me. I would've been there for you, Orin. You know I would."

"I know, beautiful. I know you have a kind heart. But why would I unload all this mess onto your shoulders? I learned about the grant program from a booklet that my *cirine* seed supplier gave me back in the City of Ravie. It was a government pamphlet of sorts, so I assumed it was a government program when I applied. It gave me hope that I might get to keep the farm after all, that I could pull through and give you the amazing life that you deserve. I only learned last night that the grants came from *him*." I stabbed my finger in Esvar's direction.

"From our foundation," Esvar corrected, as if such a detail mattered at that point.

I ignored him, keeping my gaze fixed on Ana.

"I want you, Ana, more than I ever wanted anyone in my life. I…" I loved her. There were no doubts in my heart about the powerful, all-consuming feeling I held for her. But I wasn't going to tell her that during an argument in the parking field of the hospital with Esvar standing next to us. "I…I certainly wasn't using you to get to his money," I finished in one breath.

More than anything, I wished I could kiss her now. But she kept her distance, and when I took a step forward, she moved a step back, away from me.

Did she not believe me?

Panic speared through my chest at that thought.

Did Esvar's lies ruin it all, just like he undoubtedly intended?

Esvar rubbed his neck, frowning deeper than usual, but he said nothing, and for that I was grateful. All my senses were tuned in on Ana as I waited for her reply.

"I never doubted you, Orin," she said, avoiding my eyes. "I can usually sense an asshole a mile away. Even my ex was a decent man—a wrong man for me, but not an asshole. I always knew you aren't either."

I should feel relieved at her words, but she still wouldn't come to me. The three of us formed a triangle, with Ana keeping an equal distance from both Esvar and me.

"But that doesn't change anything." Her voice came out so small, it pained me. "I can't be with you, Orin."

My breath caught in my throat, choking me. My heart seemed to stop. All I could do was just stare.

Esvar sucked in air with a shocked sound.

"I can't be with you either, Esvar," Ana added quickly, not looking at either of us. "I…I just can't do this any longer. It isn't fair to either of you. I feel like I'm leading you both on, and it's…it's wrong. You deserve better."

A soft sob fell from her lips, and I couldn't take it anymore.

"Ana." I rushed to hug her, but she still wouldn't let me, raising her hands in a protective gesture.

Esvar froze in his tracks on his way to her too.

"I can't give you what you want, Orin," she said. "I can't make your dream come true. And it kills me…" She shut her eyes tightly, tears trembling on the tips of her long eyelashes. "I can't make you happy either, Esvar. I tried so hard to manage this arrangement the best I could. I was so afraid of hurting anyone. I hoped I could stop it from getting too far, but in the end…I failed. It got too far, didn't it?" She opened her eyes, looking at us with plea. "I'm sorry if it hurts now. I'm so, so sorry. But there is just no other way. I have to end it with both of you. Right now, before it gets even worse."

"Ana!" Esvar and I uttered in unison.

"Why end anything?" I muttered. My head was spinning, and I felt the same as when the current had tossed me in the flood—completely and utterly helpless.

She kept holding up her hands in front of her as though attempting to stop an avalanche of feelings from crashing into her.

"It's better to end it now," she said with a firm nod, as if trying to convince herself with her own words. "It's getting out of control. Just look where we are now…" She pointed at my arm. "You fight each other. You keep getting hurt. And it's all my fault—"

"No." Esvar shook his head energetically.

"I'm fine," I assured her quickly. "You heard what the nurse said. It'll heal in six weeks."

This couldn't be happening. None of it was her fault. And even if it were, I'd rather break every bone in my body than lose Ana.

"He'll be fine," Esvar echoed. "Full recovery, as the nurse said—"

"It's not about the nurse. It's..." Ana dropped her hands in frustration, then finally met Esvar's eyes. "It's me. I can't choose, okay? I'm a vile, greedy woman who wants it all. I want you both. Do you want to know how bad it really is? I think about Orin when I'm with you." She turned her gaze to me next. "And when you made love to me last night, Orin, I wished Esvar was there too. How perverted is that? Do you know what I fantasize about when I touch myself?"

She glanced between us, as if inviting us to venture a guess, but we both stood silent. I was frankly stunned by her admission and unsure what to do with it. Esvar seemed shocked as well.

"I imagine *you* in the front," Ana pointed at me, "and *him* at my back. You're both fucking me at the same time. That's my favorite fantasy now. The one that makes me come so hard and so fast, I can't give it up no matter how much I try. I know it's all kinds of wrong. I'm ashamed to even say it out loud. But I believe you both have feelings for me, and I hope that since you finally learned the whole ugly truth about me now that maybe...maybe those feelings would fade, and you'll hurt less about your relationship with me being over..." She backed away from us, with her hands pressed to her chest, as if trying to keep her own heart from breaking. "I'm sorry. I really am... I hoped that getting to know you better would help me choose, but instead...instead I fell in love with you both."

She turned on her heel with a sob and jogged toward the parked emergency aircraft from Tadolia that was getting ready to take off.

"Ana!" I sprinted after her, with Esvar close on my heels.

I hadn't quite processed everything that she'd said yet, but I just couldn't let her go.

"Don't!" She waved us off, jumping into the aircraft.

Its propellers spun, raising a wall of wind between Ana and

us. The aircraft took off, leaving Esvar and me standing in the meadow alone.

My stomach hollowed, and my chest felt empty with my heart squeezed into a ball of pain.

Ana was without a doubt the best thing that had ever happened to me. And now, it felt like I had lost her for good.

CHAPTER 15

ESVAR

"Esvar," Fyna met me at the door to our office the moment I walked in after my lunchtime run. "Have you put this in the system? I can't find it there and need to make sure."

She thrust a piece of paper into my hand. I glanced at it—Orin's application for a grant.

"No, I didn't."

With the doubts about Orin's true intentions, I didn't want to process it when I had first discovered it six days ago. In the days that followed, I hadn't had a chance to come back to it.

"Good. Less work for me to do." Fyna tossed the application into the trash bin.

"Wait!" I quickly snatched the paper out of the bin before it would get shredded and pulped. "Why did you do that?"

"We got a letter of cancellation from the applicant. But since you've never inputted his information into the system, I don't have to search for it to delete it now."

"He cancelled?" I stared at Orin's name scribbled at the top of the form. "But why?"

Fyna shrugged.

"Who knows? Maybe he found money elsewhere? Or maybe he doesn't want to run the farm anymore?"

Or maybe his pride made him do it?

Knowing Orin, my assumption was the most accurate one. Orin didn't want to have anything to do with me. He certainly wouldn't want to feel obligated to me either. He probably blamed me for Ana breaking up with us, just as I blamed him for that at first.

In the days since, however, my thoughts and feelings had shifted. I was no longer angry at Orin for endangering Ana by taking her on that doomed camping trip. No one could've predicted that the dam would break, resulting in the massive flood. And frankly, had I not injured Ana's foot, she would've been able to go on the hike that Orin had initially planned. They would've walked up into the jungle and camped away from the river, likely escaping the flood completely.

So ultimately, Ana and Orin getting caught in the disaster that night was my fault, not Orin's.

Ana must be blaming me, too, because she hadn't come to the office since the day of the flood. Instead, she'd been conducting meetings with the applicants, along with the men from our office. When checking her schedule, I noted that she'd carefully chosen the meeting dates when I wouldn't be present, making sure she wouldn't have to see me at work for at least an entire month.

She now spent most of her time away from Tadolia. Yet I ran past the bakery building every fucking day, just to catch a glimpse of her empty window.

My fault was in everything that had happened, including the flood and the breakup. There was enough of it to leave me feeling guilty for the rest of my life, enough to torment me and keep the wound in my broken heart open for as long as I lived.

That didn't mean I couldn't at least try to make some things right.

"I'll be gone for the rest of the day," I said to Fyna.

I had no clear plan in my mind when I left the office with Orin's application in my hand.

In the relatively short time I'd known Orin, I'd experienced a wide range of emotions toward him, from jealousy to anger to even hate. Despite all his shortcomings, however, I believed he didn't lie when he spoke about his feelings for Ana. Whether he lied about anything else remained to be seen.

Finding Orin's farm wasn't easy. From the application, I knew its address and was able to input the location into the aircraft's navigation system. But when the aircraft arrived at that point on the map, all I could see below was an impenetrable jungle.

"Shouldn't there be a field? A garden? Or an orchard? Or wherever the fuck that *cirine* fruit grows?" I muttered to myself, peering into the purple-green canopy of the Tragulian jungle in search of any sign of life or at least a dwelling.

Much to my embarrassment, I had no idea what a *cirine* plant looked like or how it was cultivated, though I'd eaten many products made with that fruit.

Bringing the aircraft a little lower, I finally spotted the sprawling roof of a building nestled in the jungle. Covered with large green-and-purple leaves, the roof blended with the jungle's canopy almost seamlessly, making it nearly impossible to see from the air.

The building was shaped like three rectangles, with a court-yard in the middle that opened to a landing pad in the front. Except that the landing pad was now almost completely over-grown with shrubs and vines. It'd gotten possibly worse in the past six days since Orin had lost his aircraft in the flood and no longer used the pad. But I suspected it hadn't been perfectly cleared or groomed for much longer than that, allowing the jungle to almost fully reclaim it now.

I swerved to the right of the house where I finally saw a cultivated patch.

Two *marids* were harnessed to a wide piece of equipment meant to weed the field. But they weren't working. Braying frantically, the animals beat the ground with their hooves, trying desperately to escape their harnesses. Orin wasn't there.

Had he abandoned his *marids?*

A wide path of crushed vegetation led from the jungle. At the end of the path, a large mass of gray flesh undulated at the edge of the field.

A *fescod?*

I'd never seen one before. Even from a distance, the creature looked repulsively terrifying.

I grabbed the controls, unsure whether to land or to flee. Then I saw Orin. With a long blade clutched in his left hand, he slashed at the *fescod* while trying to evade the attack of the creature's numerous dangerous appendages.

The Ravil was fast and vicious. Like most of his countrymen, he had undoubtedly killed many *fescods* before. But he currently had only one functioning arm—the left one. His right arm was still in the cast and suspended in a sling.

No longer hesitating about what to do, I landed my aircraft on the field, next to the terrified *marids*. After a hurried search through my emergency kit, I grabbed the first thing that looked like it could pass for a weapon—a long metal bar of some sort.

"Hold on, Orin!" I ran into the fight, wielding the bar over my head.

At full speed, I slammed the bar against the thick, gray body of the *fescod*. My weapon bounced right off, nearly hitting me on the head.

"Fuck." I ducked, barely evading a snap of the *fescod's* sharp pincers with spikes.

Its massive body wobbled with thick rolls of flesh. Slim appendages emerged from its mass, equipped with sharp spikes and toothy claws.

"How do you fight these bloated sacks of shit?" I cursed under my breath.

"Cut and stab, Esvar. Don't punch," Orin panted, slashing with his blade.

He left long gashes in the *fescod's* thick skin, but they weren't deep enough to slow the creature's attack. Even worse, the cuts quivered and moved, sealing themselves shut shortly after Orin had inflicted them. The *fescods'* flesh had the ability to regenerate, which made incapacitating them so much more difficult.

Cut and stab.

I had no weapon that cut. So I grabbed my bar and jammed it into the *fescod's* side. Dark blood burst out, but only briefly. The *fescod's* flesh constricted around the bar, tightening and thickening around it. I tried to pull the bar out, but it was now fully seized by the *fescod's* body, stuck in his muscle tissue like in a firm grip of a fist.

"What the fuck?" I let go of the bar, stunned.

"Yeah, these fuckers are nasty." Orin blew away a lock of his hair that had fallen over his eyes, then ducked to avoid a snap of a *fescod's* claw.

I pulled at the bar, trying to pry it out. But to no avail. The creature rolled forward, snapping its claws and pincers at me. I retreated step by step, racking my brain about what to do next.

Orin sliced another long gash in the *fescod's* flesh. Tossing his weapon aside, he then grabbed one side of the wound.

"Help me rip him open!" he yelled. "Quickly, before it seals shut."

I remembered reading somewhere that to kill a *fescod*, one had to reach inside and rip its heart cluster out. Never in a million years would I have thought I'd end up needing to do that in real life.

I leaped forward, but the *fescod* jerked sideways, knocking Orin off his feet. The massive shapeless blob of skin and flesh threatened to crush the Ravil under its weight. With only one functioning hand, Orin could do nothing to keep the wound from closing.

The *fescod* rolled over Orin's dropped blade, burying it under its gray body. We had nothing to cut with anymore.

But I always had something to stab with.

Taking a step back, I rammed forward and speared the *fescod* with my horns. I jerked my head back quickly, yanking my horns out, then dug my fingers into the wounds promptly, preventing them from closing.

"Perfect spot," Orin approved.

He climbed to his knees as the *fescod* tried to roll away in an attempt to shake us off. I wouldn't let it get away, though, tearing at its flesh and widening the wounds just enough for Orin to reach inside.

"Hold it!" Orin yelled, sinking his entire arm up to his shoulder into the *fescod's* dark mass under its thick skin.

The flesh convulsed with a splash of dark blood. Orin yanked his arm out, holding a quivering heart cluster in his hand.

"Got it!" he cried out triumphantly, then tossed the bloodied organ aside.

The *fescod's* body spasmed with a shiver rippling through its flesh, then stilled, dropping to the ground like a giant, half-deflated balloon.

"Thanks." Orin plopped down on his ass, resting his left arm on his bent knee while catching his breath.

My knees gave in, and I sat on the ground next to him. My hands shook. I fisted them tightly, but it hardly helped. I'd never killed anyone before, even if it was just a mindless *fescod*...

"Are you alright?" Orin gave me a close look, then nodded in understanding. "First time for you, isn't it?"

"Yes." I tried to smile, but my facial features just wouldn't cooperate.

"I'd like to say that it gets easier, or some other crap like that but…" He stared at his good hand, making a fist, then flexing his fingers open. "Let's just hope you'll never meet another one ever again."

Orin was younger than me and often acted his age. Right now, however, there was a maturity well beyond his years in his hard look.

I glanced over my shoulder at the lifeless mass of the dead *fescod*.

"What an ugly creature," I spat through my teeth.

"Ugly, disgusting, and hard to kill, especially with one arm." Orin gestured at his cast. "Looks like you got here just in time. Now you can add killing a *fescod* to your life experiences."

I blew out a breath, finally managing a semblance of a smile.

"I sure gained a new appreciation for everyone who had to go through this, both during the war and now."

"During the war, it was harder. They never attacked on their own like this. There was always a whole army of them crashing through the jungle at once."

"Are you sure there aren't any more nearby now?" I peered into the trees with concern.

Orin shrugged.

"There may be. But without their central mind, they no longer move or attack in packs. I've never had more than one attack in a day here since the war ended."

"Are you saying they've attacked you here before?"

He nodded. "Not as often lately. The last one came by more than a month ago. Their numbers are dwindling, which is a good thing for Ravie. *Fescods* aren't true animals. Even as mindless creatures, they bring no value to our planet, just destruction."

The fescod's blood dripped from my horns down onto my face. Cringing, I wiped it off, then rubbed my hands on the grass, trying to clean them off.

Orin squinted at me, giving me a close once-over.

"Those horns are sure handy. You make me wish I had a pair too. You know what?" He pushed to his feet. "I'm done with work for today. By the time the *marids* calm down enough to work again, it'll be dark anyway. Let's put them in the barn and go to the house. You'll need to wash off all that blood before getting into your pretty aircraft. We both deserve a beer too."

"Sorry, I parked on top of your crops," I said, after Orin and I had washed the blood off our hands and faces under a water hose in the courtyard.

"It doesn't matter now." He handed me a massive clay mug of dark beer, then took a seat in an old wicker armchair next to me.

Once upon a time, the courtyard must've been open to the fields beyond. The family would gather here, around the large river-rock fire pit in the middle. Children would be playing on the wide, wraparound porch of the house shaded by the leafy jungle canopy.

At some point in time, however, probably during the war, the porch had been fitted with thick wooden spikes. Sticking out at an angle, they were meant to prevent *fescods* from rolling onto the porch and destroying the house. The courtyard was now fully enclosed, cut off from the fields by a tall log fence with a sturdy gate in the middle.

"I'm just tending that field mostly out of habit now," Orin

said with an awkward smile. "No one needs it, but I don't have it in me to let it all go to waste. I won't be around to harvest it, anyway."

That came as a shock to me.

"Are you going somewhere?" I asked.

He nodded. "I'm moving to the City of Ravie as soon as the farm is sold."

I nearly choked on my beer. "You're selling it?"

He nodded again, not looking at me directly, then took another swig of his beer.

I knew Orin only for a short time, but in all this time, two things had been unwaveringly strong about him—his love for his family home and his passion to bring the farm back to life.

The question *"Why?"* was on the tip of my tongue. But I believed I already knew the answer.

Even with my limited knowledge about farming, two *marids* weren't nearly enough to clear and restore the vast fields that used to surround the farmhouse before the jungle had reclaimed them. From Orin's application, I knew the exact size of this property. The cultivated patch where Orin had been working today before I showed up represented probably one-tenth of the land he owned.

Orin simply didn't have the resources to do everything that had to be done, especially while also having to fend off the attacks of *fescods*. I didn't need to pressure him into voicing his financial troubles out loud. I got the picture.

"My seed supplier already has a buyer for me," he said in an upbeat voice, but he couldn't quite mask the somber expression that settled over his eyes.

I put my beer mug on top of a stack of patio stones that served as a side table in the sitting area by the fire pit. The stones must've been brought here to replace the missing and broken ones in the patio, but Orin hadn't gotten around to it yet. Grass and shrubs had taken over the porch and the patio, poking out from between the rocks. Everything grew exceptionally fast in the warm, humid climate of Tragul. It was impossible for one man to stay on top of it if he had no outside help and only one working arm now.

"Listen, Orin." I rested my elbows on my knees, leaning forward. "I heard you withdrew your application—"

He scoffed with a sharp lashing of his tail.

"Believe it or not, Esvar, I honestly didn't know it was your foundation that provided the grants. I knew Ana worked for you and that you owned an investment business or something. But I had no idea that these two were connected."

I raised both hands.

"Hey, I believe you. I'm sorry I threw those accusations at you. It's just that even the slightest possibility of that happening…" I ran a hand over the fur on my head, letting my voice trail off.

I didn't come here to rekindle an old fight.

"Anyway," I said firmly. "Who cares where the money comes from if you're perfectly qualified to receive it?"

"I don't want your money," he said resolutely.

"It's not *my* money. I mean, not all of it and not anymore. I have my personal investments of course, but the grants come directly from the accounts of the foundation."

"Same difference." He shrugged.

What a stubborn man he was! The obstinate Ravil would rather give up his home than accept any help from the foundation just because it was associated with me.

I was partially at fault in his resentment toward me. It didn't come just from us being rivals for a woman's affection. I'd tried to tarnish his good name in front of Ana. Orin had every right to kick me off his property, instead of inviting me in and giving me beer.

If it weren't for the *fescod* and the unexpected bonding that our fighting its attack had brought to Orin and me, I'd probably have a rib or two broken by Orin now, and I would've deserved it too.

"Orin." I leaned closer. "If you refuse the grant, it'll go to someone else. Hopefully to someone just as deserving as you are, but I'd be hard pressed to find a more suitable candidate than you."

"There are plenty of deserving people in Ravie," he dismissed.

"True, but you're definitely one of them. This farm is exactly what we're looking to support—a long-standing Ravil family business with an owner who has a strong personal connection to it and a deep desire to bring it back to life. You grew up here. You've worked this land yourself. You know what needs to be done. All you need are the resources to make it happen."

He stared straight ahead, saying nothing. But his silence gave me hope that he was at least considering my words. At the same time, his frown didn't look very promising.

"Listen," I said carefully. "Even if you were pursuing Ana with the intention of getting the grant—"

"I fucking told you I was not!" he snapped, slapping a hand on his chair's armrest.

Fuck, that had been the wrong thing for me to bring up.

"I know. And I'm sorry," I said in an even and hopefully calming tone of voice. "What I mean is that it doesn't matter. You qualify for the grant either way. I just got scared that day. When I saw your application... The mere idea of someone using Ana that way made me lose my mind. I didn't think rationally when I accused you. I know you genuinely like Ana."

"I love her—" he cut himself short, as if regretting voicing his feelings out loud. "I kind of hoped to say it to *her* rather than to you, but here we are..."

He sighed heavily.

"Ana is impossible not to love, isn't she?" I smiled as a warm, light feeling spread through my chest at the thought of her. I missed her so much my heart ached.

He blinked, glancing away.

"How…how is she doing?" he asked softly.

I grabbed my mug again and took a long swig of beer to quiet the unconquerable longing before speaking.

"I haven't seen her since that day, in the hospital."

Orin stared at me, stunned.

"Why the fuck not? Do you not work together?"

"I believe she's purposefully avoiding me." Heaving a heavy breath, I rested my mug on my knee. "I haven't seen her, but I know she isn't happy. She spends most of her time outside of Tadolia now, flying out to the interviews in this part of the country. The coworkers who accompany her say she schedules as many interviews as she can cram in a day. She then processes the information collected, goes to her rented room, and stays there until the following morning, when she then does it all over again. She doesn't socialize with anyone outside of work. They say she eats all her meals in her room too. But I'm worried sick that she may not always eat at all."

I ran a hand through the fur on my hand, wincing against a painful stab of worry in my chest.

"That's not like Ana," Orin said in a hollow voice. "Not at all. Ana enjoys being with people. She loves to laugh, to dance." Agitated, he rose to his feet abruptly, then plopped back into his chair. "What the fuck have we done, Esvar? And how do we fix it?"

I knew how he must be feeling at that moment because I'd been dealing with the same helpless and hopeless sensation sinking heavily into my stomach from that day in the hospital.

I remembered the day Ana arrived on Neron. I had barely found a few minutes to spare in my busy schedule to come to the spaceport to meet her. I was tired, stressed, and overworked. She walked out of the spaceship unsteadily after the five months of cryosleep during her journey from Earth. She looked weary, too, with her wild curls disheveled and her clothes wrinkled a little, but she beamed as she took in the greenery under the vast glass dome of the spaceport. Excitement lit up her eyes. She buzzed with it when I greeted her. Chatty and bouncy, she burst with anticipation for an adventure. Her enthusiasm proved infectious, making me see this trip in a new light too. I basked in her light.

And now… Now I was the one who had dimmed it.

Orin was right. We were responsible for all of it.

"We have to fix this," I said firmly.

I didn't know how or even *if* we could make things better for her. But I felt determined to try. For Ana, I would do anything.

An idea rose from the back of my mind. It wasn't a new idea. A selfless, emotionless, rational part of me had considered it before, from a strictly theoretical point of view, but I'd shoved it away with anger and possessive determination. I had buried it in the back of my mind and never looked at it again because I knew it'd break my heart. More than that. It would outright kill me.

But what was my life when Ana's happiness was at stake?

I drew in a bracing breath, as if ready to jump off a cliff to my death.

"I'll tell you what…" I exhaled in one breath. Every word felt like I was cutting off a limb or…slicing my own heart open. "You will renew your application, Orin. It will be approved—"

He stirred to protest, but I raised a hand, stopping him. I had to say my piece quickly and in one go before I could think about it too much, before I could *feel*.

"It will be approved," I promised, "not because of anything that I'll do or say but because you are the right candidate for this grant. There will be no objections from anyone, trust me. You will keep your farm, bring it back to life, and make it a great place to live…for Ana."

"What?" His mouth fell open.

"Wasn't that your dream while you courted her? You wanted her to live here with you, didn't you? She'll love it here," I spoke quickly. "She's no stranger to farm life. She loves Ravie and its people. This is the perfect place for the two of you to raise your children—"

"Wait a minute. What children?"

He blinked at me, bewildered, but the dreamy expression had already set behind his eyes. I recognized it easily, because what I was saying would've been my dream, too, if Ana had chosen me.

But she hadn't.

I swallowed, holding on to the remnants of my composure with everything I had.

"Yours and hers," I croaked through my tightening throat. "Because *you* can give her children. It's been proven."

Voranians could not reproduce with humans, but there was a living, breathing proof that humans and Ravils could. Emma Nowak, the first human woman on Tragul, had naturally conceived a healthy baby boy with her Ravil husband. I hadn't even considered that fact before, consumed by my burning desire to claim Ana at all costs. Ana and I hadn't spoken about children yet. I didn't even know if she wanted to have any. But if she did, it made perfect sense for her to choose Orin over me.

"Are you giving up Ana because of some hypothetical children?" Orin looked more doubtful than excited about my plan.

"No..." I searched for words to express what I was feeling so strongly. "I can't, Orin... I can't watch Ana wither in misery. I can't live my life knowing that it's because of me—"

"Not just *you*," he interrupted decisively. "I fucked up too."

"Maybe. But that's not the point now. You asked how we were going to fix it, and I want to fix it. I'll do anything for Ana's happiness."

"Even give her up?" He squinted at me.

"Even let her go," I exhaled, feeling as if life itself left me with that breath.

The weight of a mountain compressed my chest, making it impossible to say another word.

Orin sat quietly for a moment, not moving a muscle. Even the tip of his tail lay flat on the cracked patio stones, like a discarded fur duster.

"Is that why you came here?" He shook his head in disbelief. "You, the fucking strong-headed, conceited, possessive Voranian came here to tell me I can just have the woman you've wanted so desperately? The one you've fought me for so fiercely? The woman you still want just as much, I'm sure."

I hadn't come here with a firm plan in mind. But what I'd said was true. There was nothing I wouldn't do for Ana's happiness. Even if that meant life-long suffering for me without her.

"I don't just *want* her, Orin. I love her. But… Anyway, I've seen the way she looks at you. She loves you, so…" Pressing my hands into the armrest, I pushed to my hooves to get up.

My resolve was not infinite, and neither was my composure. I'd done what I had to do for the woman I loved, and it was by far the most difficult thing I had to do in my entire life.

Now, I needed to be alone before my heart burst to pieces. I'd never been through a heartache like this before. I didn't know what it'd do to me once my self-control waned, and I certainly didn't want Orin to see me when that happened.

"I should go."

"You should do no such thing," Orin drawled, getting up from his chair too. "Did you ask Ana if this was what she wanted? Or did you just make your noble decision all by yourself on behalf of all of us? How do you know that Ana even wants to be with me?"

Did he have to do this to me?

He wanted me to convince him to accept what I had given up?

With my heart wrenched out of my chest, I was on the verge of either murdering someone or bawling my eyes out, preferably without Orin being present at either of those events.

I tossed a longing glance at the gate—my escape route.

"Of course she does," I said, willing my voice not to shake. "She said she fell in love with you. I saw the way she looks at you—"

He raised a finger. "I distinctly remember her saying she fell in love with us both."

"Right. But the problem was that she couldn't choose between us. The kind, sensitive girl that Ana is, she didn't want to hurt anyone. Now that I've removed myself from the equation, she doesn't have to choose. You see? Instead of all three of us being miserable and alone, at least the two of you can be happy."

He tilted his head, his tail now flipping side to side.

"Except that I don't think I can make her completely happy, Esvar. I don't have everything needed for that. And neither do you."

"What do you mean?"

Was he walking away too?

But that solved nothing.

"I mean," he said, "that I saw the way she looks at you too. She loves you too. Ana wants us both, you and me. She stated it very clearly, actually. But the two idiots that we are, we just let it fly right over our heads, didn't we?"

No, I didn't. I had absorbed Ana's every word. I remembered everything she said. Except that to me, it sounded like she was stating the problem, not providing a solution to it, like Orin seemed to think.

"She can't have us both," I replied, utterly confused.

"Why not?" He fixed a hard stare at me with a challenge.

Was he joking?

"Because…" I spread my arms wide, momentarily lost for words. "How can that even be accomplished?"

He smirked. "She told us exactly how. You in the back, me in the front, both thrusting into her in perfect sync."

"But that's…that's just her fantasy."

"A fantasy that only you and I *together* can make a reality for her. Esvar, I can't make Ana's dream come true without you."

"What exactly are you saying here, Orin?"

A hefty dose of doubt joined my confusion. Fantasies were fantasies for a reason. Not all of them were meant to come true, and some were simply impossible to bring to life.

But Orin seemed enthusiastic.

"Come on, Esvar, just for a moment, stop being the cranky grump you always are."

"I'm not cranky at all. And I'm hardly a grump," I protested.

"Take your clothes off," he blurted unexpectedly.

"My clothes?" I glanced down my body.

Both my shirt and my pants were covered in *fescod* blood. It had dried by now, leaving dark, crusty spots and smudges all over the fabric. It stank and felt disgusting.

Orin had already washed his arm, the one he'd inserted inside the dead *fescod*. Now, he only had a few stains on his pants, and I wondered if one of the reasons why Ravils never wore shirts was to have fewer blood stains to get out of fabrics.

"Come on." Orin snapped his fingers at me. "Take them off. I'll put them in the wash. May as well while we're at it."

He reached for his belt too, looking like he was about to take his pants off right in front of me.

"Are you changing? Here?" I muttered.

"Yes. Do you have something against that?" He unbuckled his belt and tossed it aside, then opened the closure of his pants.

Did he lose his mind?

I took a step back. I'd never been in the presence of a naked male before. I'd only ever seen three women naked in my life, all of whom I'd had sexual relations with.

"I'm not into males," I clarified, just in case.

He laughed, probably at the shell-shocked expression on my face.

"Neither am I," he said. "But Ana is. And—lucky us—she is into both of us. But we can't give her what she wants if you can't even undress in front of me. How are you supposed to fuck her with me if you don't want me to see you naked?"

He grabbed the waistband of his pants, clearly intending to disrobe while I watched.

"Here? Now?" I reached for my belt hesitantly, actually considering removing my clothes.

I obviously lost my mind, too, just like Orin.

"Who'll be here to see us? Other than *fescods* occasionally, no one ever comes by this place. And *fescods* already paid their monthly visit today. So…" He yanked down his pants.

"Um…" I glanced aside quickly.

I had never planned to be connected with Orin in any intimate way. But if we both tried to be in a relationship with Ana, we had to get considerably closer to each other too. Orin was right. At the very least, we should get comfortable being naked together.

I would do anything for Ana. But if I wanted to be a part of this for the rest of my life, I realized I had to do it for myself too. If I was uncomfortable about this possible arrangement, I needed to know it now.

Slowly, I turned my attention back to Orin. I'd dreamed about being with Ana, just the two of us. Now, I tried to fit Orin into that dream.

Would it work?

Could I do it?

The Ravil grinned at me, with his hands propped on his hips and his pants gone.

My doubts and questions must've been written on my face because he nodded and said, "I know. Spending the rest of my life in your company didn't enter my mind right away, either. Since Ana mentioned it that day, however, I admit I've thought about it. I didn't believe it would work because you clearly hated me. But now that you came here with that noble plan of selfless sacrifice of yours, then helped me fight a *fescod*, I think we might be on to something here. Ana is a smart woman for refusing to choose between us. Why settle for one man and push away the other when two of us can take care of her two times better? You think my farm is a place where Ana would love to live and raise a family? Then stay here and make this family, *our* family, with us."

He hiked his chin up defensively, as if expecting me to fight him. Or laugh at him. But I didn't feel like either. Instead...I felt included.

I'd spent all my life on the sidelines of love and relationships, watching couples form and families grow with none of them being mine. I had friends and colleagues, but at the end of the day, I went home alone, slept in my bed alone, and woke up to another day with no one to share it with.

"How is that going to work?" I wondered, genuinely intrigued by Orin's idea now. "We'll all have our bedrooms and take turns?"

Orin shook his head.

"That's not what Ana said, is it? She doesn't want turns. She wants us both. So, we'd better get used to seeing each other naked."

He looked so confident, standing in front of me in nothing but his short fur that left nothing to the imagination.

"Have you done this before?" I asked, fiddling with my belt buckle without actually opening it yet.

"Sharing a woman with another man? No. That'd be a first

for me too. For better or for worse, we all will be starting at the same point, from zero."

That was good to know, but I hadn't even gone that far in my mind yet.

"I meant undressing in front of another man," I clarified.

"Oh, that… Yes. A million times. We used to bathe in rivers at war camps. All warriors at once. It's not a big deal. Don't you have communal showers at those fancy academies in Voran?"

The academy I went to had private bathrooms with individual bathtubs, but that was irrelevant at this point. There was but one way to find out if I could do it.

"Well, alright…" I finally unbuckled my belt, then opened the buttons of my shirt.

"How does it feel?" Orin asked. "Are you embarrassed? Tense? Awkward? Is it too much? Because if you push yourself too hard into doing something you don't really want to do, it may not work. Or at least, it won't work for long."

"I'm fine. Just let me try." I took off my shirt.

"So far, so good," I thought.

The breeze ran through the fur on my chest, tickling my skin underneath. It wasn't a commonly experienced sensation for me, but it wasn't unpleasant. I could certainly take the next step.

I blew out a breath and pushed my pants down, then straightened my back, facing Orin, who slid a quick glance down my naked body.

"You have furry balls!" he blurted with a burst of laughter.

It was so incredibly childish of him, I couldn't even get mad at him for it.

"So do you." I smirked, pointing at his crotch.

"Nah." He shook his head. "Mine aren't nearly as fluffy. Just look at those two fuzzy little fur balls!" He caught my unimpressed stare and lifted his hands up in a gesture of surrender. "I'm sorry, I'm sorry. I'm not making fun of you. Actually, you have an advantage over me in this area. Girls generally like cute fuzzy things, don't they?"

"If we really end up living together, I fear it'll be a challenge for me not to try to strangle you with your own tail one day," I muttered under my breath, planting my hooves in a wider stance with my pants bunched around my knees.

Orin tossed his head back in another bout of hearty laughter. I had to give it to him, his merry mood had its benefits. Humor drained the tension from my shoulders and eased the awkwardness of the situation for me.

"But it's not just you and me who will be living together, my friend," Orin murmured, wrapping his fingers around his cock. "Ana will be with us. Every day. And every night. Sharing the bed with us…"

"What are you doing now?" I squinted at his fist sliding up and down his hardening shaft.

"How well can you perform in my presence? Can you give Ana what she wants? Can you fuck her fantastic ass while I ram my cock into her sweet, wet pussy?"

Fuck.

My cock stirred at his words. Never before had I been aroused by a man's horns. But this… Well, this was more about Ana than about either of us. It didn't take long for my imagination to conjure her naked, trapped between Orin and me, and moaning.

Her little whimpers when she came on my tongue had imprinted in my mind forever. I'd never taken a woman the way Ana imagined me taking her in her fantasies. Thrill filled me when I envisioned it now.

"I'd have my tail on her clit," I rasped, fisting my cock. "She'll love that."

Pleasure spread through me from the contact. I squeezed harder, imagining Ana's little hole tightening around my shaft.

It felt fantastic. I dropped my eyelids halfway, moving my

unfocused gaze away from Orin. He was there. I was fully aware of his presence and of his hand moving energetically up and down his cock. But the image of Ana now stood firmly between us. I could almost smell her scent again, taste her skin on my tongue... The thought that I might get a chance to do it all to her again and more spurred my arousal.

"She'll hold on to my horns," I took over the narration from Orin. "She loved holding on to my horns when I ate her out."

"Fuck, I'm getting really envious of your horns," Orin groaned.

Orin had many things I could be envious of, too, from his stunning good looks to his effortless natural charm. But if Ana loved us both, there was no reason for me to envy him. She didn't need to be his or mine. She could be *ours*.

Our joint fantasy had taken over my mind and my body. Desire heated by blood as I stroked my cock.

"I'll be in a better position to play with her tits if I'm behind her," I said, savoring every detail of this vision. "But you have to use your fluffy tail to stroke her skin. Human skin is very sensitive. And Ana is so...so sensual..." I panted, struggling for breath with lust gripping every muscle in my body.

"I love...kissing her—" Orin's voice broke off abruptly.

I remembered Ana's pussy spasming with climax around my tongue, and that was my undoing. I came hard, my cock pulsing in my hand. My release shot out, splattering onto the broken patio stones.

Orgasm rocked through my body, making my knees buckle. My hooves slipped on the hard stones, sending me on my ass into my armchair.

"Fuck..." I slumped in the chair, trying to catch my breath.

With his head tilted, Orin squinted at me. A lopsided grin curved his lips. A puddle of seed on the ground between his feet proved that he'd come too, probably just before me.

"Do you still hate me?" he asked unexpectedly.

"Hate you? No. I don't think I ever did."

"Yeah, right," he drawled sarcastically.

"Alright, fine," I admitted. "I *disliked* some of your actions and certain qualities I attributed to you, which I've since discovered weren't actually true. Now, I'm willing to give you a chance."

"Aww, that's nice." His grin grew wider. "You've been growing on me too, Voranian. I think I even like you now. And it's not because we've just fucked."

"We didn't *fuck*." I rolled my eyes.

He laughed, clearly enjoying pushing my buttons. By now, however, I'd gained some understanding and even an appreciation of his silly kind of humor. Orin used it to soften the harsh realities of life. It probably helped him survive on many occasions. And right now, it definitely made life seem a little easier.

Standing over me with his shoulders spread wide, his hands on his hips, and his impressive cock halfway up again already, he presented quite a sight.

I could see why Ana wanted him. But she wanted me too. And now, I might not have to give up the woman I loved. I might get a chance to make her happy by staying with her instead of letting her go.

If only she agreed with Orin's crazy idea of all three of us forming a family together.

CHAPTER 16

ANA

It was my fault. I had no one else to blame for the misery gnawing at me. I brought this mess on myself and on the two men whom I cared so deeply about.

People often had a difficult time finding one decent person to fall in love with. I was so incredibly lucky to find two. And I lost them both. The loss crushed me. I hadn't expected to fall in love so soon after my divorce. I certainly never envisioned being torn between two men.

And now...

Now it hurt twice as much.

During the day, I kept myself busy. I made sure to have my work week solidly booked, with the out-of-town trips even spilling into my weekends whenever possible. I loved meeting the Ravil people. I'd heard so many life stories, I could probably write a long book series with the information I'd collected during the interviews. There were struggles in people's lives, but also hope for a better future.

I carefully documented all the information for the committee to determine the grants' recipients and their amounts. It thrilled me to know that many of these people would get the means to keep their businesses going, and it was all because of Esvar. He chose a worthy cause in life. Except that his admirable dedication didn't make it any easier for me to fall out of love with him now.

I missed him. I missed Orin too. So much that every reminder of them devastated me. I thought I did the right thing by breaking up with them. But it didn't *feel* right. It felt painful.

Returning to Tadolia after my latest two-day trip was like coming home. Only no one was waiting for me here. I had dinner on my own, like I did most evenings. I could've had it with Zaen and Natlea or with any of my coworkers, but I didn't feel like I deserved their company. What I deserved was this crushing, miserable loneliness, and I made sure to deliver it to myself in spades as a punishment for my inability to choose a man and stick with that choice.

I took a bath, then put on the shorts and tank top I slept in. I've been sleeping a lot lately, but it was too early for bed, barely past dinnertime. The Tragulian sun hadn't even fully set yet. I didn't feel tired. Or sleepy.

I felt nothing.

Wandering over to my kitchen area, I stared at the tea kettle. Maybe a cup of herbal tea would help me fall asleep?

Then I remembered how Esvar always had a cup of tea ready for me the moment I came into the office. The tea kettle wavered and blurred in front of my eyes, obscured by tears.

Dammit, I'd cried every single night this week.

The last bouquet of flowers that Orin had left by my door the morning before our doomed camping trip on Razor Ridge still stood on the table. It'd been just over a week since I got the flowers. The vase had almost run out of water during my last work trip, but the flowers still looked luscious and smelled amazing.

Orin's flowers lasted longer than my relationship with him. And it ended not because I'd fallen out of like with him but because I'd fallen in love…

Now, I was bawling full force. Big, ugly sobs tore out of my chest as I crashed face down onto the couch.

I barely heard the knock on my door over my crying, despite it being a rather powerful knock.

Oh no.

Zaen must've heard my wailing and came to see if he could restore the peace in his bakery.

I put on a robe over my pajamas and wiped my face with my sleeve. The last thing I wanted was to talk about my heartache with my landlord, but I had to provide some explanation for my meltdown.

"Ana! Are you alright?" It wasn't Zaen's voice.

"Orin?" I froze in my spot in the middle of the room.

For a moment, I believed that my distress resulted in hallucinations, making me hear one of the two voices I'd heard only in my dreams lately.

"Please open the door, sweetheart, or I swear I'll break it. I can't stand hearing you cry," the second of the two beloved voices I missed said.

"Esvar?" I rushed to the door and flung it open.

My heart melted at the sight of them. I didn't even ask them why they had shown up at my door so unexpectedly. I was just glad that they had.

I'd forbidden them to seek my company. I was going to reiterate it to them in just a minute. I was going to tell them to leave. Soon.

But for now…

For now, I just rested my eyes on the most wonderful sight

in the world—Esvar and Orin standing shoulder to shoulder in front of me.

"What happened, my beautiful?" Orin frowned, fisting his good hand as if ready to fight whatever or whoever had upset me.

"Ana, darling, why are you crying?" Esvar took my face in his hands, searching my eyes for answers.

"I-I just...miss you," I sniffled, losing my resolve to send them away.

"We're here now." Orin gently hugged my shoulders with his left arm, kissing my hair. His right arm remained in a sling.

"How are you? How is the arm?" I asked, swallowing my tears.

I'd been worried sick about him. I'd even called the hospital, asking for updates that they couldn't give me anyway.

"I'm fine," he dismissed with a grin. "Better than ever."

"Can we come in?" Esvar asked.

I shouldn't let them in. Sooner or later, they would have to leave again anyway, and I feared I wasn't strong enough for another goodbye.

"We need to talk to you," Orin said.

We?

That was new.

I'd thought they would fight again, trying to convince me to change my mind and somehow choose one over the other. I had not expected them to show up at my door hand in hand, with a joint mission in mind.

Esvar brushed his thumbs over my cheeks, wiping away my tears.

"Let's go in, sweetheart. I'll make you some tea. It'll calm you down." He gently led me inside my apartment and toward the couch.

His kindness was almost my undoing. It took everything in

me not to break down again and collapse sobbing on his bare chest.

Bare?

Since when did Esvar stop wearing shirts?

"What happened to your shirt?" I asked as Esvar lowered me onto the couch while Orin entered after us and closed the door.

I'd never, ever seen Esvar topless before, and it…it made him dangerously appealing right now.

"It's a long story," he muttered, suddenly looking uncharacteristically shy, then walked over to the kitchen counter to make me tea.

"Not *that* long," Orin laughed, plopping down on the couch with me. "You only lasted for like a handful of strokes."

Esvar set a tea mug on the counter with a clank. "Hey, you came first. Far ahead of me."

I moved my gaze from one man to the other, utterly confused. "What are you two talking about?"

"We had sex," Orin explained casually. "He's wearing my pants, too, by the way. His are still wet, and so is his shirt."

My mouth fell open. "I had no idea you two liked each other that way."

"We don't!" Esvar protested, returning to the couch with the tea for me. "Fuck, I'm still trying to process the notion that I like him in *any* way at all."

With the mug in my hands and my mouth agape, I just sat there, waiting for either of them to explain what was going on.

Orin hugged me from behind, gently leaning my back against his chest.

"My beautiful Ana," he murmured in my ear. "Esvar and I want to bring your fantasy to life."

"Because as it turned out, it's our fantasy too," Esvar added.

He sat down at the other end of the couch, then lifted my feet onto his lap. After sliding my slipper off my right foot, he gently massaged my sole. I'd read that Voranians often felt repulsed by human feet. Apparently, our toes and especially our ability to wiggle them looked freaky to those who were born with hooves. Yet Esvar rubbed the tension from my foot with a blissful serenity on his face, clearly savoring the physical contact with me.

"Um…which fantasy exactly are you talking about?" I asked.

Frankly, sipping a fragrant cup of tea while being hugged by Orin ever so gently at the same time as Esvar peacefully massaged my feet was already a dream come true.

"Ooh, do you have many?" Orin growled excitedly, then winked at Esvar. "She has more than one."

"Then I'm looking forward to bringing them *all* to life. In time," the Voranian man echoed.

I shook my head, amazed by how in sync these two suddenly seemed to be, when all they could do before was fight and argue.

"You finally seem to be in agreement here," I said. "Only I'm still confused about how you've reached it."

"You see, sweetheart," Esvar started. "Orin and I realized that despite all our differences, we have one very important thing in common."

"We are both in love with you," Orin finished for him.

My breath hitched in my throat. I'd both wished for and dreaded this happening. Happiness spread through me in a warm wave, making me feel lightheaded. But anxious worry quickly doused it, though.

"I'm so sorry…I didn't mean for this to happen," I half-whispered.

"Why?" Orin tightened his good arm around me from behind, sliding his hand under my breasts.

Esvar wound his tail around my ankle possessively, the arrow-shaped tip gliding up my leg in a gentle caress. "You said you cared about us both."

"Exactly. I do. And I still have no solution to this situation. I can't choose between the two of you."

"Then don't," Esvar said simply.

Orin nuzzled my hair above my ear. "Date us both."

They were hard for me to resist even when they used to fight each other. Now that they had presented such an unbelievably united front of temptation, cuddling and caressing me from all sides, I didn't stand a chance. I struggled to hold on to any remnants of common sense.

"We tried that already," I said. "It didn't work."

I knew I should get up from the couch, but Esvar was massaging my calf and Orin was gently kneading my breast through my robe, and I enjoyed it all too much to put an end to it.

"We did it all wrong, darling," Esvar said, letting his tail slide higher under my robe until I felt its tip nudge the edge of my shorts. "You dated each of us individually while trying to decide which one of us to keep and which one to let go. No wonder it caused you so much stress and anxiety."

And guilt. I constantly felt guilty, wishing and trying to do the right thing, but so confused about what that "right thing" really was.

"We believe that all three of us dating together will work much better. Because we all want the same thing," Orin said brightly.

"Which is what?" I asked tentatively.

"To stay together," both men replied in unison.

I arched an eyebrow, eyeing them skeptically. "You two want to stay together?"

"With *you*," they said at once again.

God, I loved that idea. It thrilled me how in agreement they were on it too. But...

"How is that going to work?" I asked.

I'd never even heard of anyone dating two men simultaneously. To my knowledge, even the Voranian women didn't do that. How did one have two dates at once?

Would all three of us go to the same movie together? Sit at the same table in a restaurant? Go camping together and sleep in the same tent?

So far, I had to admit, I loved the sound of every single one of those dates.

But how would my two aliens like sharing my time and my body with each other?

Orin hugged me tighter, fondling my right breast. His caress had moved past relaxing and turned invigorating as he teased my nipple through my thin robe. Heat throbbed between my legs, making me squirm.

"And…how exactly are we going to go about sex?" I asked breathlessly, shifting my hips to accommodate the progress of Esvar's tail up my leg.

"You told us *how*." Orin kissed my neck. "I'm in the front. Esvar is in the back. You're in the middle, coming on our cocks."

Oh, my God.

My inner muscles spasmed at that image, my arousal dampening my pajama shorts. I moved my legs apart, allowing Esvar's tail to slip inside my shorts.

"Oh…that sounds fantastic," I moaned at the nudge of his tail just where I needed it.

"Have you finished your tea, Ana?" Orin asked in a raspy voice. "Because I want to take that robe off you."

He took the mug from me, then slid my robe off my shoulders.

"I can't wait to have my hands on you, my sweet." He kissed my neck, tugging down my tank top.

I freed my arms, allowing him to take off my robe and slide the tank top all the way down to my waist. Orin leaned me back against his chest again, and my gaze fell on Esvar.

He seemed frozen, staring at my bare chest, and I couldn't

tell whether he was mesmerized and aroused or stunned into silence by jealousy and anger.

"Look at these, Esvar," Orin purred, lifting my breasts one by one in his hand. "Look how gorgeous our woman is."

He ran his hand from the base of my left breast to the tip, slightly pinching my nipple at the end, then did it again to my right one, fondling me openly under Esvar's full attention.

Desire spread through me in ever-increasing swells, spiking with every pinch of Orin's fingers. But I was afraid to move, waiting for Esvar's reaction with bated breath. He watched Orin's fingers playing with my nipples. His magenta eyes darkened to such a deep burgundy, they looked almost black. A deep rumble came from his throat, and I worried he might be in pain seeing another man's hands on my body.

If so, none of this was going to work. I couldn't subject Esvar to this torment, no matter how much I enjoyed Orin's touch.

I moved, trying to get up. My foot shifted in Esvar's lap, with my toes sliding along the hard erection in his pants.

He was hard. But did he want to be?

Orin didn't seem concerned. He winked at Esvar, teasing him with the sight of my nipple peeking between his fingers while he toyed with my left breast again.

"Do you want Esvar to fuck you, my beautiful?" Orin murmured in my ear. "He said you haven't seen his cock yet. He has a nice one. Show her, Esvar."

Amazingly, Esvar obeyed Orin's command. Of the three of us, Orin seemed to be the most comfortable in this unusual situation, making it easy for Esvar and me to simply follow his lead for now. It must also be a relief for Esvar to release his straining cock from his tight pants. Rising to his knees on the couch, he quickly unbuckled his belt.

"You're going to love it, Ana," Orin said excitedly, loudly enough for Esvar to hear. "He has the cutest pair of furry balls."

Esvar blew out an exasperated breath, but I noticed a smile

tugging at his lips. He appeared more amazed than annoyed by Orin's playful humor this time. Something had definitely happened between these two. Or maybe it had been happening all along? Just as my relationship with each of the men had grown, the one between them had a chance to develop and strengthen too.

Esvar yanked his pants down, freeing his cock. It stood hard and proud over a pair of testicles that were indeed covered by thick gray fur, a shade darker than the rest of him.

I couldn't help myself and reached for them.

"Oh, my goodness, they're so soft and fluffy." I smiled, cupping his ball sack with both my hands. Soft and fuzzy on the outside, the two firm spheres rolled inside under my fingers.

"Fuck." Esvar groaned, gripping the back of the couch with his left hand.

"Go easy on him, Ana," Orin warned. "He looks like he's about to come already. And I can't blame him. Just seeing your little fingers playing with him makes me want to come too."

He was looking over my shoulder, and I rubbed the side of my face against his velvety cheek.

"We can't forget about you, either, can we?" Before I even reached behind me and touched the bulge in Orin's pants, I knew he'd be hard.

Esvar slipped my shorts off while I opened Orin's pants and released his straining member too. Esvar gripped my hips, yanking me to him. With a soft giggle of surprise, I grabbed on to the first thing I could, which happened to be Orin's cock.

Orin sucked in a breath. Holding me with his arm under my breasts, he growled, "Give it to her, Esvar. Give her what she wants, what she dreams about."

Leaning closer, Esvar dragged his tongue between my legs and over my hot, throbbing clit. Sadly, just once. I moaned in protest when he withdrew, but he grabbed my thighs, positioning himself at my entrance.

"Ready, sweetheart?" he asked under his breath.

"So, so ready, Esvar..."

He moved forward, sliding into me in one firm thrust.

My desire spiked. Pleasure rippled through my body. I arched my back, squeezing Orin's cock in my hand.

"Fuck, you feel so good, my darling." Esvar's voice came out strangled and strained. "I've had my fantasies, too, Ana. And this...this is better than any of them."

He held back for a moment, as if to savor our connection or maybe to regain his composure, but lust got the best of him. With a deep growl, he rammed into me again.

Orin held me during the punishing pounding of Esvar's cock. The Ravil's tail caressed my skin with its soft tassel on the tip. Esvar pressed the tip of his tail against my clit, moving it in rhythm to his thrusts.

I squeezed my hand that was wrapped around Orin's cock, making my handsome Ravil groan in pleasure with Esvar's every thrust.

"You too, Orin..." I said. "Give me what I want too."

Tossing his head back, Esvar roared through his teeth. His cock jerked inside me. His tail rubbed harder, setting off my release. I whimpered in pleasure, my eyes drifting closed from pure bliss of the best orgasm I'd ever had.

Orin's large hand wrapped around mine on his cock to strengthen my hold on him. With two energetic joint pumps, he came too.

"Fuck...this was..." Orin gathered me in a one-armed hug, pressing my back to his chest and burying his face in my shoulder from behind.

With a long, deep exhale, Esvar leaned forward and rested his head on my thighs, carefully tucking his horns under my forearm.

I closed my eyes, feeling like I was floating in a never-ending ocean of bliss and comfort. For me, this was heaven. There was nothing more I wished for and no one else I wanted when the two men I loved were here with me like this.

I didn't want this to end. Ever.

But were Orin and Esvar feeling the same thing I did?

I opened my eyes, but before I could ask anything, my tablet dinged with a message. Without looking up from my lap, Esvar took it from the coffee table and handed it to me.

"Anything important?" he grumbled. "Or should I toss it out the window for interrupting the most amazing evening of my life?"

I glanced at the screen and huffed a breath. "Lucas wants to know how to roast a turkey…"

"What's a turkey?" Orin glanced at the screen over my shoulder.

"A large bird that people roast and eat," I explained.

"Do you not have recipe books on Earth? That's how I learned how to cook," Orin said.

"We do. But instead of buying a cookbook or looking up a recipe online, Lucas chooses to keep bugging me…"

"May I?" Esvar took the tablet from my hands.

"Please don't toss it out of the window," I quipped. "Or you'll have to deal with my boss, since it's the company's property."

Orin snorted a laugh at my words. But Esvar remained serious. Sitting up, he poked at the screen energetically a few times, then gave it back to me.

"I think it's time, Ana," he said.

A dialogue window was open with the question in both English and Voranian, "Are you sure you want to block this contact?"

Block Lucas?

I balked at the idea. What if there was an actual emergency with Lucas one day?

Then I remembered that even if there were one, I wouldn't be able to do anything about it anyway. There were other ways for him to reach me if he really needed me, through social media or through our common friends. He didn't need to have easy, direct access to me like this anymore.

Esvar was right. It was time for Lucas to find a new emergency contact and learn to live without me. It was time for me to let him go too.

I clicked "Yes", removing his ID from the list of my family and close friends, which automatically blocked him.

There was no sadness in me from that action. It felt liberating to finally sever that nagging thread from my past.

"So," I looked at the two men who were my present and, hopefully, my future. "What's going to happen with us now? How is it all going to work?"

I tried to keep worry out of my voice. Now that I got them both right here where I wanted them, I couldn't bear to even think about them leaving.

Orin kissed my cheek soothingly. "We'll figure it out as we go."

"But what if it doesn't work? What if it doesn't last?" Now that I'd tasted true happiness, the fear of losing it wrecked me.

"It will work," Orin replied with carefree conviction.

"No relationship is guaranteed to last," Esvar observed pragmatically. "But if something doesn't go smoothly, we'll talk. We'll figure it out together, and we'll make it work. The important part is that we all have a very strong motivation to make it last. We've learned that the three of us are far happier together than apart."

He was right. No relationship was guaranteed to last, but we all wanted this one to endure. That was a good start.

I smoothed the disheveled fur on Esvar's head, and he smiled, leaning into my caress.

"We should move to my bed," I murmured, arranging his fur into neat swirls around his horns. "It has more space for all of us if you want to stay the night. Are you staying the night?" I turned my head to catch Orin's gaze.

"I'm not going anywhere, for as long as you have me," he assured me with a quick kiss on my lips.

I glanced at Esvar next.

"Neither am I." He smiled, hugging my hips. "I'm here to stay, sweetheart."

I released a long breath of relief, stretching in their arms.

Yes, this was heaven.

EPILOGUE

ANA

10 YEARS LATER.

"Oh, these smell so good, Orin." I leaned over one of the trays with freshly baked *cirine* tarts. "I'll have to keep some at home for us to eat after the parade."

Orin placed a picnic basket on our large dining table for me to pack the tarts in, then hugged me from behind.

"These are for the community table for Family Day in Tadolia. I'll bake more for you tomorrow. Promise." He kissed my cheek.

"Nope. I'm keeping some. But feel free to bake more any time." I got a plate and put five tarts on it, then set it aside.

Five tarts, one for each member of our not-so-small family that included myself, my two husbands, and our two children. It was an unusual arrangement—not just in Ravie, but possibly in the whole known universe—but it worked for us.

Esvar and I had moved to Orin's farmhouse less than a month into our triple dating arrangement. It was easier that way. We no longer had to search for time to see each other when we all lived under the same roof.

The first thing that Esvar did before we even moved in was build a security system along the entire perimeter of the farm. No *fescod* had ever caught us unaware since. As reluctant as Orin was in accepting help for himself, he never argued with Esvar on anything that benefitted me. Both my husbands made my happiness and well-being their lives' missions.

Shortly after our first successful harvest of *cirine* fruit, Esvar and Orin proposed to me, right here, in our courtyard. They had decorated the newly renovated patio with flowers and colorful ribbons that I spotted from the air when returning from a shopping trip to town that night. Then they both got down on their knees as per my homeland's tradition that they had researched in every detail.

Of course, I got two wedding rings.

Esvar had his ring made from *shalel*, the rarest mineral found only on the planet Aldrai. He said he had been on a waiting list for that stone for a month before he was finally allowed to buy it and make it into a ring in time for his proposal.

The other ring, Orin had made from his mother's pendant, the only surviving piece of her jewelry he had left. I cried when he told me that. I still got misty eyed often when I looked at it, thinking about the woman I never met but deeply admired for the loving memory her son kept of her.

Orin, Esvar, and I got married a few months later, also here in our courtyard, because it was important for us to mark the official start of our family in the place where we'd made our home.

Almost the entire population of Tadolia and many people from other towns had come to our wedding. Even Governor

Eehie and his wife attended the celebration. Having more than one husband was unusual, but there was no law dictating how many a woman could have. So, both my beloved men became my lawfully wedded husbands on the same day.

For our honeymoon, we traveled around Ravie, visiting every stunning landmark and taking in as many sights as we could. We even made a stop in the remote border town where Emma Nowak lived with her family, and I finally got to meet the legendary human warrior woman who helped win the brutal war.

I used to imagine Emma Nowak as a tall, fierce, muscular woman who fought *fescods* alongside the massive Ravil men, and I was shocked to discover that Emma was actually a petite, smiling blonde, shorter and slimmer than me. The more she spoke, however, the more her inner strength and quiet confidence became apparent. By the end of the dinner shared by our two families, I no longer doubted that this woman could easily kill a *fescod* on her own, and she wouldn't even make a big deal out of it.

Having two husbands hadn't been without challenges, of course. Orin said things without thinking at times. Esvar, on the other hand, would often keep his dislikes and frustrations to himself, allowing them to build up sometimes to the point of an eventual temper explosion. Occasionally, I would lose my patience with them both. But all those things were minor and, like Orin had predicted it ten years ago, we were figuring them out as we went.

Our son, Itan, was born less than a year after our wedding. Half-human, half-Ravil, Itan inherited his dad's sandy-blond hair and my dark-brown eyes. To my delight, he also had a real Ravil tail with a cute fluffy tassel on its tip. The tail was also the only part of his body where Itan had fur. The rest of his tawny skin remained fur-free, just like mine.

Itan's younger sister, Mellae, was a full-blooded Voranian, conceived from a donor egg. She had everything her dad had—horns, hooves, and tail, as well as the Voranian temper. When she was a toddler, it proved a challenge to keep her from head-butting her brother with her small but sharp horns or from kicking him with her hooves when she got angry at him. Thankfully, that didn't happen often. Most of the time, Mellae adored her older brother, ready to attack anyone who threatened to hurt him.

Both our kids loved their dad Orin's *cirine* tarts. But no one enjoyed them more than I did.

"I think I'll have one right now," I teased Orin. "Just to make sure it's good enough to eat."

I twisted in my husband's arms to face him and caught his next kiss on my lips.

"*You* look good enough to eat," he murmured, dropping his voice dangerously low.

The velvety note in his voice resonated through my chest, spreading through the rest of my body with ripples of desire. Holding me around my waist, Orin pressed me against the table. A bulge in his pants nudged against my belly.

"You know, the tarts could use some time to cool off before you pack them up." He cupped my breast while trailing kisses along the side of my neck.

"Esvar will be here any minute to take us to Tadolia," I reminded.

My other husband had already taken our children to the town for an arts-and-crafts class before the parade.

"Good," Orin responded. "Then he can join us soon."

He tried to lift me up onto the table.

"Careful! Tarts," I reminded, shoving one of the trays aside.

"Right." He pressed me to him instead, holding me under my butt. "Couch it is then."

With excitement rushing through my body, I tugged at the ends of the scarf I wore around my breasts in the Ravil fashion.

"But we can't leave the children waiting," I pointed out for the sake of reason.

He lowered me onto the round couch in the middle of our spacious living area. "The children are busy making silly hats for the parade and decorating the floats. Their class is for two hours. And even without the class, Zaen and Natlea are always happy to have them over to play with their grandkids."

That was true. Itan and Mellae loved going to Tadolia. All their friends lived there. One of the most amazing things about living in a small town like Tadolia was that everyone knew each other. The children in the community were looked after by all the parents of the community.

Our children were safe, but nothing could save me from being thoroughly ravaged by my husband now.

Orin spread me on the couch, hiking up my skirt.

"Let's see if I can make you come before Esvar gets here," he muttered while kissing the swells of my breasts above my scarf.

The soft tassel of his tail fluttered over my exposed skin, spreading ripples of pleasure through my body. He tugged the scarf down, exposing my breasts, then dragged his tongue over my nipple.

"Mmm, you taste better than a *cirine* tart." He grinned, licking his lips.

"I doubt it," I laughed.

He playfully nibbled on my nipple in retaliation, making me whimper in need. Trailing his kisses between my breasts, then along my belly, he shifted down my body and buried his face between my legs.

"Definitely better than anything I've ever tasted," he murmured, finding my clit with his teeth through my panties.

"Oh, Orin..." I moaned in pleasure, thrusting my hips up toward his mouth.

"Shhh," he soothed, sliding a finger under the fabric of my underwear. "Look at you, wet already, my wife."

"I...I don't think I'll last until Esvar gets here," I confessed, moving my hips in rhythm with his finger sliding in and out of me.

He frowned with a teasing pout. "Oh, we can't let that happen, can we?"

His finger left me at once.

"Orin?" I rose on my elbows. "Don't stop."

"But we have to, my beautiful. Esvar wouldn't want to miss watching you come for us."

Need pulsed between my legs with an urgency I could not deny.

"He'll live," I grumbled, reaching with my hand between my legs.

"Nuh-uh." He lashed out with his tail, catching my arm.

His tail looped around my wrists, tying them together, then yanked them up and over my head. Orin's usually soft, caressing tail flexed like a rope around my wrists, firm and unyielding.

"Nooo, let me go..." Writhing in my restraint, I pushed my foot against Orin.

He slid off the couch, laughing.

"I'd love to, sweetheart, but you'd be pouting at me again, like the last time when we let you come too quickly, remember?"

Oh, I did remember that. I knew I got the most explosive orgasms when my two husbands played with me a little longer before finally letting me have them. But right now...right now I just wanted to come so badly, my knees shook.

"Oriiin," I whined.

"Aw, my poor little beautiful wife," Orin cooed, kneeling by the couch. "Let me make it a little more bearable for you."

He gently squeezed my breast, running his hot tongue over

my nipple. With his other hand, he caressed my inner thigh. I jerked my hips up, searching for contact with his hand. His thumb slid over my most sensitive spot, spiking my desire.

But with a teasing smile, he promptly moved his hand away. "Patience, beautiful."

I groaned in frustration. He rolled my nipple between his teeth. Lust rolled through me in a hot, sweaty wave, and I thought I would come right then and there, simply from Orin caressing with my breasts.

The soft whirring of an approaching aircraft came from above, and I released a breath with relief.

"Oh, Esvar is here," Orin announced brightly, tugging at my underwear. "Let's take these off you now. He'll love to see you bare and dripping."

He slid my panties off and tossed them aside. The underwear slid across the tiled floor and stopped next to my other husband's hooves—Esvar stood in the doorway of our living room.

He took in the scene—Orin kneeling by the couch with his tongue dancing over my nipple, me with my wrists trapped in Orin's tail, my breasts on display, and my skirt up to my waist.

"The best sight to come home to," he growled.

With his legs crossed at the ankles, he leaned his shoulder against the door frame and reached for the buttons on his shirt.

After all these years in Ravie, Esvar still wore shirts in public. But I loved it when he took them off at home. I followed his hand from button to button, holding my breath in anticipation.

"Show her to me," he rasped, sauntering closer.

"With pleasure." Orin grinned, getting hold of my knee.

He moved my legs apart, exposing me to Esvar. My inner muscles spasmed, my body quivering under his intense dark gaze.

"Beautiful," Esvar approved, taking off his shirt. "So delightfully wet already. You've done a good job, Orin."

"He wouldn't let me come, Esvar," I complained.

He bent over and placed a sweet, tender kiss on my forehead. "Thank you for waiting for me, sweetheart." Taking his pants off, Esvar nodded to Orin. "Go ahead, make her scream."

Orin beamed, finally sliding his hand between my legs.

I cried out in pleasure. Lust spiked, flushing my body with heat. I arched my back, lifting my ass off the couch.

Orin worked me with his fingers as Esvar watched. With all his clothes now off, he stroked his cock slowly, not touching me yet and not taking his eyes off me. I held his intense stare as long as I could before my eyelids fluttered closed with the approaching orgasm.

"Stop," Esvar bit out, and Orin immediately withdrew his hand.

"Orin, no!" I screamed in frustration, panting and writhing with a hot, unfulfilled need that flooded every part of my body down to the tips of my toes.

Overwhelmed by the sensations rocking me, I strained against Orin's tail holding me captive.

"What a beautiful sight you are, my darling." Esvar sat on the couch between my spread knees, then trailed soft kisses along my inner thigh.

Orin licked the finger that had been inside me. "Just like I said. Better than *cirine* tarts."

He loosened the noose of his tail from around my wrists. And I immediately reached between my legs again, desperate for release, but my fingers sank into the thick fur on Esvar's head.

"Just a taste," he murmured as if to himself.

His enormous tongue descended between my thighs. The tapered tip flattered over my hot, throbbing clit before plunging deep inside me.

I released a long moan as he swirled it around my inner walls.

"Please, Esvar…Orin, please," I begged them, turning into a hot, needy mess.

Orin sat on the couch, sliding my upper body up onto his lap and gently kneading my breasts.

"She said *please*, Esvar." He took pity on me.

I looked up, meeting Orin's gorgeous emerald eyes.

He winked at me. "Ready to ride me, beautiful? Because you know I'm ready for you. Always."

I nodded eagerly, both breathless and speechless too.

Orin helped me to turn around and climb on top of him, with my knees on each side of his thighs. My long, wide skirt fell over my legs and Orin's hips, concealing them from view. Esvar growled, disgruntled.

"This has to go." He pulled my skirt off over my head.

Esvar then straddled Orin's legs behind me, reaching around me to take my breasts into his hands. I released Orin's hard, straining cock from the confinement of his pants, and my Ravil arched his back, rising into my touch.

"Oh, how I love your hot little hands on me, Ana," Orin moaned with a radiant smile.

"Are you really ready for him?" Esvar slipped his hand between my legs, then moved his fingers in a widening circle inside my opening, stretching me for Orin's thick cock.

I leaned my back against Esvar's fur-covered chest.

"I can take him," I assured him, my breath halting with anticipation. "I want to take him. I need to… I've been taking him for years just fine."

"Because I always make sure you're ready for his giant cock." Esvar kissed the side of my neck tenderly.

Orin exhaled a laugh. "She loves my giant cock, don't you, my beautiful Ana?"

"I do…" I wiggled my hips, trying to trap his cock between my legs, but Esvar held me.

"Slowly, sweetheart, we don't want you to get hurt," he murmured, reaching for a bottle of body oil in the drawer of a side table.

Always protective and often bossy, Esvar frequently took the lead in our games. At the beginning of our relationship, he used to be mostly silent, sitting back, observing and learning. We were all learning things about each other. Now, we knew exactly how much he enjoyed taking charge, and Orin and I were happy to let him lead us.

With one arm around my waist, Esvar dripped the oil on Orin's cock, and I quickly spread it over my Ravil's velvety skin. Esvar then finally lowered me onto Orin's massive member. It was a big one, I had to admit. Even after a decade of fucking Orin in every position imaginable, I felt the tingling burn of the stretch. It temporarily eased my need until the delicious sensation of being filled so completely urged me to move.

Orin tossed his head back, sighing in bliss as I took his entire hard length. "Fuck, you feel so good, Ana…"

His tail danced over my skin, sending a shiver of pleasure through my body. My inner muscles clenched, coating his cock with my arousal. I moaned, arching my spine and resting my head on Esvar's shoulder.

"Good girl." Esvar kissed my cheek, fondling my breasts.

His tail snaked around us, the arrowhead tip flicking my hot, throbbing clit. My body went limp with a wave of warm pleasure.

"Ahhh," I exhaled, collapsing over Orin's broad chest.

"Come here, sweetie." He wrapped his arms around me, catching my lips in a kiss.

Esvar's tail prodded between my butt cheeks. I gasped, sliding up Orin's cock a little, but he tightened his arms around me, holding me in place.

"Hold still, sweetheart, or you'll make me come right away, which would be a shame. We don't want to have all the fun without Esvar, do we? Lean closer to me, lift your pretty bottom for him. Yes, just like that." He adjusted my position, pulling my chest down to him for my butt to rise higher for Esvar.

"What a gorgeous view you are, my darling wife," Esvar hummed with approval, palming my ass. The oiled tip of his tail swirled inside the rim of my back opening, stretching and widening me for him.

Desire rocked through me so hard, my entire body trembled.

"I…I need…" I pleaded, trapped in Orin's arms.

He stroked my back soothingly, kissing my hair. "Hush, sweetheart, almost there now."

"Help her," Esvar instructed.

Orin eased his hold on me, finding my clit with his fingers. I felt Esvar's cock pressing between my butt cheeks, but I got distracted by Orin's fingers playing with me in the front. Lost in pleasure, I moved my hips, rotating them slightly. Orin groaned. His body tensed under me. Esvar gripped my hips, slowly pushing in deeper with a low, guttural groan of need.

This was the moment I loved the most, when all three of us were connected and teetering on the brink of ecstasy.

I ran my fingers up Orin's chest, then cupped his face.

"I love you…" I whispered, breathlessly.

"I love you, too, my gorgeous, beautiful wife." He thrummed my clit with his fingers, rendering me speechless.

Esvar pounded harder, sliding me up and down Orin's cock with each powerful thrust. Squeezing my breasts, he trapped my nipples between his fingers.

Pleasure surged higher, then exploded through me. My thighs trembled. My breath caught in my chest. My mind seemed to float as a mind-blowing orgasm rocked my body.

Spearing his fingers through my hair, Orin cupped the back

of my head, bringing my open mouth to his in a gasping, all-consuming kiss.

He and Esvar came almost simultaneously, trapping me between their large, hot bodies while I rode the high swells of my climax.

"I love you, darling," Esvar whispered above my ear.

"I love you too," I exhaled, catching my breath. "I love you both. So, so much."

My body felt boneless as the afterglow set in. I rested my head on Orin's shoulder.

Esvar leaned over me, carefully making sure not to crush me under his weight. Bringing his arms around me in a gentle embrace, he splayed his left palm on Orin's chest, and Orin rested his hand on top of Esvar's, giving it a firm squeeze.

This was heaven. Warm and comfortable, with both their cocks still buried deep inside my body, I felt like I could stay like this for the rest of my life.

"I need a shower," I stated, not moving a muscle.

"Only if we all have it together." Orin stretched, letting his cock slip out of me.

Esvar exhaled a laugh. "You know how *that's* going to go."

"The children are waiting," I reminded.

"The children are having the time of their lives," Esvar assured me with a kiss on my bare shoulder. "They barely waved me goodbye, running off to play with their friends when I dropped them off. Trust me, they won't even notice we aren't there, not until dinnertime at least."

"Shower it is then." Orin playfully slapped Esvar's naked butt, urging him to get up. He then threw me over his shoulder, making me squeak in delight, and got off the couch too.

With my ass up in the air over Orin's shoulder, Esvar used the chance to kiss my butt cheek.

"One more time, sweetheart?" he asked.

Happiness bubbled inside me as Orin's tail tickled the soles of my feet.

"Always." I laughed, unable to keep in my delight. "I'm always up for one more time with you two."

If you liked My Tails, you should see My Horns too.
Flip the page to take a look.

SEVEN HORNY SINS

CHAPTER 1

Pushing on the bag to compress the garbage inside it, I tied the ends, then heaved it out of the bin. It had been another busy day at the restaurant. If things continued moving this way, I might be able to move this place into the black this year.

Of course, with more customers, the amount of work increased too. It was nearly midnight already, but Claire and I had just finished cleaning the kitchen.

"You can go home," I said, dragging the bag to the back door. "I'll finish here and lock up."

"Are you sure?" Claire grabbed her purse from the counter but lingered, not rushing for the door as she usually would. As a single mother of a teenager, she always seemed to be in a hurry.

"There isn't much left to do," I assured her. "Just to take out the trash."

Taking the garbage out to the dumpster behind the restaurant was not in the job description of the Head Chef, or the General Manager, or a few other positions I held as the owner of this place. Sam was supposed to do it, but his shift ended hours ago.

I really needed to hire more people. It'd be nice to have this place open for lunch and dinner seven days a week, including Mondays. But good employees weren't easy to find, and I had no time to look for them. Meanwhile, I ended up picking up the slack, not just cooking and running the kitchen, but also doing everything else that needed to be done.

Claire shifted her weight to her other foot, still not leaving. "Maddy, sweetie, can I borrow a hundred or two until payday?" She put her palms together in a pleading gesture and sang, "Pleeease."

I set the bag on the floor by the back door and shoved my long, dark hair out of my face. My high bun had all but exploded during the vigorous cleaning.

"I'll give it back when I get paid," Claire promised. "You know I'm good for it."

She was. Mostly. Sometimes it'd take Claire far longer than "until the next paycheck" to repay it. Often, she simply forgot, and I never reminded her. Claire was a good friend and a loyal employee. The last thing I wanted was for money to stand between us.

"Sure. How much do you need?"

"One...um, no." She winced. "Make it *two* hundred. Josh needs new shoes. Again." She rolled her eyes. "I swear this kid grows too fast for me to keep up. And you know how teenagers are, he wouldn't wear just *any* shoes out there." She sighed. "I can't get away with buying secondhand for him anymore."

"Okay, but I don't have that much cash on me," I'd dropped whatever we had in the till at the bank that afternoon. There wasn't that much to begin with as most transactions were cashless nowadays. "I'll stop at the bank on the way to work tomorrow, after I drive my mom to the dentist. Unless you want me to do a transfer?"

"Nope. Cash is good. Thanks." Claire beamed, grabbing me into a quick hug. "Don't stay too long. Work isn't everything." She rushed to the door, talking over her shoulder. "You really should meet my neighbor. He's a long-haul truck driver, always on the road. You guys are made for each other. With him, you can work as much as you want. He'd just fuck your brains out once in a while whenever he's in town."

If only I had any time to date even such a low-maintenance truck driver as Claire's neighbor. I spent every waking minute here. Even on Mondays, when the restaurant was closed, I had plenty of marketing and admin stuff to do every week. No one had "fucked my brains out" for over two years now.

Claire blew me a kiss before disappearing behind the swinging kitchen doors. "You're a lifesaver."

A lifesaver.

That was exactly what Sam had called me today when signing me up for a contribution to his second cousin's wedding gift.

"Can I put you down for five hundred?" he'd asked. "They don't have a lot of money but have this amazing honeymoon planned. It's like a once-in-a-lifetime thing."

Not that I had a lot of money either. I'd spent every penny of my grandma's inheritance to lift this place off the ground. After two years of struggling to get our name out there, the restaurant had just started making some real money. The word about our tasty food had come out. There were lots of glowing reviews all over social media. We had waiting lines for each dinner service. Yet the more money came in, even more went out.

People often assumed I was "a woman of means" just because I owned a restaurant. In reality, there was a lot of debt to pay off before I could even think about moving out of my mom's basement one day.

But Sam, and Claire, and every one of the eleven people who worked for me were vitally important for my business. More than that, my employees were my friends, and I couldn't refuse helping friends, could I?

"It's just money." I brushed off the concerns and dragged the trash bag out into the dark alley behind the restaurant.

Squeezed between several high-rise buildings, the alley remained in the shadows even on a sunny day. At night, it was nearly pitch dark, especially since the light above the back door had gone out again. Or maybe some kids broke it. I sighed. Another thing to add to my "fix-it" list that already had plenty of things to fix both in the restaurant and back at home.

Thankfully, there was just enough light coming from the windows and from the street at the end of the alley for me to find my way to the dumpster.

A weird purple-green glow appeared from behind the dumpster as I approached, as if a bright neon sign was hidden there. People often dumped things here illegally. It wouldn't surprise me to find a broken storefront sign. Except that this one clearly wasn't broken. How was it even on?

"This world does not look the same as in Pandora's box," a deep, grumpy voice said suddenly, coming out of nowhere.

I squeaked in shock, dropping the trash bag, then turned around, frantically searching for the source of the voice.

"And it smells," it complained with a strangled cough. "What the fuck is this stench?"

"The human world always stinks, some places worse than others," another voice replied, sounding just as low and eerie as the first one. "Now that I've got what I came here for, let's head home."

"Wait, Avar. It's my first visit in decades, and all you let me see is this dark, stinky place? What is it, anyway? Where are we?"

The surreal voices echoed all around me, but I couldn't see anyone in the alley. There was only darkness and the weird pulsing purple-green light coming from behind the dumpster.

Would they attack if I ran back to the restaurant?

Fear chilled my limbs. I grabbed the bag again. It wasn't much of a weapon, but it was all I had. Backing away in the darkness, I stepped on an empty soda can. It crushed under my foot, then rattled away as I jumped aside.

"Did you hear that?" the first voice asked.

I froze mid-step with my foot in the air.

"There is a human here." The second voice stated the obvious.

I'd been discovered. Now what?

Run?

What if they chased me?

And who the fuck were *they*, anyway?

"Who's there?" I shouted, trying to sound firm and assertive, and definitely not scared out of my wits.

"We should leave. You said it stinks here, anyway."

"Wait, let me see the human," the other voice insisted eagerly.

The green glow grew brighter, expanding from behind the dumpster and molding into an oblong shape.

My heart jumped into my throat.

Aliens!

What else could they be?

I stumbled back, tripped on a piece of trash, and fell on my ass, the bag landing on my lap.

"I have a security system here," I warned in a shaky voice, using the garbage bag as a big, stinky shield. "Leave now or I'll sound the alarm. The police will be here right away."

"A live human," a voice said breathlessly as the green light grew. "It's been a while since I saw one up close. Isn't she precious?"

The purple glow extended from behind the dumpster too. The mix of both proved blinding in the dark alley. I squinted, unable to see a thing.

"I know who she is," the other voice said with undisguised animosity. "Trust me, Invi, she isn't a good soul."

The accusation was unfair and simply outrageous.

"Hey!" A flash of indignity burned through my fear. "You don't even know me, asshole."

"See?" The voice said triumphantly, as if I had proven his point. "I may as well take her with me."

The purple glow grew brighter, flooding the ugly dumpster with a brilliant shimmer that was hard to look away from.

"Oh, hell, no!" I tried to scramble to my feet, but the garbage bag got in the way. I tripped over it in a hurry and fell on all fours. "No one is taking me anywhere."

"Her body won't survive her soul's journey, Avar, will it?" the other voice asked calmly.

"All humans die." The reply came serene and gentle, as if it wasn't a life-and-death situation they were discussing, *my* life and death. "She'll just get a chance to amend her ways a little sooner. And I will get a real human body for my collection."

"Is it *my* body you're talking about?" I jumped to my feet and swung the garbage bag at the approaching purple glow. "Stay away from me!"

The shimmer spread like ink through water.

Holding the bag in front of me, I backed all the way to the door until my butt slammed into it. I hurriedly felt with my hand for the handle behind me. One push, and I'd be safe. They wouldn't break through the fireproof metal door, would they?

A thick, undulating tentacle stretched from inside the purple light, and my insides dropped with terror. A scream stuck in my throat.

"What a rare treasure her body will make," the ethereal voice growled with anticipation.

Then, the world went dark.

AVAILABLE NOW

MORE ILLUSTRATIONS

For more art for this and other books by Marina Simcoe, including NSFW illustrations, please see the author's Patreon: https://patreon.com/MarinaSimcoe

ALSO BY MARINA SIMCOE

My Holiday Tails

Married To Krampus

My Tiny Giant

My Birthday Getaway

New Year, New Planet

Mail Order Mom

My Pumpkin

What Makes an Alien a Dad?

My Family Day

Dark Anomaly Trilogy

Gravity

Power

Explosion

Standalone Novels

Experiment

Enduring (Valos Of Sonhadra)

THE WORLD OF THE RIVER OF MISTS

Joyless Kingdom

Somber Prince

Joy Guardian

Pleasure Trader, coming 2026

Wingless Crow (Duet)

Wingless Crow – Part 1

Crownless King – Part 2

Fire in Stone (Duet)

Fire in Stone – Part 1

Hearts on Fire – Part 2

Serpent's Touch (Duet)

Serpent's Touch – Part 1

Serpent's Claim – Part 2

<u>*Madame Tan's Freakshow (Trilogy)*</u>

Call of Water

Madness of the Moon

Power of Rage

PARANORMAL ROMANCE BY MARINA SIMCOE

Demons (Complete Series)

Demon Mine

The Forgotten

Grand Master

The Last Unforgiven - Cursed

The Last Unforgiven - Freed

Stand Alone Novels Set in Demons World

The Real Thing

To Love A Monster

Midnight Coven Author Group

Wicked Warlock (Cursed Coven)

ABOUT THE AUTHOR

Marina Simcoe likes to write love stories with characters, who may or may not be entirely human, because she firmly believes that our contemporary world could always use a little bit of the extraordinary.

She has lots of fun exploring how her out-of-this-world characters with their own beliefs, values, and aspirations fit into our every-day life.

She lives in Canada with her very own grumpy brute, their three little kids, and a cat, who is definitely out of this world.

For updates on her future books please visit Marina Simcoe Author page on Facebook or www.marinasimcoe.com.

instagram.com/marinasimcoeauthor
facebook.com/MarinaSimcoeAuthor
bookbub.com/profile/marina-simcoe
goodreads.com/MarinaSimcoe